PRAISE FOR THE GUARDIANS OF ASCENSION SERIES BY CARIS ROANE . . .

"Caris Roane powers into the paranormal _____ enre with a sexy, cool, edgy romantic _____ the dark wings and letha _____ ion vampires. Prepare to _____
—*New York* _____

"Roane's world-buildi _____ _____ .triguing, and in addition to her compe _____ otagonists, she serves up a slew of secondary characters begging to be explored further. The Guardians of Ascension is a series with epic potential!"
—*Romantic Times* (4½ stars)

"A super urban romantic fantasy in which the audience will believe in the vampires and the Ascension . . . fast-paced . . . thrilling."
—*Alternative Worlds*

"A great story with a really different take on vampires. This is one book that is sure to be a hit with readers who love paranormals. Fans of J.R. Ward's Black Dagger Brotherhood series are sure to love this one, too."
—*Red Roses for Authors Blog*

"*Ascension* is like wandering in a field of a creative and colorful dream. There are many interesting, formidable, terrifying, beautiful, and unique images. They surround and envelop you in a story as old as time."
—Barnes and Noble's *Heart to Heart Romance Blog*

"Incredibly creative, *Ascension* takes readers to another level as you learn about two earths, vampires, ancient warriors, and a new twist on love. I felt like I was on a roller-coaster ride, climbing until I hit the very top only to come crashing down at lightning speed. Once you pick this book up, clear off your calendar because you won't be able to put it down. Best book I have read all year."
—SingleTitles.com

BORN IN CHAINS

Book One: Men in Chains Series

CARIS ROANE

St. Martin's Paperbacks

NOTE: If you purchased this book without a cover you should be aware that this book is stolen property. It was reported as "unsold and destroyed" to the publisher, and neither the author nor the publisher has received any payment for this "stripped book."

This is a work of fiction. All of the characters, organizations, and events portrayed in this novel are either products of the author's imagination or are used fictitiously.

BORN IN CHAINS

Copyright © 2013 by Caris Roane.

All rights reserved.

For information address St. Martin's Press, 175 Fifth Avenue, New York, NY 10010.

ISBN: 978-1-250-03529-5

Printed in the United States of America

St. Martin's Paperbacks edition / October 2013

St. Martin's Paperbacks are published by St. Martin's Press, 175 Fifth Avenue, New York, NY 10010.

10 9 8 7 6 5 4 3 2 1

To Jennifer Schober for her tremendous support over the past four years.

ACKNOWLEDGMENTS

Many thanks to Rose Hilliard and the team at St. Martin's Press for creating and supporting the *Born in Chains* vision!

CHAPTER 1

Chained to a cavern wall, Adrien hung forward from his shackles, arms shaking. The short length of the wrought-iron loops prevented him from falling to his knees, but after hours of torture he couldn't stand up straight and his shoulder joints were loose and screaming.

The torturers had come and gone.

Through his pain, he heard his half brothers calling to him, shouting his name, forcing him to concentrate.

He tried. But something else snagged him. The power that always hovered just at the edge of consciousness, the power of the Ancestrals that he rejected every day of his life, whispered to him, *She's here.*

The vision came over him and his heart seized. He could feel the future in his bones as the images pressed in on him, of a beautiful woman with soft highlights in her light brown hair, gold earrings sparkling and dangling past her chin, a warm smile on her lips. She wore a deep burgundy velvet gown, the color of blood, trimmed with what looked like gold crystals over a bodice that revealed a deep line of cleavage. Her shoulders, arms, and back were bare. And he felt something for her, something that called to his vampire soul, something that made him strain against his manacles.

He needed to get to her, to be with her, to keep her safe.

The vision rolled.

Let's go, she said. She extended her hand to him. He took it, then just as he felt the softness of her palm and fingers, the vision ended, dissipating like dust in the wind.

But not the sensations left behind, the need he felt to be with her, to get to her. He strained harder in his chains, hurting himself all over again.

Suddenly his stomach cramped and his body seized. He cried out in agony. He heard his brothers shouting at him but he couldn't respond.

The vision of the woman had ignited his blood-hunger.

Getting just enough blood while chained up had been another form of torture. He and his imprisoned brothers suffered the agonies of blood-hunger, the cramps, the saliva that thickened in his mouth, the dreams during the daylight hours of piercing a vein.

If some act of fortune didn't break in his direction soon, blood-madness would follow.

"Adrien, talk to us. Adrien."

He recognized the voice. Lucian, his oldest half brother, the one who carried the sins-of-the-father in his soul. He'd been the one to break them out of their father's compound, leading them into a new life of shedding years of intolerable pain and channeling all their ensuing rage into fierce fighting skills. They'd become peacekeepers in their world.

"Adrien, come back to us, brother." Marius this time.

The pain ratcheted up, from both deep bruises and surface cuts. He'd been lashed with a whip then beaten with its stick end. He wasn't sure which hurt worse.

"Adrien, answer us." Lucian again.

He tried to speak, but his throat felt washed with fire. In the middle of everything, he'd shouted his pain and his rage.

Fortunately his blood-hunger began to dissipate, and he opened his eyes. Man-made dry-stone walls separated him from his two brothers, so that they were lined up on one side of the cavern like horses in stalls.

"Adrien?"

"I'm here." His voice was barely a whisper.

But vampires had excellent hearing, so Lucian and Marius shouted their joy that he was still alive. They'd been in this Himalayan hellhole for the past year, sent here by the Council of Ancestrals, now ruled by Daniel Briggs, the monster who had chained them up personally, adding a touch of his preternatural power to the manacles so none of them could escape.

Lucian called to him again. "Adrien, repeat the vows."

The vows. Yes, the vows had held them together all these centuries, from the time of their escape from the monster's experiments on his young.

Adrien tried to join in. His lips moved, but he couldn't make the sound come out.

"In times of chaos, what feeds the will?" Lucian shouted the words.

"Blood!" His brother's voice resounded through the cavern, catching Adrien's soul and easing his pain.

"What feeds us in the midst of destruction?" Lucian once more.

"Blood!" Marius cried.

"Throughout our lives, what serves the body?"

"Blood."

"Blood," Adrien whispered, trying to do his part, but a thousand whip marks all over his body still trapped his voice.

Pain. So much pain.

His turn to recover today. They'd each been put under the whip once a week, beaten and sliced up repeatedly. Sometimes the women who performed the torture brought clubs and battle chains just to mix things up.

"Adrien, do you hear me?" Lucian called out strong and loud. "Give the response. We're waiting for you."

Adrien blinked back the stinging sweat that dripped into one of the cuts on his cheek. His dark hair hung in damp clumps in front of him. The humid air, the torture, and his sweat created a cloud of wet stink and pain. Hanging as he was, his shoulders ached as though fire burned in each. He needed to draw himself back, but he could barely move.

"Adrien," Lucian called out again, his voice sharp and commanding. "Give the ritual response. Now."

"Blood," Adrien said, the word like a soft scratch against wood, a mere hush in the dark vaulted cavern. A metallic taste filled Adrien's mouth.

He spit on the floor and tried again. "Blood." Still a hoarse whisper. "Blood." Louder. "Blood."

He repeated the word until his vocal cords decided to function again and now he shouted into the jagged stone walls.

He kept shouting until his brothers joined him. "Blood, blood, blood."

His strength returned slowly until at last he reached back and grabbed the heavy links of black wrought iron. He drew himself upright, his cut feet bearing his weight and causing a new round of agony. But at least his arms weren't threatening to pop out of their sockets. He hooked his elbow in the slack loop of the chain and laid his head down on his arm, the only way he could sleep.

Yes, sleep was what he needed, but just as he might have drifted off his thoughts snagged on Daniel and the

Council he ruled, which had allowed him to send Adrien and his brothers to the vampire prison in the Himalayas.

Over the past two years Daniel had ripped the vampire world apart, removing authority from the five smaller local courts and transferring it to the weak-willed, poorly governed Council of Ancestrals. He was growing in wealth in a heinous, soulless manner, by dispossessing well-to-do vampires of their fortunes and selling off extensive mineral rights to a human named Harris Kiernan, a typical man of his species, full of greed and little else.

Adrien wanted both Kiernan and Daniel dead so that they could do no more harm against the vampire world. But mostly he wanted Daniel dead, his body burned, bones ground to dust, and every last element salted.

He nodded against the chains, his body aching head-to-toe. So help him God, yes, he'd see Daniel dead.

And with his determination shored up once more, he fell asleep.

As darkness fell, and with a lantern in hand, Lily Haven moved up the path that led to the secret cavern prison.

She walked behind one of the jailers, a female vampire of Indian origin, her skin slightly paler than that of her human counterparts. The woman flicked the black leather handle of a whip, a sign of preference, ownership, usage.

Lily couldn't believe she was here, that any of this was happening, that vampires existed and she would soon be bound to one.

The blood-chain around Lily's neck, the tool she'd be using to take control of a large male vampire, vibrated almost painfully.

She could feel him now, and the terrible pain he endured, the one whose blood had been forged into the metal that now hung in thin loops around her neck.

Harris Kiernan had warned her what the female guards did to the prisoners, torturing the men to the point of death, each of them once a week, something that had been going on since shortly after the prisoners' arrival a year ago. He'd told her to prepare herself for a rough ride on every front—that her job here in India, to take charge of the vampire known as Adrien, would only be the beginning of a difficult trek.

Difficult didn't begin to describe her journey of the last two years. It had started with an attack on her neighborhood while she'd been visiting her sister in Oregon. A vicious group of vampires had gone through her neighborhood on a rampage, killing, raping, and stealing, an event the US government still called "an unparalleled gang-related attack." That night she'd lost what was most precious to her: a beloved husband, a daughter Jessie, just five, and her son Josh, who had been eight at the time.

She'd grieved without cessation until two months ago when she'd learned that her son was still alive. Josh, now ten, still lived, which is what had brought her here. Kiernan had held her son captive for two years, though well cared for, she'd been assured. And all Lily had to do to get him back was take charge of a powerful vampire and use him to find what was called an extinction weapon. Then Josh would be returned to her.

Lily carried a damp washcloth in her free hand, intending to hold it to her nose given the terrible conditions in the cavern-turned-prison. As she drew near the opening, she saw that the doorway was lined with intricately carved stone blocks, a sign that she had entered a secret vampire world.

The first hint of the stench inside reached her and she jerked her wrist, bringing the washcloth to her face.

The woman glanced at Lily. "Some say it smells like a

garbage bin behind a restaurant, only a hundred times worse. I don't smell it, of course. I've got a nose like a hyena." Then she laughed, whipped her head around, and moved within. "Like the prisoners inside, anyone can get used to the smells."

Lily remained for a moment near the entrance, breathing through her mouth as much she could, the washcloth pressed over the bridge of her nose. Finally she lifted the lantern high and followed, watching as dirt gave way to a floor made of stone pavers.

Crossing the threshold, she saw that the space rose to at least fifty feet in height, a typical-looking cave made of jagged dark rock, although portions of the walls appeared to have been worked with chisels at one time. Maybe there were even patterns but given the dim light, she couldn't tell.

She hadn't gotten more than fifteen feet when a wave of dizziness washed over her and she stopped.

The dizziness again. From the time she'd put the chain on, her senses had come alive in a way she'd never experienced before, as though she could know things if she just focused.

But this time the feeling of knowing became more and more specific until the space in front of her shifted, moving fast all around the edges. A vision emerged as the women brought one of the prisoners from his individual space, an open cell separated from other cells with walls of stacked stones. She recognized him from the dossiers she had on each vampire. He was the one called Adrien, the one she'd be taking with her.

He was naked, the state all the men were kept in, and his dark hair, not quite black, hung in lank, filthy strands almost to his shoulders.

He stared from beneath tight brows as he walked forward, a kind of soft light illuminating her vision. The chains between his manacled feet dragged against the stone, making a scraping sound she wouldn't soon forget. Male guards stood nearby with Tasers, one of the most effective weapons against vampires. Something about the vampire metabolism made them susceptible to electricity.

Adrien was tall, six-six according to the file on him, and much paler than the resident Indian counterparts, clearly descended from European stock. Despite the length of his captivity, he was well muscled, and in this vision he didn't have a single wound or scar on him. He was incredibly handsome, his cheekbones strong, a shallow indentation in his chin, his lips full, his brows straight. She had seen pictures of him, but she hadn't been exactly prepared for the breadth of his shoulders or the flexing of his powerful thighs as he moved.

She was drawn to him, something she didn't want to be feeling at all given that he was what she despised most: a vampire.

Now she sensed the time sequence. Two hours ago. He'd been tortured only two hours ago.

The vision continued as the guards threatened to use the Tasers unless Adrien did as he was told. He obeyed, backing up to the wall. The guards slipped the loose chains from each manacled wrist over hooks on the wall.

When the whipping began, Lily closed her eyes, but the vision didn't care and showed her everything anyway, straight into her head, each strike on Adrien's flesh, each cry from his lips, blood flowing from wound after wound until his flesh peeled away from his body in a hundred different places.

The women took turns flaying him, eyes glittering, nostrils flaring, sweat flowing from the work it took to wield the whip and make the cuts as deep as possible.

Not until Adrien passed out did the vision begin to fade.

"Hey, human, you in some kinda trance?"

Lily blinked and her eyesight returned; her sense of smell as well. Somehow in watching the vision, she'd taken the washcloth from her nose. She returned it now and only with tremendous effort kept from vomiting.

"Take me to Adrien," she mumbled behind the terry cloth.

"You're in luck. He's still hanging from the obedience hooks." The woman laughed once more. "These prisoners never learn."

Lily wasn't far from Adrien now. She could *feel* him, as though she already knew him, but the sensation rankled. Adrien, and all his kind, deserved to disappear from the face of the earth, so why should she care about his pain? He was a vampire, like the ones who had destroyed her family and her neighbors.

As she turned the corner of one of the high walls made of flat stones stacked neatly on top of one another, there Adrien was, just like in the vision, cut up and beaten. But because two hours had passed, he was well on his way to healing. Like the rest of his kind, he had a powerful ability to recover from the most severe wounds within hours.

He rested his head on the chains, but with his eyes closed, he held himself upright, feet planted over a foot apart.

She set the lantern on the floor. "Where does he go after a whipping?"

"Back to his stall, not much different from this. Smaller."

With the damp cloth still pressed to her face, Lily glanced at the stone floor at his feet. He stood in a pool of dark blood, his blood, and what she assumed were layers of dried blood beneath.

She tore her gaze away and lifted her chin. The chain-based visions wanted to return, sweeping over her, but she pressed them back. She had seen enough for now.

"Leave this cave," she said to the woman.

"What?"

"You heard me. I want to be alone with the prisoner."

The woman opened and closed her mouth, then shrugged. She slapped her whip against her hand and muttered something about human bitches that needed to be drained dry.

When she was gone, Lily drew close to Adrien, standing only four feet away. She continued to breathe through her mouth and held the washcloth close. Even with half-healed cuts all over his body, he was magnificent, like something sculpted from marble. His brows, however, were pulled into a tight knot.

But as she stared up at him the chains hummed, and she knew a deeper truth about the vampire: He was trying to figure out not how to escape, but how to murder someone. She felt his determination as though it released in his sweat.

Adrien returned to consciousness, but he didn't know why. He was only partially healed, and his body throbbed with pain. Usually he'd sleep for hours to complete his healing process as quickly as possible.

Yet something had awakened him, but what?

Above the usual filth of the cavern, he smelled a scent different from the vampires who usually took shifts—a human smell, one that filled him with rage.

He despised the world of humans, always taking what they wanted no matter who got hurt, or robbed, or dispossessed; the way they traded, for a few miserable dollars, the flesh of their kind into the forbidden sex-slave rings of his world, never to be seen again. And the way they illegally purchased the mineral rights of the caves Daniel Briggs stole from his fellow vampires.

And now a human was here, a woman, in the Himalayan prison.

Small sparks flew through his mind, as though part of him registered what was happening though the other part stayed sunk in denial. The muscles of his arms reacted, flexing in deep pulls then relaxing as if displaying his biceps. His abs knotted up in the same way.

With his eyes still closed, he lifted his head, leaning forward, straining against his manacles, pulling at the chains that bound him. Strength flowed into his arms, and a profound need swept through him to get out of his restraints. He needed to be free to protect his brothers from the enemy, from the human.

He groaned.

"What's brewing, Adrien?" Lucian called to him.

"The enemy is here." His voice sounded raspy again. He opened his eyes, but he couldn't see very well. He'd taken a lot of blows to the head and face this time.

"You mean the human? We can smell her, too."

He blinked several times and there she was, staring at him from a pair of large hazel eyes.

He breathed in and yes, she was very human, a stench more heinous to him than the putrid smells of the cavern. She had a lantern near her feet but he could see her easily as he adjusted his vampire vision.

The moment she came fully into view, however, he stalled out. His rage left him, flowing backward, and something else rushed toward the woman, something he didn't want to feel. It was her, the woman in his vision.

A strange combination of desire and need boiled within him. He felt as though he knew her on some level he couldn't explain.

Then the anger returned, at her kind, for their greed.

"What do you want?" he called out.

"Adrien, what the hell is going on?" Lucian's voice, louder this time, more urgent, bounced off the jagged stone ceiling.

Adrien couldn't respond, partly because he didn't know what the hell was happening and partly because time had just drawn to a hard standstill.

His brothers called to him, but he couldn't quite hear them. He watched the woman's lips move, so she must have been speaking as well, but his ears had shut down.

He saw her as though sunshine cascaded over her long, light brown hair. What would her hair look like pulled up high on her head? Did she own a burgundy gown dotted with gold crystals? He wanted her. He needed her. But he couldn't be feeling this way, not about a human.

His thigh muscles contracted and his knees bent. He tilted his head back and shouted into the heights of the cave, a sound that roared in his ears. His brothers shouted as well, joining him.

When he looked back at the woman, she'd covered her ears with her hands, her face twisted in pain, which caused him a certain amount of pleasure. She should hurt, this short-lived mortal, a representative of a race he abhorred.

He struggled harder against the chains and manacles, bruising and cutting his wrists and ankles as he tried to get to the woman, wanting her to pay.

She moved toward him, tears now running down her cheeks. Why was she weeping? His arms flailed and the chains clanked as he reached toward her. Her expression looked windblown, and he knew he needed to stop all the shouting, but he couldn't quiet his voice, not until her hands landed on his chest.

His back arched and he cried out one last time. He took short puffs of air into his lungs, but he began to calm down.

Only then, with the touch of her hands easing him, did he realize he was in a full state of arousal.

What the hell was this human doing to him?

* * *

Lily's heart pounded so hard that she'd grown deaf from the sound of the rhythmic rush through her ears. Her fingers felt the split of skin beneath her hands and even wetness from Adrien's open wounds, but it just didn't matter. All that mattered was quieting the vampire so that her ears would stop feeling like knives were slicing them up.

He thrashed in his chains, hurting himself even more. His wrists and ankles now bled in long red rivulets. His eyes had a red hue and he'd bared his fangs. She could feel his hatred of her as much from the chain around her neck as the power emanating from his body.

He looked like a madman, his body gyrating, his muscles from stem to stern flexing and rippling as he tried to pull away from the wall to get to her.

And yet he was aroused, which told her the other part of the story, that he had a powerful drive toward her he didn't want to have. This had all the makings of a nightmare.

She ignored that his erection pressed against her stomach. He didn't even seem to notice his sexual state. Instead, his eyes bored into hers, and as she kept her hands flat against his chest, he finally grew still, though his nostrils moved like bellows with each breath.

The other vampires in the cavern grew quiet as well, as though sensing Adrien's growing calm. The three men were half-brothers, though she knew little else about them except that they served as a type of policing force for their kind.

As she stared up at him, chills raced over her shoulders and down her arms. Her chest tightened as a strange sensation gripped her deep in her stomach, something that emanated from the chain around her neck. Kiernan had told her it would recognize Adrien since the specialist—something called an Ancestral in the vampire world—had used Adrien's blood to create the chain.

She opened her mouth to tell him about her current mission and what she needed him to do, but all she could seem to focus on was the shade of his eyes, an exquisite shade somewhere between blue and green, almost a teal but quieter, softened with faint brown flecks.

She realized that she could see really well in the dark, another result of the blood-chain. Essentially, once connected, she'd be siphoning more and more power from the chain and from Adrien himself after she'd bound him with the matching chain. In the meantime, she could already feel the chain at work on her. The vision alone had told her that much.

She looked at his lips, full and sensual. He strained toward her, leaning into her. "You're my enemy," he hissed.

"And yet you desire me."

"I want you on your back, human, then I'll make you feel just how weak you are compared with my kind."

"You speak of my weakness, but I'm not the one hanging from massive chains in a prison. You are. How did you get here, vampire? What brought you to this cavern?"

"Treachery," he muttered.

"Of course. Your kind always has an excuse. But at least we seem to understand each other, I hate your kind and you despise mine. We ought to at least be on an equal footing when I take charge of you."

"What does that mean?"

She backed away slowly, and as her hands left his chest his gaze fell to the chain at her neck. His eyes narrowed.

"I'll be taking you out of here."

"You've got a blood-chain."

"I do."

"And you've got the matching one?"

She nodded. "I was hired by a private individual to take you into my custody and make use of your powers."

He scowled. "Daniel would never allow that unless he'd sanctioned the release."

"Who exactly is Daniel?"

Adrien snorted. "Daniel Briggs, the vampire in charge of everything right now, including this lovely prison."

"I report to Harris Kiernan, no one else."

The vampire hissed. "He and Daniel work together, a little married couple."

"I've been told to explain a few things to you. First, you'll be bound to me and we'll be unable to get more than a few feet apart at any given time. Second, for either of us to remove the chain will mean death to both. Finally, you'll have to do as I say. And just to be clear, I'm more determined than you can imagine to see my mission through. I've got a lot at stake and I will get what I've come here for. Or die trying." She lowered her chin. "Do you understand?"

"You're saying you're putting your life on the line for your mission."

"That's right."

"Have you considered that once bound, I might decide to do the same? That I might find living in this state a worthless venture?"

"Yes, but it doesn't matter. I've made the decision to bind myself to you and if death follows, so be it."

He nodded slowly. "All right, I believe you. So what's your mission?" His eyes flared suddenly. "Wait, I can sense something from you, *about you*. You're a locator, aren't you?"

"That's what I've been told. That's why I'm here."

"And if we form this bond, you'll be able to find things, is that it?"

"Yes." She watched as he started putting the pieces together.

"Shit. You're after the extinction weapon."

She drew in a deep breath, vaguely aware that she no longer held the washcloth, nor did it seem to matter. "I am."

"Do you understand the ramifications of this weapon?"

"That it has the potential to destroy the entire vampire race."

The other vampires shouted suddenly for Adrien to refuse to go with Lily, but he called out, "The human has already said that Kiernan—and therefore Daniel—has turned me over to her. If he has his hand in this, we can be sure he won't be far behind in trying to get the weapon for himself. Imagine the control he could exert over our race. I have to do this thing." He met and held her gaze.

Lily saw the strength of him in that moment, his basic intent—and that the last thing he'd ever do was turn over the weapon once he had it in hand.

Great.

She drew a deep breath and set her shoulders once more.

Okay, one problem at a time.

"I'm glad you're being reasonable." Lily began backing away from him. "I'll get your bath ready."

She turned, picked up the lantern, and headed out, but the farther she moved away from him, the more the stench returned like a furnace-blast of odor. Somewhere, she'd dropped the washcloth.

She picked up her feet and ran the rest of the way.

Once outside the cavern, now fully dark, she jogged back down the path. The vampire who had led her to Adrien waited for her by her tent.

Furious all over again that she was even here, forced by circumstances as heinous as they were outside her control, she delivered her orders, her words clipped. "Give him another hour or so to heal, then get him clean. I don't care if you have to use pumice on every inch of his skin, just get him clean."

"I'll see that he's bathed." The vampire turned and headed back into the main camp to round up her forces.

When Lily went inside her tent, she quickly stripped off her clothes. She moved into her makeshift camp shower, wondering if she'd ever feel clean again. As she soaped up, she shuddered at her memory of Adrien, that she'd found the enemy beautiful, that she'd desired a vampire.

The thought felt unholy as she scrubbed from head to foot.

She would order her clothes burned, especially since they had Adrien's blood on them. She wanted no visceral memory of her time here if she could possibly help it.

Although the water was just barely warm, even after the staff added hot water to the tank, she stood beneath the shower and shampooed her hair, scrubbed her skin raw, and only quit when she couldn't smell the cave any longer.

Afterward she wrapped herself up in a thick robe and reviewed the latest email from Kiernan. Her first step was simple: bind Adrien with the matching chain, then take him back to his Paris apartment to get prepped for the mission. Once he was ready, she was to contact Kiernan, who wanted to know every step of her progress.

Sighing heavily, she opened a small case to her right and removed a chain that matched her own, made up of the same small dark loops. Her chain vibrated as she slipped the second chain over her head.

In the box was something else, something to help her remember why she was binding herself to a vampire. She picked up a small piece of cloth, taken from Josh's shirt, stained with his blood.

As she towel-dried her hair, she heard a thumping on

the path outside. A dozen men hurried by, barely shadows in the dark. Two of them hauled a huge stainless-steel tub, which got dumped unceremoniously not far from her tent. Those men raced back up the path in the direction of the cavern.

She heard shouting in the distance.

What the hell was going on?

She moved to the tent doorway and held her robe closed. Other staff arrived and began filling the tub, some with cold water, some carrying buckets that steamed, but all those heads were also turned in the direction of the cave.

She listened hard.

About fifteen seconds later she heard Adrien's voice. He was shouting, then roaring, then nothing, at least from him.

When the shouting of the guards didn't abate, Lily got dressed in jeans and a T-shirt, and slid into a clean pair of loafers.

She left her tent and hurried back up the path. By the time she reached the group at the opening to the cave, she realized that the guards were firing Tasers into Adrien, laughing as his prone body jerked in the dust. He moaned each time he was hit.

"What the hell are you doing?" she called out. "I need him."

The men, all paled-out vampire Indians, turned to her, eyes as vicious as the women's.

"He gave us trouble," the tallest man said, swatting at a fly near his head. He glared at Lily.

A lie, of course. The manacles Adrien wore held a pre-ternatural charge and kept him from doing more than shuffling, just as he had in the cave during her vision.

When she glanced down at him, he craned his neck to look up at her.

Meeting his hostile gaze, her own rage flared, not just at him, but at the collective nature of the vampires around her, without decency of any kind. So typical, in her opinion, that they would torture a prisoner like this, one of their own.

"Take him to the bath," she said quietly. She wanted out of here as soon as possible, and the only way out was to get the vampire clean then bound to her with the second chain.

It took six men to lift that much muscle and haul Adrien back down the path to the large metal tub, now full of steaming water.

Once he was in the oversized bath, his knees pulled up to make him fit, she set them at the task of scrubbing the grime off him. Fortunately, he passed out. She ordered the water changed two more times.

When at last he was clean, she removed the bonding chain from her neck and carefully placed it over Adrien's head, working it past his thick hair that touched his shoulders, until it rested against the back of his neck and dipped down in front to his collarbone.

A vibration passed from her chain to his. Her heart beat hard in her chest, as though trying to break free. She took deep breaths. A strange tingling moved through her body, from her head, flowing in waves down to her feet then back up as the chain made the connection she'd been told would happen.

The connection solidified and she placed her hand on Adrien's chest over the chain. She sensed so many things about him all at the same time: his rage, his physical agony, and his desire to keep his world safe.

She looked up at the guard. "Get these manacles off. Now."

The guard set to work, using a special tool to pound out the bolts that locked the manacles in place. Once both sets were gone, she sent the guard away.

With the blood-chain in place, Adrien wouldn't be able to move but a few feet away from her.

Oh, God, she was now bound to a vampire.

But her reasons, yes, her reasons were worth anything that happened from this point forward.

CHAPTER 2

Adrien hurt deep into his body, as though the electricity from the Tasers had taken the recent torture and driven it into his bones. He'd finally left the cavern for the first time in a year, and though he had been completely incapacitated with manacles and chains, the guards had still fired half a dozen Tasers at him repeatedly.

His fellow vampires.

The guards weren't even humans.

As his consciousness returned, he realized he sat in a tub of warm water that felt damn good on his aching, whipped body. He couldn't imagine what he smelled like. After that many months in a closed environment, he'd lost the ability to smell what had essentially become a cesspool.

His neck hurt. His head rested on the thin metal lip of the tub but he couldn't seem to do anything about it, probably because of the semi-paralysis that still kept him immobile. Damn, those Tasers had hurt.

He drew in a deep breath and recognized the human

scent from earlier, from the one determined to get the extinction weapon.

He shifted in her direction and stared at her from beneath hooded lids. She knelt beside the tub, watching him. He'd been without sex for a year, and without a decent draught of blood. The woman would serve his needs just fine.

His nostrils flared as he smelled her sex and her blood, both scents beating at his body, firing his appetites.

"Adrien, can you hear me?"

He nodded slowly. "Yes."

"My name is Lily. Lily Haven. I've already put the bonding chain on you. Can you feel it?"

When he didn't answer right away, she picked up his hand and pressed it against his neck, and he felt the thin loops as well as a vibration beneath his fingers. "You've bound me."

"I have."

His anger returned: Even though the wrought-iron manacles were gone he was still a prisoner, just a different kind. And bound to a human.

He glared at her, letting her feel his anger.

This time, she touched the chain at her throat. "So much rage."

"Yes, at the very least, rage."

"I didn't want this." Her voice was little more than a whisper.

"But you'll be well paid for your trouble."

At that, she released a sigh. "Yes. I will."

He continued to hold her gaze, to let her feel that he didn't intend to go easy on her, that she wouldn't be enjoying her time with him, and that if it came to it, he'd destroy the weapon before he let her have it.

Her chin dipped several times in succession as though she understood his thoughts. Maybe she did, because he could feel her easily through the chains as well—he knew that she feared him but was determined to do whatever needed to be done to fulfill her mission.

And she was a locator, rare in either the vampire or the human world. But how had either Kiernan or Daniel found her? He'd heard of this kind of ability, and that it could only work if paired with a vampire of sufficient power. Through the blood-chain, she'd be able to access his power, draw it into her, and eventually gain the skill of connecting with anything she wanted to find.

In this case, a weapon to destroy his kind.

That anger toward the vampire world radiated from her didn't surprise him. The worlds had begun to clash, and it was getting harder and harder to keep the vampire world a secret.

And somehow she had run head-on into either Kiernan or Daniel, a deal had been struck probably involving a small fortune, and now she was here.

Yet really angry, as though some injustice had been done to her. That was the surprise: that she would be using Kiernan to gain a fortune, yet be almost as angry as he was by the arrangement.

Now, there was a mystery to solve.

Because she was so physically close, however, a more urgent problem surfaced as he caught the rich scent of her blood. His hunger returned and he groaned.

He felt her emotions abruptly shift to concern for him. "How badly are you hurt?"

"Not hurt. I need blood." He glared at her. But the woman ought to know what was headed her way, and that he'd hit her like a freight train right now if she didn't back off.

She leaned away from him as though sensing his thoughts. Her eyes widened, and now he smelled how much he frightened her.

The scent of fear beat at him and his fangs emerged. "You'd better move as far from me as you can right now—or offer me a vein. One or the other, human."

She rose to her feet then backed up far enough that he felt the tug of the chain at his neck, the warning that because they were bound, they were limited by distance as well.

He pressed his hand against the chain and glanced at the woman. She stood ten feet away, no more.

He closed his eyes.

Bound, again.

Chain-bound.

He'd worn a different set of chains in his youth. He'd been bound to the evil one, and couldn't leave the house or the grounds since dear old Dad had built an electric fence to keep his sons prisoner.

"Adrien."

He shifted his head toward her once more.

"I . . . this isn't who I am."

"What do you mean?"

She shifted her gaze away from him. "Nothing. Never mind. As soon as you're able, there's a shower in my tent. It'll help."

But a different kind of emotion vibrated through the chain at his neck, coming from her. He didn't understand it at first; then a roll of pain went through him and he finally got it: The human was incredibly sad. In fact, she was grief-stricken.

But the part of him that had suffered snorted at her despair. Let the human feel her pain.

What was she to him?

What could she ever be to him, but the enemy?

Lily slid both arms over her stomach as she stared at the massive vampire in the huge yet too-small metal tub. He watched her with such a predatory stare that chills kept chasing over her body.

She sensed so many things from him—his confusion, his anger, but mostly his blood-hunger—and right now she felt like the fly to his spider.

She'd never been around a man like him before. The sheer size of him was enough to make her wary. Only he wasn't just a man, but a vampire, a different race altogether, something she didn't understand, something she didn't trust, something much more animal than human.

And lethal.

Nor was it helping that the shared chain opened him up to her, revealing his aggressive intentions toward her—his desire for her blood for one thing, and sex for another. His level of determination became an itch on her skin.

Right then she felt the energy of who he was: a ball of fire, of rage. He had power as well. Formidable power. Kiernan had told her that Adrien had the potential to become an Ancestral, something rare in the vampire world and something laden with preternatural ability.

And for the first time, she truly doubted that she'd ever be able to see her mission through. For one thing, his loyalties lay elsewhere, with his brothers still in prison and with the vampire world generally, so he could never be a truly reliable partner. But given his size and physical strength, that he was a trained fighter and that he had tremendous potential among his kind, what on earth made Kiernan think she'd be able to control him all the way to the end?

Adrien stood beneath the shower attached to Lily's tent. He hadn't been clean in a year and he didn't care how many times Lily's crew had to refill the tank, he'd be damned before he took one more step into the future without getting every molecule of filth off him.

He scrubbed his hair until his scalp burned; his legs, arms, and chest until his skin felt raw; his crotch until he felt bruised.

Only then, stripped of the last of the cavern muck, did he step, naked as hell, from the shower into Lily's tent. His captor sat at a small desk.

She glanced at him and grew very still as she looked him up and down. Her lips parted, her nostrils flared. And just like that, as unexpected as anything he could have imagined, he smelled her sex, a warm, sweet flow of desire that tightened his abs. *She wants me.*

She cleared her throat, then gestured to a stack of towels on a small table to his right. "Help yourself."

She returned to review something on her desk, a small notepad. She rubbed her neck beneath her binding chain. Apparently, the fairly lightweight string of small black loops chafed her as it did him.

Good. If he had to be bound, then he wanted her annoyed and scratching to get free as well.

His jaw quivered at the sight of her, all woman, a reminder yet again that he'd not been between a woman's legs in too damn long.

He let his gaze fall slowly down her body. She stretched, her hands behind her back, which pushed her chest forward. Her breasts were large and firm. A nice handful. A better mouthful. Her narrow waist flared to womanly hips.

Her hair hung in soft waves to the middle of her back in a light brown, layered flow with subtle gold streaks, hair obviously cared for in an expensive salon. Once again he noticed the beauty of her hazel eyes. She had thick dark lashes, arched brows, full lips.

She turned toward him and he let the towel fall away from his now partially erect cock. She needed to know what he intended her to have, the sooner the better.

"What am I supposed to do about clothes?" he asked.

Her gaze dropped exactly where he wanted it. But she looked away, swirling her hand in his direction. "At least put a towel over that."

"You might as well get used to it, Lily." She jumped at the use of her name. "I haven't gotten laid in a long time and it's all I can think about right now. That, and tapping your vein."

She shook her head, color climbing her cheeks. "You've got the free use of your hand."

Oh, this was too easy. He stared at her hard as he took his cock in his fist and started stroking. "You're right, I do."

She made a disgusted sound, left her chair, and headed to the front tent flaps.

He called out, "Wait, human—"

But she'd moved too fast trying to get away from him. She got pulled backward by the chain's power and landed on her ass. He couldn't help himself: He laughed long and loud, and it felt good.

She stood up and swiped at her jeans. She turned to face him, her jaw grinding. "Would you please cover up?"

The slight note of desperation in her voice made him wonder. He leveled his gaze on her and asked, "You sure you want me to do that?"

She looked him up and down once more, blinking a couple of times.

She took a deep breath. "This isn't going to be simple," she muttered. Meeting his gaze once more, she said, "Yes, please cover up. I won't deny I'm tempted, because ever since I saw you in the cave, the chains haven't really stopped vibrating, and I've been experiencing visions as well. I'm feeling too much here, but I'm not fool enough to believe it means anything. You know how you look, how women react to you. You're a slab of meat, nothing more."

Hatred boiled in him that she would speak to him that

way. In his world, he was admired and not just because of his appearance. For her to reduce him to something found in a slaughterhouse repulsed him. She had no soul, this woman, bent on using him for her own purposes, probably to make a fortune just as all corrupt humans did in their world.

He'd met so many like her. They'd catch rumors of the secret vampire world and hear tales of making a fortune by selling their fellow humans—mostly women, but some men as well—to vermin like Kiernan. Those humans in Kiernan's mold would serve as go-betweens, approaching Daniel or a dozen other vampires who ran illegal sex-slave clubs that traded in human flesh. But it was always the humans who brought their captives to market, selling them like cattle.

Of course both Daniel and Kiernan did a lot more than just trade in human flesh, especially now that Daniel ruled the Council of Ancestrals and could do as he pleased. Daniel would forge documents and take control of mineral-rich caverns owned by wealthy vampires. Then he'd sell the caves off to Kiernan, who in turn worked surreptitiously with many human government officials, each profiting as the food chain went on and on, everyone involved obligated, by the heinous nature of the transactions, to continue keeping the vampire world a secret.

One day this house of cards would fall down, but probably not for a few years yet, maybe even decades.

All of it disgusted Adrien, and now he was bound to a human woman who had also sold her soul for profit, something apparently she was willing to die for.

Lily now hunted for the extinction weapon, at Daniel's request, forging a tracking bond with Adrien. Through the shared chain, as she siphoned his power, she'd be able to locate the weapon, at least in theory.

Though rumors had abounded since the 1950s about

the existence of the weapon, other rumors had surfaced as well: that there had been several versions of the weapon, and that the remnants of those weapons had been hidden away in hundreds of caverns all over the globe.

Hunting for a viable weapon would be the old needle-in-a-haystack pursuit.

He took a towel and slowly wrapped it around his waist.

Lily returned to her chair but shifted it to face in his direction. She dipped her chin toward another, larger chair. "Why don't you sit down and we can talk for a few minutes? Things need to be said, plans laid out." He felt the weight of her words, and at the same time the chains that bound them together spoke to him of all that sadness again.

He tucked the white terry in at the waist.

He sat down carefully in the large camp chair, hoping it would hold. He was a lot of vampire to test so little canvas.

"It's good for up to three hundred pounds," she said.

He nodded, then settled in, stretching out his legs. Damn but it felt good to move, to be free of his shackles, even to sit. He rubbed his wrists.

"The first thing you need to know is that you've been released permanently from prison. No going back. I was told it's all legal and that your release will be publicized to your world over the next few days, which means that you won't have to worry about anyone coming after you."

"I'm not worried about that."

"Why? I thought that would be your first concern, that you'd land back in prison before we even got started."

"Daniel put us there, and I don't intend to let it happen again."

She met his gaze, her expression grim. "I can feel through the chain that you mean what you say."

He nodded.

She picked up the list she'd made and flipped the edges of the paper. She drew in a deep breath then stood up. "I want you to know that while you're in my care, Adrien, I intend to be humane."

He snorted his laughter. "How kind of you. Then I should be clear as well: I'll need blood, soon. And sex. If you can't provide either, you'll need to bring someone in. Got it?"

"Understood."

"Has it occurred to you, human, that I might not want to help you find this weapon?"

At that, she leveled her hazel eyes on him. "I've thought about that, but I already know something about you because of the chains: You'll do whatever you need to do to survive, to get back to your brothers here in the cavern in order to free them. Am I right?"

He nodded. "Just short of turning a race-killing weapon over to Daniel or anyone else like him. So you work for Harris Kiernan."

"I wouldn't say that I work for him."

"But you think he's a stand-up guy, no doubt."

She leveled her gaze at Adrien. "I wouldn't say that, either. I've never met him. We've handled everything through email and the much rarer phone call. That's it."

"Well, take it from me, he's a real prick."

She stared at nothing in particular. "Yes, I would say he is."

He felt it again, a vast amount of sadness—and somehow Kiernan was connected to it. He wondered if she'd been a sex slave at one time, but she didn't seem the type, she didn't seem ruined in that way. No, whatever had caused her so much grief was something else.

She lowered her chin slightly and drew in a deep breath. "Now I have a question for you. Kiernan explained to me about how vampires can use a phenomenon that he called *altered flight*—sort of like moving at a fantastic speed but in some kind of altered reality that allows you to pass through anything solid. Is that right?"

He nodded.

"And just how good are you at altered flight?"

He lifted a single brow. "How good am I?"

"Kiernan suggested that because I'm human, we might have some trouble getting from one place to the next."

He eyed her narrowly again. The woman had guts, he'd give her that. Humans didn't enter altered flight easily, not with lesser vampires like himself. Any vampire of Ancestral status could easily take a human anywhere around the globe within minutes, sometimes seconds—they were that fast, that powerful.

But Adrien had resisted his Ancestral call for centuries, being outraged generally by that inbred, narcissistic, compassionless, and incredibly ineffective group for as long as he could remember. He'd rather eat dog shit than become an Ancestral.

No, this would be a rough ride for Lily. She knew it, too, by the look in her eye, like someone facing a tiger in the dark.

His mind shifted sideways for a moment. She stood at least five-ten, not a bad height against his own six-six. Her hazel eyes glinted in fear, but her lovely chin rose with courage. He had a sudden desire to put his hand on her face and rub his thumb along her cheekbone.

With these thoughts, his chain vibrated softly against his neck and chest. Dammit, he liked the look of her, and as much as he wanted to despise her, the blood-chain told him a different story.

He looked away from her, steeling his mind against any kind of thought that would make him sympathetic toward her.

"So what I suggest is that we head to Paris, using altered flight. I understand you have an apartment there. Or will that be too much for you?"

He snorted. "Hell, no, it's not too much for me, but you're probably not going to like it."

"Doesn't matter. Let's get going. You can get dressed and I'll alert Kiernan that I have you in my custody, then we'll see what he wants us to do next."

Adrien stilled. He hated the thought of leaving the Himalayas and his brothers—but what choice did he have?

No, this path was set. He could feel in his bones that he needed to travel this course. He would just have to trust that somehow, as he went along, he'd figure this out: how to survive, how to keep Lily alive, and above all, should they actually find the extinction weapon, how to keep Daniel or Kiernan from gaining control of it. And somewhere in there he'd get back to Lucian and Marius.

He dropped the towel and held his hand out to her. "Okay, Lily, let's get the hell out of here."

Lily glanced at his open palm, and her heart rate jumped up a few notches. She'd already touched him, but this felt different—as though a door swung wide, daring her to step through. That strange sensation reached her again, the one she'd felt in the cavern when she first saw Adrien, of a kind of strange knowing, like an echo bouncing from one jagged stone wall to the next.

But how could she really know a man she'd just met?

Her chain vibrated once more and as had happened from the first, her desire for him spiked, something she had a hard time squashing down. Of course, it didn't help that he stood in front of her with his extraordinary body on full display. She'd never seen a man like him before.

"Take my hand, Lily. We need to go."

Another deep breath and she placed her hand in his but retained her distance.

He shook his head. "No, this won't work. You'll have to come closer. Altered flight can be damn dangerous for humans. I'll need to protect you the whole way."

Her heart now thumped heavily in her chest. She didn't want to get closer to this vampire, but she didn't really have a choice. "Fine."

As she moved toward him, he drew her into his arms so that she ended up balanced on top of his feet, her arms wrapped around his neck. Basically, she was plastered against his naked body.

He slid his arms around her back and waist and held her tight—but nothing happened, at least not the altered flight phenomenon Kiernan had told her about. Instead, she felt him take a deep breath and release it slowly.

Lily hadn't been this close to a man in a long time, not since her husband died two years ago. She'd forgotten how it felt, the simple pleasure of the hard planes of a man's chest, his heavier muscled thighs, and of course she couldn't ignore his cock, which she felt firming up against her lower abdomen.

She wished there was some other way of doing this because it felt so good, even dangerous. The chains had already begun exposing the depth of her need and of her desire for the vampire, but this level of proximity wasn't helping at all.

After a moment, when he hadn't started to fly, she asked in a mumble against his shoulder, "What's wrong? Did you forget how to do this? I mean, I know you've been chained up for an entire year."

He snorted. "Just taking a breath."

His voice had a threatening edge. She couldn't imagine exposing her throat and having him sink in his fangs, but the only other choice was bringing in a third party. And from what she knew about vampires, sex usually accompanied the taking of blood.

The thought both sickened and excited her, especially the thought of this vampire throwing her on her back and taking so much from her. But she'd be feeding the same kind of beast that had killed her family if she serviced Adrien.

She felt trapped again by her situation. Yet what choice did she have if she ever hoped to get Josh back?

Thoughts of her son shook her to her core all over again, so she toughened up. She would do whatever needed doing in order to bring him home safe and sound once more.

She shifted in Adrien's arms so that she could look up at him. Maybe she scowled, but she said, "I'm prepared to give you what you need once we're in Paris. I know it's part of the deal because of the chains, but are you sure I have to hold on to you like this right now?"

"Yes. I'll regulate my speed, but this probably won't be much fun. I need to make one pass through the cavern, then I'll take you the rest of the way to Europe."

She started to argue—the last place she wanted to be was inside the stench of his former prison—but he began the altered flight, which jolted her senses.

Could she even talk to him during a flight?

The first thing she realized was that she'd left her tent behind; then the path. The next moment she was hurtling toward the wall of rock outside the cave. She cried out and shut her eyes, clinging to him harder, but nothing happened, only a soft sensation like feathers across her skin as Adrien took them through the mountainside.

The movement of the flight slowed so she popped her eyes wide and found herself flying very slowly through the cavern. What she saw, however, sickened her. Lucian and Marius hung from black chains, each in a separate stall, each standing in his filth.

They were able to see Adrien and as he passed through the cavern, each shouted, calling out his name and waving triumphant fists in the air.

"I'll get back here as soon as I can," he shouted in return, though the movement of the altered flight seemed to muffle speaking voices.

On a more positive note, she couldn't smell the cavern.

Adrien sped up the altered flight, and that's when things went haywire. Dizziness and blackness swallowed her, along with a pain in her skull that made her shriek. She'd never hurt so bad in her life.

"I can tell you're hurting but we've got to get to Paris, the quicker the better." His voice had a strange resonance through the pounding in her head.

"Okay." Even her lips vibrated with pain as something wet trailed down her lips and chin.

She clutched at him now and tried to breathe. She felt his chest rise and fall rapidly, the exertion of the altered flight maybe. She could feel that he was expending a lot of energy.

The passing seconds of the flight began to feel like an eternity. When at last he drew to a halt, she collapsed on a woven rug of some kind, facedown. She lay prone, her head on fire. She wiped at her nose, thinking maybe she'd been weeping, but the liquid had a thicker consistency than tears.

She lifted her head. She needed a tissue.

Adrien lay on the floor next to her, his hand on her back. His gaze fell to her lower face. "Your nose is bleeding."

He pushed to his feet, left her for a moment, and just as he must have met the outer reaches of the chain's tight hold on them, she heard water running.

He returned a few seconds later with a damp washcloth in one hand and tissues in the other.

She rolled onto her back, wiped her lips and chin, then placed the cool washcloth over her nose. The apartment was dark with no lights on, but right now with her head aching, she was glad of it.

She tracked him as he moved to a wall of closets, which meant she was in his bedroom. He dressed quickly in dark jeans and a tight black T-shirt.

She worked herself to a sitting position. "That was incredibly painful," she said. She clutched the washcloth with one hand while she blew her nose using the tissues.

Her stomach turned over several times and she worked hard not to throw up. She refolded the washcloth, trying to find a clean spot.

Adrien sat down in a nearby chair and put on a pair of black socks. "I felt your suffering through the shared chain. I got here as fast as I could. Shit. But this isn't good."

"Travel is going to be a problem. My head hurts so bad."

"Yep."

"Maybe I'll get used to it. It was okay at first, but when you sped up, it got worse really fast. Can we travel at the slower speed?"

"Sure, but we'd be hours getting anywhere that isn't on the other side of Paris. Also, if anyone was tracking us or watching for us, we'd be vulnerable."

"Do you expect an attack?"

Adrien met her gaze as she held the washcloth to her nose. "I have enemies. Daniel does, too. We have fanatic-based groups that—if they catch wind that we're after the extinction weapon—will try to stop us. Didn't Kiernan say anything about them?"

"No. He didn't." She looked at the washcloth. "My nose has stopped bleeding."

"You were screaming."

"I was? I don't remember. I guess I was. I can't begin

to describe what the pain was like, sort of a dagger through my head."

"How's your head now?"

"Getting better fast."

He grunted.

"What?"

"I thought the chains we shared would be powerful enough to get us through, that's all. They felt strong enough. I guess I was wrong or maybe just wishful."

She rose to her feet and glanced around. She pivoted toward him, continuing to dab at her nose. "What are you not saying?" She touched her chain. "I can feel your sudden indecision about something."

He slid his feet into heavy black shoes, not quite boots but close. "There's another type of blood-chain, a double, side-by-side arrangement, that could change things for us, but hell if I'm willing to go that far."

"You may not have a choice. I say we get the chains if it means we can travel more easily."

His gaze shot back to hers. "What the hell does that mean, that I may not have a choice? So far all that's required of me is to hunt for the weapon. And right now, I don't give a damn if it causes you this much pain."

His sudden anger should have bothered her—after all, he was over two hundred pounds of heavily muscled vampire, and he could break her in half with his bare hands if he wanted to. "I'm not giving you an ultimatum," she said. "I'm suggesting that in order to get this job done, we each may have to do things neither of us wants to do."

"We're already doing that because I sure as hell don't want to be bound to you like this." He reached down, put his hand on her arm, and leaned close. "Listen, Lily, I can get us both out of this. I know a couple of very powerful vampires who work with blood-chains. They'll know what to do, to get these off without either of us dying. And I can make it worth your while, whatever Kiernan or Daniel is paying you. I'm a wealthy man. Would five million dollars get the job done?"

She just looked at him and sudden images of burying her husband and daughter, of attending several memorials for her good friends and neighbors, rolled through her mind like a dark storm.

Josh's smiling face came next. She felt cold as she said, "Have you got fifty million?"

Adrien's nostrils flared. "No."

Fifty wouldn't have made the smallest difference, either, but she didn't tell him that. All she said was, "This mission is what I want, what I need to do."

He stood up suddenly. "I guess that's a real *fuck you,* isn't it?"

She looked up at him, way up. The vampire was tall, especially since she still sat on the floor. "I guess it is."

"I can't believe you'd turn down five million." He glared at her for a long moment, then his expression filled with disgust. "Typical human, out for what you can get, never mind who gets hurt."

She snickered. "That's rich: *who gets hurt.* And you a vampire. But let me make myself clear to you one last time: You can't even begin to fathom what I'll be given in exchange for the weapon, and it'll be worth every ounce of sweat or knife-like headache, trust me on that."

She didn't blame him for his anger. Right now she was his enemy, she had control of him, and she could say yes or no to any of his requests or demands.

He stood up and paced the length of the closets, fuming.

At least the pain in her head had finally dissipated, her nose had stopped bleeding, and she no longer felt dizzy. "Where do I put these?" She held the washcloth and tissues for him to see.

He gestured with his hand to a door to his right, beyond a long dresser. "That's the privy."

The bathroom wasn't far at all, but once inside, the chains tugged at her. "Could you come a little closer? I want to shut the door."

Though she couldn't see him, he must have moved because the tension on the chain eased. She discarded the tissues and rinsed the washcloth out.

She glanced around and realized she was staring at black marble, on the walls, the sink, the massive shower, even the toilet. The fixtures were an antique silver. The elegance seemed juxtaposed with the fierce vampire who challenged almost every word she spoke.

At the far end was a second door that probably led to a hall and the rest of the apartment.

As she finished up and washed her hands and even rinsed her face, she met her gaze in the mirror. Josh had her eyes, the same hazel color and roundish shape, which was the reason everyone said he looked like her. But the truth was, he had his father's mouth and nose, even his strong jawline.

Josh. Her heart sank into her stomach all over again. Josh alive. Her son. She had to get him back. The drive was as powerful as the orbit of the earth around the sun.

She released a sigh, needing to get on with things. The sooner she got her hands on the weapon, the sooner she'd get her son back.

When her phone rang, she drew it from the pocket of her jeans then opened the door but was startled to find Adrien standing there. He leaned against the doorjamb, and she was surprised all over again by how big he was. She also knew that his vampire genetics gave him great physical strength, incredible strength. He really could break her in half if he wanted to.

The phone rang again, but all she could do was look at Adrien.

His brows pulled together as he stared back at her. "Aren't you going to answer that?"

She nodded and touched the surface of her iPhone. "Yes, Mr. Kiernan."

"Do you have him in hand?" Kiernan's voice had a slight rasp, which always made her want to clear her throat. Maybe he was a smoker.

She glanced up at Adrien again. Did she have him in hand? Was that even possible? "I have the vampire with me, yes."

"Good, because I have bad news."

Her heart dropped. Was Josh okay?

"We've had reports that an element in Daniel's world has gotten wind of our plans and they don't like it. You need to tell Adrien to expect assassins. Fanatics. He'll understand. Now work with the vampire to get your tracker skills functioning as best you can, then have him seek out the latest rumors about the weapon and get on it."

Before Lily could ask even a single question, like how exactly her mysterious tracking ability was supposed to work, Kiernan hung up.

She met Adrien's gaze and was ready to repeat the conversation, but he pushed away from the door frame and lifted a hand to silence her. "I heard him. Damn fanatics. And Kiernan can eat shit and die, as far as I'm concerned. How you could ever align yourself with a lowlife like that, well, fuck."

Lily wanted to tell him that it wasn't by choice, but she didn't see the point of trying to argue her case with him. Still, given that he was a vampire, *a vampire,* it chapped her hide to see his disapproval of anything she did.

She huffed a sigh. "He said you'd understand, so who exactly are these fanatics?"

Adrien narrowed his eyes at her. "You do know that you're being used by two of the worst men in either species and that there's a good chance you're going to die because of it? What do you think of that?"

Lily shrugged and held his gaze. "Then I'll die."

He shook his head. "You don't care if you die?"

"Oh, I care. Believe me, I do care and I intend to stay alive. But this is what I've chosen to do."

"Is it really worth the money?"

"My reasons for doing anything are none of your goddamn business." She lifted her chin, letting all her hostility toward his kind flow through her. She wanted him to feel her opposition to his vampire world whether Kiernan was an evil human or not, or whether she was doing Daniel's bidding or not.

He took a step toward her and leaned close to her face. "Well, given that I intend to stay alive, too, I need to know what's going on in that weak human skull of yours. It might even be to your advantage to work with me."

For a long moment, probably because the chain vibrated heavily against her neck, Lily felt a powerful urge to tell Adrien everything, about Josh, about the attack on her family, about being strong-armed with Josh as the motivator, but she couldn't. Even if she trusted Adrien, and she was far from doing that, Kiernan's rules were simple: No one was to know about Josh, or she could kiss this deal, her life, and her son's life good-bye.

So for two months she'd lived in this nightmare of fear and hope, of a resurrected son who'd been gone two long years. But he was in the hands of a man who had no qualms about using him as ransom for a mission that would take her deep into the world of the vampire, the last place she wanted to be.

"Right now," she said, her chin level, "you're on a need-to-know basis. So unless there's anything else, I suggest you tell me about these fanatics and give me some idea where we should go to start our hunt for the weapon."

He grabbed her wrist and shook his head. "Soon you'll tell me what the hell is going on here, because something's not right. Maybe it has something to do with Kiernan, maybe it doesn't. But my instincts are screaming at me that we're in danger on more than one front. As for the fanatics, there's more than one group. Each is full of religious zealots intent on keeping the vampire world hidden from the human world—something I actually believe in as well."

"Why aren't you part of one of those groups, then?"

"Because they don't hesitate to kill innocent people if they stand in the way." He laughed harshly. "The stunned expression on your face tells me exactly what you think of me. You're actually surprised that I'd hold a position like that, against killing innocents."

"Yes, I'm surprised."

"Why? You don't even know me."

"I know enough." She let her hatred fill her words. "You're a vampire. I don't need to know anything else."

She watched his eyes darken, his mouth turn down, his nostrils flare. This time she felt his opinion of her, his loathing of her kind.

He stepped close and breathed in hard through his nose. "I've always hated the stench so prevalent in humankind. It has a cloying, grasping quality, a desire for money above everything—the same reason you've bound me with a chain around my neck."

"I think we understand each other pretty well now, don't you? So let's just get on with finding the weapon."

Adrien thrust his fingers into his hair and turned in a circle. She felt his rage and his frustration as the chain all but thumped against her neck.

He turned on her and for a long moment as he stood over her, she felt his desire to strike her down, to slam her into the floor. Although her heart rate had skyrocketed once more, she straightened her spine. "Killing me won't do you any good because you'll die as well."

He took deep breaths and finally calmed down. "This is Daniel's doing and you're just the fucking messenger, I know that. But I hate your opinion of my kind." He clenched his fists. "And I hate that the bastard finally found a way to force me to do his bidding."

"Daniel has asked you to go after the weapon before?"

Adrien shook his head. "No. He knew better than to ask."

"I see what it is. Through me, he has control of you now."

"Yes, and it's about as perfect a plan as he could have constructed. I can't go after him because I can't risk you dying—I'll die. And it's also true the other way around, especially since you're extremely vulnerable in our world, not hard to kill at all." He glanced around. "I need to check my security system and then I need to get armed."

He moved past her. "Come with me." He headed to the end of the hall.

She hurried after him knowing that if she didn't, the chain would tighten.

When he entered the living room, she saw him glance to his right, toward the front door. "Fuck."

"What?"

"My security system has been compromised."

Lily glanced at the panel by the door and saw that not one light was on. "You mean it's off? Right now?"

"Yep. Stay with me. My weapons are over here." He headed across the room behind a long dark leather couch, in the direction of a partially opened door.

Lily thought she saw something move inside the room

just as Adrien hurried inside. She heard a shout and a loud thump. By the time she reached the doorway, Adrien was struggling with another man on the floor, a man who wore some kind of long, hooded black robe, something a monk might wear.

She saw a blade flash. The chains began to tug at her, pulling her forward, but she held her ground.

"Lily," Adrien called to her, but not from the floor.

At first she didn't understand.

"Lily, over here by the fireplace."

Slowly, she shifted her gaze. There Adrien stood, *another Adrien,* straining in the direction of the mantel but unable to move.

Two Adriens.

"I need my weapons," he shouted. "Step into the room, toward me. Help me. For God's sake help me or we'll both die."

Shock held Lily immobile.

There were two Adriens.

Two.

How the hell was that possible, in this world or any world? Kiernan hadn't told her about this.

"Lily!" he shouted.

The desperation in his voice broke the spell and she darted forward, positioning herself midway between the battling pair on the floor and the second Adrien struggling toward the fireplace.

The chain released him and he immediately jerked forward to the painting over the fireplace, pulled it away from the wall, then punched in a code to what proved to be a safe. But grunting sounds from the floor shifted her gaze to his other self on the floor.

The dagger flashed once more in the dim light from a nearby window.

The assailant rolled Adrien onto his back and pressed

a dagger to his neck. Adrien battled to keep the sharp point from breaking skin.

She glanced in the direction of the fireplace. The second Adrien withdrew a chain, weighted at both ends, from the safe.

He blurred back to the assailant and, from behind, caught him around the neck, tightening as he pulled. The prone version of Adrien now grabbed the wrist holding the dagger, keeping the assailant's hand immobile as the chain did its work.

Lily held her fingers to her lips and watched as life left the stranger, all three bodies locked in battle.

Adrien held both parts of himself still as he focused on finishing the job.

The room was horribly quiet except for the faint rustle of clothing as the assailant struggled to get free, a fish flailing in a net.

After what seemed like an eternity, he grew limp, but still Adrien held the chain around his neck, taking the kill to its limit, making certain of death. After what seemed like an hour, he let the body fall to the floor.

Adrien re-formed, the two beings drawing together in a swift, almost invisible rush of movement, reshaping to the self prone on the floor. Another shock to her system.

He sat up, sweat pouring from him, dripping off his forehead, soaking his shirt, the dead vampire at his feet.

It was all so horrible.

He sat there for a long moment, his arms braced around his knees, his gaze fixed straight ahead, the battle chain dangling from his left hand. She remembered seeing him in two places and tried to understand the dual parts, how they might have functioned.

She stared down at the corpse on the floor. "He's dead." Such a stupid thing to say.

Adrien nodded, his gaze falling to the body as well, a frown between his brows. His lips sagged at each corner.

"I don't exactly know how to process that there were two of you and that you just killed a man. In front of me."

His gaze shot back to hers. "You mean that I just saved your life."

"And your own. This is monstrous, Adrien."

His gaze hardened. "You call this monstrous? Your race is so arrogant."

"Arrogant? We don't move in packs and destroy entire neighborhoods of innocent families."

"No, you build armies and destroy nations."

She put a hand to her chest. "I don't build armies."

He glared at her. "And I don't move in packs. My brothers and I police those fucking packs whenever we can. I give up my life every goddamn night hunting them down and slaughtering those of my kind that threaten the secrecy of our world. Or I did until Daniel gained control of the Council and threw all three of us in prison."

Lily stared at him. She knew so little of his world that it shocked her to hear him speak of policing rogue vampires. She wanted to think she might have misjudged things, but the tips of his fangs showed and she shuddered.

He gained his feet, sweat dripping down his face. He once more wiped his sleeve over his forehead. "Shit."

He moved past her, crossing to his desk. He unplugged his iPhone from the power source, tapped it a few times, and said simply, "I've had a security breach and I need cleanup." He didn't even state an address.

He pressed another button and slid the phone into the pocket of his jeans. "They'll be here in a few seconds, flying in. Just be prepared."

On instinct, Lily moved in his direction. Maybe because he felt her sudden anxiety, he drew close as well but maintained a slight, careful separation.

A split second later two young men arrived carrying a stretcher between them.

"That was fast," she murmured.

"Yeah. Phones have helped. We have a much quicker response time now."

One of them glanced at Adrien. "We're getting the security system fixed."

"Thank you. What the fuck happened?"

"Our whole system crashed about half an hour ago."

"You were hacked."

"Looks like."

Adrien scowled as he glanced at Lily. She was pretty sure she could read his mind on this one.

"You were right," she said.

"Then you'd better get ready to fight hard for the fortune you're after. This nightmare has just started."

One of the young men turned to Adrien. "Does this mean that you and your brothers are free? I mean, did Daniel release all of you?"

"No, not yet."

"I'm glad you're out. We've had a lot of problems with rogues, and some of the seedier clubs have gotten out of control. Your presence has been missed."

Adrien nodded but said nothing more.

Offering one last bow in Adrien's direction, the two men, with the corpse on the stretcher between them, glanced at each other, then moved swiftly into altered flight and disappeared from the apartment.

Adrien swiped at his forehead. "I've gotta shower again. Sorry. Then we probably should make some plans."

Lily held her arms folded tightly over her chest. She trembled, but she didn't want Adrien to see her this upset. She needed to toughen up if she hoped to see Josh again— and yet a man, even if he was a vampire, had just died in front of her.

With the short fighting chain dangling from his hand, Adrien crossed in front of her and headed in his long stride out of the office. She moved fast to keep up.

Once more he crossed the top of the living room. He paused to glance at the security panel by the door. Lily saw that the lights were now on, which apparently satisfied Adrien because he moved swiftly back down the long dark hall. He dipped into his bedroom, then returned with what looked like another shirt and jeans. He opened what proved to be, just as Lily had suspected, the second door to the black marble bathroom.

When he went inside, Lily stopped at the threshold. The dimensions of the room, though large, didn't exceed the capacity of the shared chains, so she said, "I'll be right outside."

He nodded, his expression still grim. When he started to unbutton his jeans, she quickly closed the door. She really didn't need to catch another glimpse of all his maleness.

She sank to the carpet next to the door, drew her knees up to her chest, and slung her arms around her legs.

Tears burned her eyes.

This was all too much.

She'd never seen a man killed before and if she hadn't had the presence of mind to move when Adrien needed her to move, well, she'd be dead and Kiernan would probably dispose of Josh as an asset that had lost its value.

She took deep breaths and arched her neck to stare up at the tall ceiling, at least what she could see of it. Her eyes had adjusted but the hall was very dark. A distant glow from the living room's front window provided the only illumination. The Paris apartment, while beautiful, had odd angles and fairly small windows.

Kiernan had told her that once she shared the blood-chain with Adrien, she would start siphoning his natural vampire powers. She might see better in the dark, hear better, and have a sense of his emotions, possibly even gain increased physical strength. She'd also be able to bring her tracking ability online; if she focused on the weapon, over the next few days she would develop the ability to see its location anywhere on earth just by thinking about it.

She tried it out now, thinking about the extinction weapon, but nothing happened, not really, except for a small sense that she was reaching out for something by sending tendril-like thoughts outside herself. She focused once more, concentrating hard, but again felt just strange little tendrils without much effect.

She was queasy at the thought that she was this connected to one of the walking undead. Except vampires weren't exactly the undead; that was just part of her world's mythology. These vampires lived in all sizes of caverns, more a tribal culture than anything else. They shunned centralized organization, but it appeared the vampire Daniel was working hard to establish himself as a dictator. And wouldn't a weapon like the one she sought be exactly what a hopeful despot needed to consolidate his power?

And every time Adrien spoke Daniel's name, rage boiled from him, a dark, deep hatred for the man who, by all appearances, intended to enslave his world. She could hardly blame Adrien for that.

Everything was in almost pitch blackness—which reflected exactly how she felt right now. She felt the pressure of the dark around her, the proverbial rock-and-a-hard-place.

Probably more than anything, she needed to come to terms with Adrien. He was so angry. Every breath he took vibrated with rage. Of course he had reason, since he'd been chained up and tortured for a year, and his brothers were still there. Yet she sensed there was something else eating at him, something that went very deep and probably had to do with Daniel.

And Adrien was four hundred years old and Daniel five times that, figures that still boggled her mind. The vampire world was long-lived. Adrien had had centuries to stoke the fires of his hatred for a man like Daniel.

CHAPTER 3

Adrien loved his Paris shower. He'd had the head mounted high to compensate for his height, and the strong water pressure really stripped the dirt away—or in this case the sweat. He leaned back and let the warm water flow over his hair, his forehead, nose, and chin.

Beautiful.

Other sensations struck.

He'd killed yet another fellow vampire.

He was tired of killing his own kind, but he and his brothers had been serving his world for centuries doing just that. When vampires followed the wrong path and hurt other vampires or humans, he stepped in, as both Lucian and Marius did, and others they'd trained through the decades.

The problem in his culture was simple: His kind valued individual liberty above everything, which left the whole society vulnerable to despots like Daniel. Self-direction was so prized among his species that few strong, supportable laws had been instituted to protect good citizens from those who practiced evil.

There were even heresies abroad that had so perverted the essential law of their world that those who killed humans were now being elevated in rank in certain secret societies, offered medals and prized cave dwellings for taking human life.

As he rinsed the battle-sweat off his body, he turned his mind to the here-and-now. He was in Paris after having been imprisoned for a year. His thoughts turned quickly to Lucian and Marius. He had to get them out, but if he made the attempt, and Lily got hurt or died, he'd be dead.

One final rinse and he shut the water off. He could have stayed in a lot longer; the filth he'd lived with was still too sharp in his memory. But one assassin might be followed by another or several. At least his security system was back on full force.

He toweled off in brisk movements.

So who sent the assassin? A number of sects existed throughout his world, each led by a different spiritual guide. But the largest group of fanatics followed an Ancestral called Silas, a vampire of tremendous ambition, perhaps even close to Daniel's level. Silas shared something in common with Daniel: He didn't hesitate to kill anyone if it meant furthering his ambitions.

So, yes, he would guess Silas had initiated this attack.

He stepped into a clean pair of jeans and slid a black tee over his head. He was tugging on the sleeves at the shoulders, adjusting them, when a stomach cramp gripped him hard.

Oh, shit. He didn't really want to do this, but now he had no choice.

"Lily," he called out. "I'm going to need blood, dammit!"

* * *

As Adrien appeared in the doorway, Lily saw that he was trembling, all the way from his shoulders to the tips of his fingers. She'd been warned by Kiernan of the effects of blood deprivation on the vampire, and here they were in plain view.

Another tremor.

Something was wrong.

Thunder rolled over the city and suddenly a spattering of rain hit the windows.

He winced suddenly and bent over at the waist. Through the chains, she sensed his stomach knotting as though in pain. "What's wrong?" she asked, but she already knew. Oh, dear God, how was she supposed to do what so obviously needed doing?

He rose up, breathing hard. "Time's come, Lily. I need blood and if you can't deliver it, I've got to take care of business right now. I've got to get someone. They kept us blood-starved."

Thunder rumbled overhead again and a flash of lightning brightened the cloudy October sky.

He lowered his chin and held her gaze in a hard grip, his nostrils flaring. "I'm talking sex here as well. I've gone too long without both and it's almost impossible in a situation like this to take blood but hold back the other. Do you understand?"

He took a couple of steps toward her, and she took two steps back. Her heart pounded in her chest. His gaze fell to her throat; fangs appeared.

The wall of closets hit her back. The Eiffel Tower winked through the rain now hitting the windows. She tried to tell him no, but the words wouldn't leave her mouth.

"What will it be? I'll call someone, but you'll have to watch."

"I hate this."

"Ditto."

He trembled now and his color looked really bad. His eyes had a wild look.

She almost told him to use his phone right now, to call a donor, but she couldn't. She'd desired him from the first, maybe even from the first time she'd seen a photo of him. And she was so lonely, so grief-stricken, that some sick parted of her wanted this and wanted it now.

He must have taken her hesitation as a yes, or maybe he couldn't help himself, but the next moment he moved so fast she hardly saw him. She cried out as he caught her around the waist. His mouth covered hers as his tongue penetrated her deep. She could feel him hard against her belly.

Was she really doing this? Really letting a vampire take her blood and her body?

She hated him, hated his kind for taking her family from her, and hated herself for wanting him right now.

He lifted her in his arms and carried her to the bed. He was shaking head-to-foot, and the chains told her just how out of control he was. He laid her out on her back. "I can still call someone, but I don't want to. I want you, Lily, and I want you now." His arms, planted on either side of her, trembled.

But in that moment, maybe because even in his over-wrought state he'd given her a choice, a wave of desire crashed over her, something that had been building since she'd first seen him in the cavern, in the vision before he'd been tortured, looking like a proud stallion, facing up to the pain to come.

Her breasts ached and she felt so swollen and needy between her legs that she let out a harsh cry. "I'm here," she all but shouted.

Lightning flashed from the small windows on either side of the bed and thunder rolled as he landed on top of her. She had a brief glimpse of fangs as another flash lit the room.

She turned, exposing her neck, and he used a hand to pin her head so that she couldn't move. He struck quickly, puncturing her vein, a brief slice of pain that disappeared the moment he began to suck in quick, heavy, starved pulls.

She could feel his desperation but the more he took, the more her body grew lax, melting into the down-filled silk. She wanted her clothes off since her body had lit on fire, burning deep.

She hadn't had sex in all this time, not since her family disappeared from her life. And sex was all that she wanted right now, the relief of it, the physical pounding.

Fierce sex, even with a vampire.

Adrien took fire down his throat. He rarely drank from humans, but on the rare occasion he did, it had never been like this—as though each drop carried the source of all life.

He wanted more, so much more. He wanted to drink her down tonight, tomorrow night, and every night after that. He wanted the flavor of her blood on his tongue when he woke up in the evening and the last thing in the early-morning hours when he went to bed.

His blood-starvation had made his mind a cauldron of disjointed thoughts, of profound need.

He heard her cries and moans and didn't care if he was hurting her. The hungry shifts of her legs rubbed his cock, stroking him, helping him to know that all he needed would soon follow.

He ached into his groin, a gathering of twelve months of frustration and despair. He knew that what was about to happen, especially with his blood-need satisfied, might just shake the foundation of the earth.

At last, he slowed his drinking and began to secrete the potion that would heal the fang-wounds in minutes. The same potion also carried a chemical that speeded up red cell production to replenish the supply. He'd be taking more from this human in the coming hours, the least he deserved on behalf of his kind for the wreckage her kind spewed over his world.

As he drew back, he saw her in the glow of his vision. Her pupils were dilated and her lips dark and swollen. Good. She was sexed up and ready, because what was about to come wouldn't be a gentle coupling.

"I hate you for what you are," she shouted. Her hand whipped toward his face, ready to strike, but with his usual speed he caught her hand before she connected.

He leaned down and put his lips on her mouth then drew back. "Can you taste your blood?"

Her tongue made an appearance. She winced at the taste, but her body undulated with more need.

He lifted up, holding her gaze, and stripped off his shirt.

She looked up at his chest and cried out, then her hands clawed him, her nails dragging over his skin, scraping long strips. She leaned up and took a nipple in her mouth, sucking hard.

He groaned and with one hand took off his jeans, a real test of his skill as he hovered above her, and let her suck and bite him.

Her arms wrapped around his neck to hold her steady. He started working her clothes off her, peeling away her pants and her shirt as she kicked off her shoes.

As he fell on top of her, he plundered her mouth. Her nails found his back this time and each scrape hardened him one degree more. He grunted his approval, thrusting his tongue heavily into her mouth.

He pushed her legs apart with his knees. She cried out

against his mouth as his cock found her entrance and he began to push.

The human was tight, but she shoved her hips against him, forcing him in deeper.

He needed to calm the fuck down.

Her hands roved his body, rubbing up and down his biceps, which flexed beneath her touch.

"You're so wet." And tight. My God she was tight. She hadn't been used in a long time. He hoped to hell he wasn't hurting her, but nothing in the chains told him she was feeling any pain as her body undulated beneath him and against him.

He began to push into her in short thrusts. His balls were so ready.

"Do it, Adrien. I can feel that you're ready and I'm ready. Do it."

He gave a cry and thrust into her hard, pulled back and thrust again. His hips took over, and every stroke was like a lightning strike of pleasure along his cock.

He heard her crying out and could feel her tight orgasm pulling on him as the release came, what he'd been aching for during his captivity, to be inside a woman and feeling all her flesh as his cock jerked inside her and his beautiful come filled her.

He barely heard her cries of ecstasy as he shouted his pleasure. But he could feel that she was coming again, her hips matching his thrusts.

Even though he'd come, he could stay hard for a good long time, and given the length of his celibacy he was pretty sure he could release again, so he kept working her body. He leaned down and kissed her, which somehow lit her up and she arched once more. He drove hard and fast, bringing her yet again so that she screamed in ecstasy.

The rain still beat on the windows and as another flash

of lightning and roll of thunder shook his Paris apartment, she came, crying out, a sound that matched his shouts and groans as he released into her again.

"Get off me," Lily said, her voice hoarse. How many times had she screamed while he'd brought her, but now she wanted him off her and out of her.

Adrien pulled out and flipped over on his back, throwing an arm over his forehead.

She turned on her side, away from him as a few tears leaked from her eyes, tears of dismay and rage that she'd enjoyed giving up her blood to a vampire, that she'd taken pleasure from his body repeatedly.

She hated herself for having been weak with him—but mostly she blamed the chains because from the first her attraction to him had worked on her, building her to the point that the moment he came at her needy and trembling, she'd lost her will to refuse him.

She should have insisted on a donor. He'd even suggested it and yet she'd remained mute, unable to tell him to get someone else. Her lack of willpower disgusted her. She wasn't a person to give in so easily to lust and yet she had, almost as though the chains had stolen her ability to choose anything but him.

The tears tickled over the bridge of her nose. She swiped at her face, still breathing hard from the sheer gymnastic quality of the joining.

She felt the bed tip and shift and glanced over her shoulder.

Adrien had shifted to sit on the edge of the bed and now had his phone in hand.

She stared at his back, her vision warming up because of the chains, despite the lack of lighting in the room. He had bloody streaks where she'd scored him and the sight made her smile grimly, a small satisfaction that she'd hurt him, if only a little, while he'd plowed into her.

She watched Adrien's shoulders rise and fall. He'd taken a deep breath. "I need to ask you something. Have you tried to use your tracking ability yet? Now that we're chain-bound, that ability should start coming to life."

Oh, that. "I tried it earlier. I have to say nothing much happened." She explained about the sensation of tendrils leaving her.

"I've heard it described that way. Well, just keep trying at different times. I'm sure it'll improve as we go along." He was silent for a moment, then said, "I'm going to make a phone call to a man named Rumy, a friend, a good friend, though he's well connected to our underworld. He owns a place called The Erotic Passage in the Como system, Italy, on the lake by the same name. I think it's the right place to start. If anyone knows anything, it'll be Rumy." He was silent, his head bent as though staring at his phone. "Is that okay with you?"

"You're asking my permission?"

He turned to look at her. She was surprised by how much better he looked. Her blood really had helped. "Neither of us is happy about our situation. I get that. But I want to get along with you. We'll need to work together."

"You're right and yes, please call this Rumy person."

He nodded and drew the phone in front of him, then after a moment to his ear.

"I need to talk to Rumy. Tell him it's Adrien." She couldn't hear what the other person said, but she could feel Adrien's sudden anger through the shared chain. "Get him on the damn phone or I'll come over there and twist your head off that scrawny neck of yours." Another pause, then, "That's better. Thank you."

Silence as he waited.

Rumy and The Erotic Passage. What a name for a club, but then what else should she have expected from a world of bloodsuckers.

After a moment, she heard Adrien talking quietly to the one he called Rumy. There was some laughter, chatting, queries about health, about the prison, a few jibes, the usual masculine nonsense.

Lily's thoughts turned to Josh, and she lifted the chain to her lips. Josh, her firstborn, the last of her family. Was he truly alive? How many times had she wondered if Kiernan had somehow fabricated the phone call, using the memory of her son to manipulate her into taking on this mission?

But she couldn't have mistaken her son's voice. She would have known it anywhere. He'd called out, "Mom? Is that you? Mom!" He'd wailed after that.

She clapped her hands over her ears, trying not to hear that sound, a pitiful, bellowing wail. She had to get to him. Had to find him.

She heard Adrien sigh. Her desperate thoughts about Josh disappeared, and her present reality returned.

Adrien rose from the bed, flinging his phone onto the comforter. "You need to get cleaned up and dressed." He walked to the bathroom, but the chain tugged, so she sat up, leaning toward him. Damn this chain for its short leash.

He reached inside the room and the next moment he flung a washcloth at her, which she put between her legs.

So far sex was just as messy with a vampire as with a human male, a thought that did nothing to ease her temper.

"You finished glaring at me?" he snapped.

"Sure, for now." She lifted her chin. "What's the plan? Does Rumy know where the weapon is?"

"No, but he suggested we check out a local Paris dive first." He moved past the foot of the bed, snatched her clothes off the floor, and flung these at her as well.

"What are you so pissed about?" She put on her bra and shirt, then scooted to the end of the bed, her jeans now in her lap.

"Can't I be angry, like you're angry right now? Or do you suppose I can't tell that you're mad?"

"I think you just had sex and took some of my blood, so I don't know what you have to complain about."

"You enjoyed this." He gestured with a slice of his hand toward the bed. "Your voice is still raspy from all the moaning and screaming."

As she slid off the opposite side of the bed from where he stood, she turned to face him. "And I suppose you think I should be grateful to you for giving me a halfway decent ride."

"Halfway decent?"

She lifted one brow then shrugged. She didn't know why she was poking the bear, but he didn't have to look so damn smug.

She moved in the direction of the bathroom only to have the chain give a tug because he stood too far away. She didn't turn toward him as she said, "Will you please cut me some slack? Literally."

"No."

She stood bare-assed and humiliated, her jeans in her hands. The proximity that the chains required wouldn't even allow her a decent exit. Lifting her chin, she pivoted in his direction and waited for him to move so that she could.

His eyes glittered in the dark, although her vision once more warmed up the space, an effect of the chains, and he stood in full, naked relief watching her keenly. "First, I don't like this any more than you do and I suppose I don't owe you this, but I was raised to have some manners, so here goes: Thank you for giving up your lifeblood to me. You may have just saved my life, and I have no doubt you kept me from a bout of painful blood-madness. Thank you." His nostrils still flared and his jaw ground his molars a couple of times.

Lily fought back the words because she really didn't want to say them, but they slipped past her lips anyway. "You're welcome."

"Fine. Now here's the slack you wanted." The moment he stepped in her direction, she turned and moved swiftly into the hall, then into the bathroom.

CHAPTER 4

Half an hour later Adrien's temper had eased a little as he flew Lily slowly in the direction of the Paris club called La Nuit, or The Night. He was still angry that he'd been forced to use his captor for his blood-and-sex needs, and even more so because she was human. But the chains had made the whole aftermath worse because he'd felt her humiliation, which then triggered a sense of guilt about the whole damn thing.

As for La Nuit, the club had a bad reputation.

Hundreds of vampires around the world owned profitable businesses, open at night to serve the clubbing clientele and to give those vampires disposed to either having fun at a night scene, or tasting humans, the opportunity to do so.

Paris had a few clubs, running the gamut from chic to seedy. And there was at least one sex club he and his brothers had raided, freeing a number of human slaves each time.

A variety of enthrallment skills kept the vampire clubs

below the radar. Adrien often marveled that more incidences of vampire world exposure didn't occur given how much interaction there actually was between the species.

Adrien had never cared much for the human-oriented clubs, since he preferred his kind, but there were many vampires who'd acquired a taste for human blood and sought it regularly.

And he had to admit that after Lily's blood, he understood why. He still didn't get it totally, though. He'd tasted humans before, once as an experiment but more often than not when he was stuck out in the world, policing some extremist group, and couldn't get back to his kind for days on end. So yeah, he'd tasted human blood, but between his prejudice against the greedy human race and the usually weak nature of the blood, he'd never once been tempted to go back.

Now all he could think about was sinking his fangs into Lily's neck again, or into other more exotic regions, and taking her once more. Desire rippled through him, but he clamped it down. The damn chains would expose him if he kept it up.

He'd been furious with Lily after the blooding, but only because the whole experience had left him craving more.

And the bonding chains weren't helping, because each hour he stayed bound to her, he grew more sensitive to what she was feeling at any given moment. Sure, she felt a mountain of rage against the vampire world, but laced through her fury ran ribbons of pure desire, something that happened just about every time she looked at him.

He wasn't exactly surprised. He knew what he looked like and he pumped iron to keep himself fit, so he understood her interest in the same way that her toned body, narrow waist, and full breasts kept his cock in a state of inappropriate movement.

As he flew her slowly in the direction of La Nuit,

therefore, he focused on what he might find at the club. He packed a Glock beneath his leather coat, along with a couple of fighting chains and a dagger. He was sufficiently armed, but his greater concern was for Lily, keeping her alive if things went south, remaining free enough to move given the short functioning length of the blood-chains.

He set up a disguising cloak as he dropped to earth in a darkened side street and set Lily to walking as soon as he touched down. He said in a low voice, "Movement helps give the impression we've been here as the disguise dissipates."

"I figured."

Well, she didn't lack for intelligence. He'd give her that.

"You feel queasy or anything?" he asked, because he didn't sense anything from her.

"My head hurts a little, but otherwise I'm fine."

"Good. And remember, if this gets ugly—"

"I've got it, Adrien. I'm to find a place to hide, preferably beneath a table or something. But do you really think we'll face fanatics at this place?"

The club he took Lily to catered to the darker elements of the city. Rumors of drugs and rival gangs made it the last place he'd usually take a woman, even a human.

His size helped. As he led Lily into the club, the crowd parted for him. He went straight to the bar and spoke to the bartender in French, asking to speak with Rumy's friend Hardesty.

The bartender jerked his head to Adrien's left. Across the room, Adrien saw a bouncer, similar in size to Adrien. Taking Lily's hand, he wended his way through the smoky room and among about a dozen tall round tables until he stood chest-to-chest with a vampire he'd never met before.

"I need to see Hardesty. Rumy sent me."

The bouncer glared, but extended his fist to the door he protected. He rapped three times with his knuckles, never once taking his eye off Adrien.

"Entrez."

The bouncer opened the door and let them into another smoky room. Lily coughed and waved her hand through the air.

When the door closed, a tall thin man sat down in a chair near the fireplace but said nothing.

"Rumy said I should see you, that you might have information. Are you Hardesty?"

A slight inclination of the head. The vampire took a drag on a cigarette then released a thin stream of smoke. "What is the famous Adrien doing in my club? This is the kind of establishment you're usually famous for shutting down." His accent was British.

"I have no complaint with you, or any club that keeps our world safe. You've never crossed that line."

"You and your brothers continue to perform this tireless service, but aren't you weary of battling forces bigger than yourselves? Daniel owns the Council now, and I've always had the feeling he's been intent on opening up our world to human interaction for a long time."

"Daniel will only do what he believes will benefit him. Right now, I don't think he's prepared to go that far."

Hardesty glanced past Adrien. "You have a woman with you. A human. That's singular. Let me see her."

"She is of no concern to you."

But Hardesty's gaze fell to the chain at Adrien's neck. Though he had it tucked inside his shirt so that only a small portion showed, Hardesty laughed. "What has happened to you that you got bound to a human? Never mind. I see the whole thing unfolding in front of me because last I heard you and your brothers were hanging from Himalayan chains. Lucian and Marius still there?"

Adrien ground his back teeth together. He didn't like or trust Hardesty, and he sure as hell didn't want to get into a chat about his recent imprisonment. "I need information."

Hardesty rose, pulling in a long drag as he did so. He moved to the side of the chair as well, farther into the room, his gaze fixed on Lily.

Adrien felt a growl form at the back of his throat. His breathing grew ragged. For a skinny bastard, Hardesty was being damn aggressive.

Hardesty lifted both hands. "Ease down, vampire. I only want to have a look. I guess the chains really do work, because I know how much you despise humans."

Adrien stepped back beside Lily and slid his arm around her waist. The emotions that pummeled him right now, both his own and Lily's, made it tough to concentrate. Maybe because her blood was inside him or maybe because he'd taken her to bed—but whatever the case, he hated the way Hardesty looked her over.

He felt her hand on his arm, gliding up and down. She turned into him; that much he registered. "Adrien, what's going on with you?" He heard her voice, but he couldn't make sense of what she'd said. He felt his fangs on his lower lips. What the hell was happening to him?

She got in front of him and placed her hands on his chest. "Hey! Can you hear me?"

He met her gaze, staring into her large hazel eyes. He might have blinked a few times; he wasn't sure. "Lily?"

"You kinda got lost there for a minute. What's with the fangs? Pull 'em in, would you? You're kinda freaking me out here."

Adrien kept looking at her, partly because she calmed him, partly because he didn't want to look anywhere else. He focused on breathing. He had to do better than this or these primal, uncontrollable feelings would put them both in danger.

"I can get rid of those chains, if you want."

Lily turned in Hardesty's direction, but Adrien slipped his arms around her, drawing her closer still. She seemed to understand because she didn't protest. "What's involved?" she asked.

"About half a million dollars. You got that kind of money?"

Lily nodded.

She did? Adrien's hold on her relaxed.

Hardesty smiled. "Anytime you bring me the money, I can break the bond on the chains."

Adrien felt relief swell through Lily so profound that it left him dizzy. "I want nothing more than that," she said. "But for now, Adrien and I have to stick together."

At that, Hardesty paced in front of his chair, still smoking. He looked like the kind of vampire who never put a cigarette down.

"So you're after something else, then. Rumy only sends me vampires in trouble, but it will cost you, whatever it is that you need from me."

"We need information about the extinction weapon."

At that, Hardesty grew very still, including the ever-moving cigarette. Only his gaze shifted, from one to the next then back to finally land on Adrien. "You want to know the whereabouts of the rumored weapon? You? Doesn't make sense." He started pacing, smoking, and continuing to talk, "Unless of course you're under duress. That can be the only reason. Daniel?"

Adrien said nothing. As did Lily.

"I wouldn't give up my reasons, either. So what's in it for me?"

"How much do you want?" Lily asked.

"More than you can give."

"I've got a lot."

"Have you got half a billion?"

"What?"

Adrien tensed up. Something wasn't right here. Once more he pulled Lily up against him, but this time kept his right hand free to retrieve his Glock. "What are you talking about, Hardesty? How the hell is anyone giving you half a billion?"

Hardesty laughed. "Wishful thinking. I'd love half a billion. I'd retire to an island somewhere. The weather here has been dreadful this fall. So much rain in Paris."

"So do you know anything about the extinction weapon or not? Rumy seemed to think you might know something."

"What I know is pitifully small, about experiments done here, in at least one of the French cavern systems, in the north I think, a few decades ago. An accident left about half a dozen scientists dead so the Council shut down the whole operation, the papers burned, the equipment destroyed."

"What kind of accident?" Lily asked.

Hardesty shrugged. "I've never gotten any details. But there is one thing I've wanted to say to you, Adrien, for a long time. My animosity toward you isn't personal, but I have resented the policing work you and your brothers do."

Adrien glanced around the room and made several swift calculations: no windows, one door at the back, possible shielding to prevent altered flight through the walls.

"What's going on?"

"That half a billion I mentioned? Ownership in an Arizona casino, something new we're doing in the States, but it will involve some specialists, human, if you catch my drift. My partners will be glad for this night's work, and I'm going to have to send Rumy a thank-you card for accidentally sending you to me."

He couldn't quite read Lily's emotional state, but she

turned into him and half sobbed, half cried out as she slid her hand beneath his coat.

The door behind Adrien opened. He turned and saw the original bouncer enter with another big vampire. He watched as they reached for their weapons. Simultaneously, he slid his hand down his thigh and withdrew a dagger. If Lily hadn't decided to get hysterical, he could have reached for his Glock.

He took her with him as he backed up against the wall. When he saw a knife and two guns, he spun Lily around so that his body would have a chance to protect her once the gunfire started.

Everything happened so fast.

He heard the shots, one after the other, at least thirteen rounds in quick succession. He expected to feel the bullets slam into his back. Instead, he felt Lily pushing at his chest. At least she'd stopped screaming.

Turning around, however, he couldn't figure out what had happened. He saw that both the bouncers and Hardesty were down. Two of them still moaned. The newest vampire lay still with his eyes wide open, pupils dilated, blood coming out of his mouth.

He glanced down at Lily, who now saw what he realized was her handiwork. "Wait, you did this?"

"Yeah, I just had this feeling and went with it. But I think you'd better get us out of here. Now."

Shock held him immobile for about two more seconds. He tested his ability to pass through the door, or any other wall, but he couldn't. He reached down and pulled the dead vampire away from the door.

He shoved Lily through then followed after.

The club was small and he had to get outside and into the air quickly, before reinforcements arrived.

He turned toward the back hall and, pulling Lily against him, flew toward the back door. Once there, he kicked it wide and without looking back flew into the night sky, making a hard right, then spiraling high.

Lily hugged him hard. She shook, and his speed caused her pain, he could feel it.

Once they had passed above the Eiffel Tower and were nearly back to his apartment, he slowed down. He heard Lily moaning. Damn altered flight. Damn weak human.

He passed through his building, back into the hallway outside the bathroom.

As soon as he touched down, she dropped the Glock, ran to the toilet, and threw up.

He took off his coat and saw the bullet holes. She'd made Swiss cheese of some really fine, expensive leather. He had to admit, she'd been smart about the business because she'd caught all three vampires by complete surprise. He'd dropped his dagger the moment he'd turned to protect her with his body.

Without thinking, he started to head to his office to reload the Glock, but the chain snagged him and Lily cried out, "Hey. I can't move yet."

"Sorry," he called back.

He returned to sit down on the carpet outside the hall, setting the gun beside him. He pulled his knees up and rested his elbows on top but ended up with his head in his hands.

His world, his goddamn disorganized world. Lily had saved them both tonight with her smart shooting and quick thinking. With that much firepower aimed at him, he'd probably be dead, she'd be dead, and that would have been the end of the story.

Lily appeared next to him, wiping her face.

He looked up at her. "How's the head?"

She nodded. "More like a cantaloupe split into two parts instead of merely exploded. I guess that's better."

He stared at her wondering who the hell she was. "You saved our asses back there. I owe you one."

She met his gaze. "I wish we'd gotten more information than what Hardesty delivered."

"You still intend to go forward with this, even after almost getting killed?"

She met his gaze, her lips clamped together for a long moment, before responding. "Sure, why not?"

"You said something back there that doesn't make a lot of sense. Hardesty asked how much you had and you said *a lot*."

She didn't look at him as she responded, "Kiernan has a lot, but he wouldn't pay half a billion."

Adrien took hold of her wrist. "You have money, don't you?"

"I have some."

He narrowed his eyes at her. "Then, why?"

"None of your goddamn business, vampire."

Adrien frowned at her. He could tell she was lying about something, but what? Then again when it came to humans and greed, lying was part of the bargain.

"I need my clothes," she said. "My soap, shampoo. I can tell this little journey of ours is going to get messier by the second. Any chance I can get some of my stuff brought here from India?"

He stood up and pulled his cell out of his pocket. He made a phone call then glanced at Lily. "From the campsite?"

She nodded. "Everything." Then, "Please."

After he gave his instructions, he said, "You'll have your things in about half an hour. In the meantime—"

"Food," she said. "I can see how this is going to unfold for us and I'm starved. How about you? Oh, wait, you already had your meal." Her sarcasm dripped.

He returned her glare but he didn't rise to the bait. He

searched her gaze because he couldn't believe she'd just been in a shoot-out but seemed so calm.

He touched the chain at his neck and frowned at her. What he sensed was something like a profound determination to see her mission through, no matter what. For this split second, despite his general dislike of humans, he almost respected her.

Maybe he didn't understand her motivations, maybe she had some serious debts to pay, he didn't know, but she'd shown cool under pressure, she'd gotten them both out of an impossible situation alive, and instead of falling apart, she pressed on, asking only for food.

He led the way to the kitchen. Some of his staff had been by while they'd taken their jaunt to La Nuit. He had cheese, fruit, and bread in the fridge, so he pulled them out and set them on the counter.

Lily took up a bar stool and started to eat.

She didn't say anything, she didn't look at him, she just scowled at something unseen and chomped on slices of apple.

Lily ate in silence. She felt no particular need to make small talk with a vampire. Anyway, she doubted Adrien would want to talk and she sure as hell didn't feel like it.

She'd almost died tonight but felt strangely disconnected from that fact except for one thing, of course: her son.

The moment those two vampires had come into the room, guns in hand, she knew exactly what she meant to do and had positioned her hand on Adrien's Glock, all the while feigning a full-blown freak-out.

She'd been right that her squeals and sobs would distract the men, including Adrien, long enough to fire a few shots. Adrien turning her into the wall had been the perfect maneuver since she could fire through his coat without alerting either of the assailants.

She glanced at him now. He cut a slab of cheese, laid it on a slice of French bread, and shoved the whole thing in his mouth. She was still surprised to see a vampire eating regular food. His gaze skated past her, into the living room. He appeared to be thinking hard, maybe about their next move.

"Wait a minute, why did you turn your back to the room?"

He glanced at her, brows lifted. "To shield you. It was an instinctive response, but useless. Given the nature of the blood-chains, if I'd died, you would have as well."

"So you didn't turn because I had your gun?"

He shook his head. "I didn't know you'd taken it."

"Huh." She bit off another piece of apple and popped it in her mouth.

Josh liked apples and hated pears, couldn't stand the grainy feel of them in his mouth. Two years had passed. What had he eaten in that time? What had he been doing? Had he been cared for well enough? Kiernan had said that Josh had a caregiver, a human woman, so apparently he'd wanted Josh in one piece, but why? Of all the children in their neighborhood who had been killed that night, why had her son been spared, and provided with a caregiver?

This was the big question she'd been unable to answer. She was almost positive that taking Josh hadn't been random. She felt the purposefulness of it in every cell of her body.

Adrien reached forward and grabbed her wrist. "What are you thinking about? Right now? You feel sad to me."

She released a heavy sigh and pulled her arm away from him. "That my son liked apples."

"I'm sorry that your family died."

She glanced up at him, chewing slowly. "It doesn't change that vampires killed them."

"No. It doesn't."

"Why are you staring at me?"

"I'm trying to understand you, that's all."

She shrugged and cut a chunk of cheese, sliding it onto her tongue from the back of her knife. "What's the plan from here? I'm not sure I'd trust Rumy again, if I were you."

"He wouldn't have known what Hardesty was up to, but a casino in Arizona?"

"Your world seems hell-bent on exposing itself to my world. And it sure doesn't seem to like you very much."

"No, not much, at least not the parts intent on illegal and reprehensible transactions."

She snorted.

"Oh, that's right. We're vampires, so there can't be anything decent about my world."

"Pretty much."

"What do you base that on?"

"Oh, let's see. Your pal Daniel, who's been selling off property that belongs to your kind, Hardesty is a real peach, and you've already said that Rumy knows every slimy element to be found between Italy and Shanghai and all the way to New York. I have yet to meet a vampire I could admire. Then there's you, happily demanding my blood like it belongs to you, but that's a quality I've come to expect from your kind: Take, then maybe ask questions later."

He cut another slab of cheese, planted it on more sourdough, and shoved it in his mouth. After chewing and swallowing he said, "You screamed a few times, if I remember, and you weren't exactly in pain."

She offered a half smile as she said, "Just like a man to make a big deal about his cock when he hasn't got much else to offer."

He rounded the bar and before she knew what he meant to do, he'd hauled her off her seat and pulled her against him. She tried to push out of his arms, but he was too damn strong. He started sucking on her neck and grinding his hips into her.

Damn the vampire!

The chain vibrated heavily against her throat. She could feel his desire like flames against her skin, and his lust ignited her own. But she struggled against all the sensations—of her incomprehensible desire for him, her lust, her need, which seemed to be multiplying as each hour met the next.

When he kissed her, she bit his lower lip, drawing blood.

He drew back, but his eyes had darkened and instead of releasing her, he settled in on her neck again, suckling and plucking, licking along her vein.

At some point her hands stopped pushing at him and instead her fingers kneaded the flesh of his arms, tugging at his biceps that flexed at her touch. He plastered himself against her, his hips undulating slowly. Her breathing grew shallow and her eyes closed; maybe they rolled back in her head.

When he kissed her this time, she let him, despite the blood on his lips.

His tongue dove deep as he rocked his pelvis against hers, the hard length of his cock rolling over her flesh, working her into a frenzy. Her moans filled the air.

She hated him, but she wanted him desperately.

She was about to suggest they return to the bedroom when he let her go. She fell back, almost making it onto the stool, but because her limbs had loosened she slid off and fell to the floor, landing on her butt.

She sat there, looking up at him.

He lifted a harsh eyebrow. "And sometimes, human, a cock is the only thing a woman wants."

He rounded the bar. As she rose to her feet, she watched

him slap another slab of cheese on yet another slice of bread and stuff the whole thing in his big fat mouth.

Damn vampire.

Adrien washed up the plates, packed up the fruit, cheese, and bread, all while Lily sat on her stool and glared at him.

He ignored her. He hoped he'd made his point that for all her complaints about *his kind,* she wanted him.

The trouble was, he ran hot for her as well, hotter than made any logical sense despite the blood-chains they shared. If she glared, he responded in kind, because the last thing he wanted was to desire his captor.

The chains, essentially, had become a nightmare of sensation. He felt worn out, and the hour was just a few minutes past midnight. And they still had work to do.

His brothers came to mind, his driving need to bust them out of that Himalayan hellhole. But how? If he failed to produce the extinction weapon, Daniel would have them killed, he was sure of it.

Even if he could find the damn thing, though, how could he ever turn a machine like that over to Daniel, the vampire without a conscience, the one who would sell his soul for just one more brick of gold?

His phone rang.

He reached into his pocket, pulled it out, and checked the screen. Rumy.

He thought for a moment, then answered, saying nothing.

"Adrien, you there?"

"Rumy." He didn't say anything more than that. He needed to hear the man's voice, hear his inflection to determine the level of the man's guilt. Had Rumy helped out at La Nuit?

He met Lily's gaze. The glare had turned into a suspicious scowl, a perfect reflection of how he felt.

Rumy cleared his throat. "Hardesty just called. He's still alive. I've sent a few visitors to his bar for what he just pulled on you, I want you to know that. He'll be shut down for weeks."

"Okay."

"His bouncer's dead. That might be payment enough for the incident."

"I'm weeping in my beer, Rumy, big salty tears."

Rumy laughed. "Just wanted you to know I had no hand in this."

"I didn't think so. You value your skin too much to make an enemy of me."

"Don't I know it. So, did Hardesty give up anything usable?"

"He mentioned a connection to one of the northern cavern systems, here in France. Know anything about it?"

"No, not really. You thinking about going up there?"

"Maybe. Not sure." One of his favorite tribes lived in the northernmost system, called Trevayne, but he didn't like the idea of introducing a human into their world. The more private cave tribes, usually located at a distance from human cities, lived quiet tribal existences with deep, layered shields to keep humans at bay, and essentially never allowed humans inside. They held more traditional values and often had a number of children in their midst, babes they protected with a vengeance.

If it weren't for the chains, he'd head north right now, without taking Lily along, to see what he could dig up about the extinction weapon. The vampires who lived at Trevayne had inhabited that system a long time and probably knew every inch of the tunnels. If experiments had been done, any attempts made, secretly or otherwise, to concoct a killing machine, someone would know about it. There might even be evidence, or a lead to another location.

"I've been asking around," Rumy said, "as casually as

I can, about the weapon. If you do head up there, you need to see Sebastien. You know him, right?"

"I do. He's a good man."

"Word is, he was on the Council of Ancestrals fifty years ago when they shut the whole thing down. Unfortunately, that's all I've got for you right now. But if I catch wind of anything, I'll let you know. Is it true you've got a woman with you, a human, a tracker, and you're blood-chain-bound?"

"No one's business."

"Understood. But there's one more thing. You might have trouble with our fanatic element. A couple of my spies tell me those rumors are making the rounds as well—that there's a hit out on you."

No shit.

Adrien didn't see any point in telling Rumy about the assassin who had already visited his apartment. Besides, the less real information out there, about him or about Lily, the better.

"Unless there's anything else . . ." He let the words hang.

"Take care of that soft hide of yours, vampire."

Adrien chuckled as he ended the call, returning his phone to his pants pocket.

"Soft hide?" Lily asked.

He glanced at her. "Wait, did you hear the entire phone call?"

"Sure. He was talking loud enough."

"No. He wasn't. Not for human ears." Absently, he touched the chain at his neck. "How's your vision?"

She glanced around. "Huh. There are no lights on but I can see everything, like there's a soft glow in the room. Well, Kiernan warned me that I might siphon some of your powers. I guess your hearing and being able to see in the dark are coming along nicely for me."

"You want the chains off? Hardesty isn't the only one who can do it."

"You mentioned that before, but the truth is as much as I'd love to be rid of this unwelcome connection to you, I want to fulfill my mission more. To get the extinction weapon, then to get the hell out of your world."

He felt it again, something she held back, something big. "What's going on, Lily? What aren't you telling me?"

She shifted her gaze back to him, more glaring. "None of your goddamn business, vampire. Need-to-know, remember?"

He settled his forearms on the bar and slid forward in her direction, getting up in her face. "You ever going to trust me?"

Her eyes widened. "Hell, no. You're a vampire. You going to trust me?"

He snorted and drew back. "Not in a million years."

"I'll be dead in about sixty, so it would never really be an issue for you, even if we were stuck for life."

"No, I guess not." He leaned back. He felt a tremor go through him, and his stomach cramped, so he turned away from the bar.

Shit, he'd be needing blood again soon. The starvation level demanded that he refill several times in the coming hours. Once his body had gotten a taste, and knew a supply was near, the cravings would demand replenishment often, especially given current stress levels.

He drew air in through his nose and shuddered. He could smell her blood now, maybe because of the chains they shared, maybe because he'd taken a hit so recently. And she could donate again. Her complexion had warmed up.

He sipped his wine and stared at her over the rim of the glass.

"What's going on?"

"I'll need blood again soon."

"What? But you just had some."

"It's a result of starvation and nothing I can help."

She put a hand to her throat, her gaze shifting around, almost frantic. "But I just gave you some blood. You'll end up depleting my supply, probably killing me."

"That won't happen." Should he tell her the truth, what he'd already done to her, that *his kind* had the ability to prompt speedy blood reproduction by releasing chemicals into his donor's vein?

"You're not the one giving it up. How do you know?"

He just looked at her.

She sought his gaze, scowling. "You're able to build up my supply, aren't you?"

He waited for a moment, then nodded.

She snorted. "I'm your blood cow, is that it?"

"If the vein fits, human."

"Not gonna happen a second time tonight."

"Fine. I'll get a donor over here."

"Looks like you'd better."

He made his phone call.

While he waited for the donor to arrive, Lily sat on her stool staring straight ahead. Her jaw moved a few times, but she said nothing.

He felt the tension in her like a slow crawl over the surface of his skin, and beneath that tension her desire for him. He stayed put as well, waiting for the knock on his front door, the chain almost a thump against his neck.

When the donor arrived, Adrien headed toward the door to let her in, forgetting again the short leash he was on.

When he reached the middle of the living room, he halted mid-stride as the chain pulled on him. He didn't look back at Lily; he was too aggravated by the whole situation.

He heard her slide off the stool, then the sound of her

shoes on the hardwood floor. He crossed to the door and looked through the peephole. He extended his senses, seeking anything in the hall that might be out of the ordinary, but he saw only a woman he'd used a dozen times in the past.

Maybe he shouldn't have called this particular female, but Lily had caused rage to flood his head.

He opened the door and the vampire-donor, a professional by the name of Night Candy with a high price tag, entered his house, levitated into the air, and threw herself around him so that his face was buried between her large and suddenly very bare breasts.

"Adrien, my love. How I've missed you. I couldn't believe it when I got your call. How long have you been out of jail?"

Several things happened at once.

His blood-hunger rose to a maddening level.

His cock responded.

He started to throw Night Candy on her back, but movement in the air stopped him.

A shrieking sounded from two female voices at once since Lily had landed on Night Candy's back.

And from all the unexpected movement, Adrien fell on his ass.

He stared up as mad midair whirling ensued, Lily hissing in a strangely vampire way, Night Candy grabbing at her arms while screaming and spinning.

Adrien feared that the human would get hurt once Night Candy got serious about the catfight. One hard vampire slam against a wall and Lily would be dead.

Just as Night Candy threw her arms wide and started to launch backward, Adrien whipped into the air, grabbed Lily, and pulled her off the woman.

He hovered above the floor, holding Lily in a tight grip as she flailed, arms and legs thrashing wildly. "I'll strangle her. Let me go, Adrien. I'll kill her for touching you like that!"

By now Night Candy stood by the door, shaking as she put her top back on. Her red wig was askew so that her fake hair covered one eye. "What gives, Adrien? Oh, my God, she's bound to you. What the hell did you call me for when you've basically got your own permanent donor?"

Lily had started to settle down, though she released a hiss now and then. "Sorry, Candy, my sweet. Send me the bill, double the usual fee, but you'd better leave. She's winding up again."

Night Candy smirked. "'Cuz you called me 'my sweet.'" She laughed as she blew him a kiss. "*Au revoir,* my sweet."

As soon as the door closed, Adrien crossed the room with Lily now hanging from his arms, still facing away from him, and panting hard. He reset the alarm then turned to lean his back against the door.

This was not what he'd expected. He'd thought to punish Lily a little; instead he'd set off some kind of crisis that involved Lily taking on more of a vampire persona than he would have ever predicted.

She'd acted like a jealous girlfriend, ready to fight any woman who dared to get near her man. Very vampire.

And the whole damn thing turned him. He looked down at the back of her head and knew exactly what he was going to do. "You'd better get ready for me, human."

CHAPTER 5

Lily sat on the floor, her body on fire. Heat coursed through her veins, and her temple throbbed. She couldn't blink. She could only sit and stare at nothing, her body a cauldron, her vein thumping in her neck as though, despite every human protest her mind threw at her, nothing mattered right now, not one damn thing, except feeding Adrien, in any way he needed to be fed.

He grabbed her beneath her arms and jerked her to her feet, then whirled her to face him. He started ripping her clothes off.

She grunted and helped, tearing at his shirt and sinking her teeth into his shoulder as he worked his pants down.

Once they were both sufficiently undressed, he pushed her up against the wall, shoved her legs wide, then penetrated her. She took him in, as hungry as he was, needing him deep, needing the sex, and needing it now.

He thrust to seat himself and once he fit inside her, she bared her neck. He licked the skin over her vein in long, wet sensual swipes. She didn't think she could ache more than she did right now.

"Do it."

He ground his hips against her and she groaned.

His fangs struck, and he drank her down while he thrust into her, moving his hips faster and faster as he sucked on her neck. His speed, vampire-fast, caused her to cry out. She threw her arms around his neck and held on as ecstasy grabbed her and took her on a ride, her body writhing against his, pleasure sweeping through and taking her into the stratosphere.

She hated him, who he was, but she needed him, needed this, because she was bound to him, because she felt the depth of his starvation and need, and she wanted to be the one to satisfy him.

Though the rational part of her brain told her this made no sense, this giving of her blood, this allowing his body to possess her, she couldn't blame the chains alone for what she was experiencing, the bald nature of her need, the depth of her desire. From the first, even before she'd put the chain on him, she'd experienced a profound attraction to the man.

He slowed his movements, and that's when she felt that he trembled from head to foot and drank from her unsteadily. He was still hard. He hadn't come.

Your blood. Lily, your blood. My God.

Had she heard him? Was that his voice, his words, in her head?

Adrien? she responded with her mind, wondering if she was just hearing things.

His body stilled completely and he drew away from her, his lips red-rimmed, his brows drawn into a tight frown.

He met her gaze, his hips quiet though he remained inside her.

What did you say? His mind to hers. *Did you say my name?*

She hadn't been mistaken then. *I spoke your name because you called to me. You said, 'Your blood. Lily, your blood.' I heard you.* Aloud, she said, "I heard all of that. Say it out loud so that I know we're talking about the same thing, that I'm not just imagining this."

"From my mind to yours, I said, 'Lily, your blood, My God.'"

"Yes, you did."

"You shouldn't be able to do this telepathically."

"It's the blood-chain. It has to be."

He nodded. His gaze fell to her mouth and she forgot her animosity. She just wanted him, wanted Adrien.

"Kiss me," she whispered.

He leaned down to her and touched his lips to hers, tenderly, the way a man would normally kiss a woman if he liked her.

He began to surge into her once more, but this time he kissed her while he thrust and it felt like heaven, like more than she had ever expected it could be with him.

She didn't understand what was happening to her, why she was feeling so much for Adrien whom she didn't know, why her arms snaked around him, feeling the muscles of his back, her hands rising until she drove her fingers into his hair.

His trembling settled down and power returned to his thighs and his arms. He surrounded her, holding her closer, bending his knees to angle up and into her. *I want you to come for me.* His voice in her head brought a deep groan from her throat.

Adrien, yes, she responded.

His hips pistoned faster and she fell into the quick rhythm, her body tightening deep within, her skin tingling over her chest and arms. *So close.*

Faster he moved. *Come for me. Come for me.*

Her body spasmed as ecstasy poured through, taking the fire in her veins and spreading it over every inch of her.

Adrien, now, do it now, release now and I'll come again.

He groaned heavily against her mouth and his entire body shoved against her, his hips moving fast again, so very fast. She strapped her arms around his neck, holding on for the ride.

He moved quicker than a human and her body responded clenching hard. Then more pleasure streaked through her and she could feel or sense his own pleasure rising, so she rode it as he shouted into the air, pumping hard.

The experience reached into her chest, expanding her lungs. She could hardly breathe as so much feel-good passed through her, waves of lush sensation, of ecstasy peaking, falling, and peaking again, over and over. And he kept pounding her.

I'll come again if you keep this up.

Oh, God, so will I.

Vampires could do that? There was so much Kiernan hadn't told her.

Once more she exploded deep inside, screaming her pleasure, gasping for breath, savoring each pummeling of his hips against hers. He shouted with her, driving his cock deep.

At last he began to slow. Her heart pounded in her chest, and her face felt flushed with passion.

He drew back, sweat gleaming on his forehead, his lips swollen and parted as he drew in deep breaths as well. "It's never been like this."

"The chains," she whispered, unable to catch her breath.

"I don't know." He searched her eyes.

She stared back wondering about him, who he was, why she could do this with him and not be repulsed, why she felt so much so quickly. The chain at her neck lay oddly still on her skin.

Slowly, he drew his hips back, sliding out of her, their combined fluids dripping down the insides of her thighs. He picked up his shirt and planted it between her legs.

"Thank you."

He nodded, frowning. She could feel his uneasiness, almost a wariness, certainly his distrust. Her own doubts intruded.

She shaded her face with her hand.

Adrien was a vampire. She needed to remember that, to remind herself that very little about her current predicament could ever carry over into her real life, the one she would resume with her son as soon as she got herself out of this mess, as soon as she had the extinction weapon in hand, as soon as she could hire someone to get rid of these chains.

And the last thing she should ever do was start to care for Adrien. Damn sex, anyway, because it was so easy to get connected with a man through sex. She knew the science behind it. And the chain wasn't helping.

"You're humiliated?" he asked. "Because you had sex with me a second time, you're ashamed?" He made a disgusted sound at the back of his throat.

She looked up at him. She opened her mouth to correct him, to reassure him that it wasn't shame. But what was it, then, if not shame?

A pure hatred and distrust of *his kind*?

Or the knowledge that she could never make a life for herself in this world, so what was the point?

Maybe it was a little bit of everything.

She had to keep her distance, so what did it matter whether she regretted the moment because of shame or because she couldn't risk trusting him. They were different species, and his kind had destroyed her family.

"Of course I'm ashamed."

He picked up his pants and punched a foot through each leg, glaring at her in turns.

She drew a deep breath and found her clothes or what was left of them. She slipped on her shirt just to be covered a little.

"Back to the bedroom," he said, sounding weary.

"I'm not tired."

"I wasn't suggesting sleep. We have work to do, but you need to get cleaned up, and your clothes and things from India are in there now."

She followed behind him, which suited her since her pants weren't fit to wear anymore. He'd ripped them down the back all the way to the crotch.

Once in the bedroom, she unpacked a change of clothes. Because he barred the way to the bathroom, she moved to stand in front of him, refusing to make eye contact.

"I'm not evil, Lily, whatever you may think."

She glanced up at him, her mouth ready to agree with him to say she knew at least that much, but what was the point? She needed to keep her focus, to remember that Josh waited for her, had been waiting for two years. My God, would her son even know her anymore?

"Please, Adrien. We just need to get through this, the quicker the better."

He stepped aside and she went into the bathroom. She took a quick shower, hoping by the time she opened the door Adrien would have some idea where they should go next.

"We need to go see a man in the north?"

Adrien sat on the floor outside the bathroom, still in his jeans and nothing else. He stared up at Lily having forgotten how pretty she was, with her large haunted hazel eyes staring down at him. His chest squeezed up, making it hard to breathe.

"A vampire?" she asked.

"Actually, he's a half-breed, and an Ancestral, rare in our world, but it happens." Just like Adrien actually. His mother was human, but the vampire genetics were dominant in his father's line and though he didn't have Ancestral status, and never wanted it, he had the potential.

"Half-breeds? As in human and vampire?"

He rose to his feet and narrowed his eyes. "Sure. Has been throughout history. Where do you think all your lore came from? And men of wealth? A lot of them are half-breeds."

"But far less powerful than a pure vampire."

"Not necessarily."

"That doesn't make sense. We'd know about them. There would be reports throughout the entire history of the world."

"Think about it, Lily. Most of the world still lives deep in superstition, but imagine just a few centuries ago when witches were burned at the stake. Do you honestly think a long-lived human would ever make his parentage known? He'd never have survived. The human population not so long ago wasn't mobile like it is now. Nowhere to hide."

"Then you've protected your half-breeds."

"You could say that."

"Why are you smiling?"

He sought about for a reason not to tell her about his parentage. On the other hand, it would be enjoyable to see her reaction. "You want the truth?"

"Yes. Of course."

He'd give her that much. She stood up to things. "I'm a half-breed. My mother was human. She was a good woman."

Her mouth fell agape. "You're kidding."

"Which part? That I have a few human genes kicking around in me?"

"That and how is it if you're part human, you hate us so much?"

"Because we're headed on a collision course with your world. It's inevitable and human nature tends to exploit, to grab, to destroy an entire population to get at its wealth."

"But vampires are more powerful, physically and you have so many other abilities that we don't."

He chuckled, but even to his own ears it wasn't a pleasant sound. "Look at the numbers, Lily. We have under a million in our entire population, spread out over the globe, and no central government to speak of. You're seven billion and growing. What are the odds of survival for us?"

She grew very quiet and very still. The chain was strangely silent against his neck.

He'd given her a lot to think about.

"Adrien, what happened to your mother?"

"She died when I was very young. Murdered."

"Oh, God, I'm so sorry."

He felt her swell of empathy but shook his head. "It was a very long time ago. Remember, I'm long-lived."

"Four centuries then." She frowned, and he could almost feel her thinking it all through. "Was she trafficked?"

"No. I mean, that's a new word these days. She was kidnapped, stolen from her life in Paris, which is one reason I have a place here."

"I'm sorry," she said.

"There are worse things."

"I don't think so."

He shrugged. "Maybe not." The information was four hundred years old yet somehow, with Lily asking the questions, suddenly he was a little boy and his mother was put in a long wooden box and lowered into the ground.

This was not exactly useful given his current situation. He gave himself a shake. "All right, I'm going to shower now, then we'll head north, at a snail's pace for your sake."

"Okay, that's fine."

He stepped aside and she dropped to the floor to wait, having already grown accustomed to their routine because of the chains.

He showered quickly, dried off, then passed by her to return to his bedroom. When he felt the chains tug, he called to her, but she was already moving and his chain grew slack.

He pulled a pair of black fighting leathers off a hanger, one with plenty of weapons sheaths so he could get better armed. One gun and a dagger wasn't going to cut it.

The pants were specially designed with slots for battle chains and several daggers. He wore a snug black tee, tucked in, another harness for his Glock, and a black leather jacket, free of holes. Travel at night in black was the only way to go. "Have you got any dark clothes you can wear?"

She moved to the bed and searched in her satchel. She changed out of her clothes, all in black, now wearing a turtleneck, jeans, and loafers. She plucked at her shirt and turned to meet his gaze. "We almost look like a couple of ninjas."

He smiled. He didn't want to but he couldn't help it. "Sorry, Lily, but the last thing you look like is a ninja." Her hair flowed over her shoulders. She was so beautiful, with sudden unexpected laughter in her eyes.

He cleared his throat and inclined his head to the door. He spoke in a sharp voice. "I need to get some more weapons, ammo for the Glock in case you decide to use it again, then we'll leave here." He narrowed his gaze and asked, "What does your locating ability tell you right now?"

Lily focused on the weapon, and as before, he could sense her reaching out. The tendrils of her tracking skill headed in several directions at once, but were unable to connect to an end point. He felt the level of her concentration and saw the lines of tension around her eyes, but nothing happened.

Glancing at him, she shook her head. "I'm sorry. I can feel the ability there; I know it exists. But it's as though I just don't have enough power to propel the search forward, if that makes sense."

"It's new to you. I'm sure in time it'll come. For now we'll just keep following our leads."

As she set her jaw once more, he brushed past her, leading the way back to the office and his armory.

Lily buried her face in Adrien's shoulder. She still didn't understand how the process worked, how she, as a human, could pass through anything solid. Though she kept her eyes closed, she could feel the difference between air and a mass of any kind, but it felt more like the difference between dry air and fog, the solid parts a soft clinging to the skin.

Adrien flew slowly for her sake, and though her head pounded, no sharp stabbing pains threatened to split her brain apart. Even the nausea at such a slow speed remained a faint queasiness. Still, she took deep breaths and tried to relax.

They must have left Paris behind, because for several minutes she'd felt only the texture of air. Though retaining her tight hold on Adrien, and her left foot balanced on his right boot, she set her gaze across his broad chest to see what they passed by.

Not much since it was the middle of the night, but as she looked up through a now thin layer of clouds she caught the occasional star, more wisps of clouds, more stars.

At one point she relaxed against him and his hand shifted on her waist, circling her even more fully. She felt his need to keep her secure and maybe that's why she let loose with a sigh and permitted her head to actually rest on his shoulder.

In this moment, the reality of her situation stunned her: that she flew in a state of mass that could pass through other masses, that a vampire built like a tank held her in his arms, that she watched clouds and stars pass like it was any other nighttime outing.

We're almost there. And now his rumbling voice in her head. He had an interesting voice, very deep and resonant. Her husband's voice had been like that. She missed him so much, the comfort of his arms around her, making love, even arguing with him about how to raise their children.

Now she was alone, trying to save her son if she possibly could, trying not to get killed in the process.

Don't be sad, Lily . . .

What did you say? So he knew she was sad and didn't want her to be.

Nothing. More gruffly this time, even in her head. *I didn't mean to say anything.*

Fine.

Fine.

She felt the descent and as she looked down, her acquired vampire vision warmed up the country setting below: a small French town, a nearby river, trees, lots of trees, farm country in broad stretches surrounding the town.

Adrien shifted direction, and as buildings raced toward her she closed her eyes. She felt them pass through a few buildings. Finally his boots hit a solid spot and the warmth of the air told her she was indoors.

We're in a home at the edge of town. Oh, my God.

She stepped off his foot and opened her eyes.

The house had been ransacked, papers strewn everywhere, furniture overturned. Adrien moved toward a doorway to the left, and she followed behind quickly.

Once more, he spoke straight into her head. *Someone got here before us.*

No kidding.

For now, stick with telepathy.

I sort of figured.

Good. At least you don't lack for brains. Then, *Oh, God, no.* He picked up his pace.

She saw the body lying in a twisted mass.

The Ancestral? she asked.

No. His servant, though, a half-breed who's been with him a long time.

She stayed on Adrien's heels as he put his feet in motion again. She ignored the body on the floor, holding her breath as she moved by. Surely death had an odor, and she didn't want to smell any of it.

One hallway led to another room, another hall, a narrow staircase, a real rabbit warren.

Lily stuck close, resisting the urge to hold on to the bottom of his coat. Her back itched with the thought that someone could attack her from behind. She felt jumpy and as her chain vibrated, and she reached out to sense what he was feeling, she knew Adrien felt the same way.

When she stepped into what had to be an attic, she heard the sound of movement on the rooftop above, someone walking or sliding on tiles. Then a thump and a harsh cry.

Adrien caught her arm and met her gaze, his jaw tight. *We have to go up there. When we flew in, no one was on the roof, but I think Sebastien is there now and he's in trouble.*

She nodded. *Let's go.* She stepped onto his foot and slung her arms around his neck.

Hold on tight.

You got it.

She felt him dip down and heard the faintest sliding sound and knew he'd just armed himself. The next second he shot into the air, passing through the roof at a wide angle so that they went about thirty feet into the air off to the side.

Four men on the roof. When I land, roll away from my right foot, but catch hold of the tiles. You can do this.

Lily's heartbeat went into overdrive as he flew down once more and landed. She rolled and caught at the tiles, but slipped, tried to catch, slipped some more but finally held fast. Her arms and hands were scraped up. She thought she'd be bruised—then she felt it, vampire healing because of the chains. But the tug of the chains told her she had to get closer to Adrien, especially since he battled three hooded, robed figures.

Fanatics.

She looked up and watched as another man, the Ancestral in striped pajamas and a dark silk robe, stood at the edge of the roof.

She turned and crawled in Adrien's direction because the blood-chain still tugged hard.

Adrien whipped into the air, moving closer to her and faster than the other vampires. She watched him use his battle chain first, whipping it to his right and catching the forearm and therefore the dagger of one of the attackers. He jerked hard, which flipped the man in the air and brought him down on his back. He grunted but stayed there.

The other two rushed Adrien. She couldn't make out all his moves because he was so fast, but by the time they reached him, he had a dagger in each hand. Then she saw it, how he separated and became two different men. The act alone gave him an advantage, since the remaining attackers paused, probably stunned by the maneuver, which gave Adrien the opportunity to move with swift jabs and quicker retreats.

The attackers took up more defensive positions, working the two Adriens farther apart.

Once more Lily felt the tug on the chains and began working her way back up the roof, scrambling each time, scraping up her hands all over again, but she didn't care.

Adrien had to survive, and she had to do everything she could to help.

The Ancestral remained at a distance as Adrien battled the other men. She glanced in his direction. He appeared to be concentrating hard, his arms held wide—and that was when she noticed how the night air seemed wavy and strange all over the roof and several feet above.

The waves emanated from the Ancestral. She realized she was watching the creation of the single most important element vampires used to keep themselves hidden, the disguising ability of the Ancestrals.

A world of power, of violent factions, of fanatics and Ancestrals, and of certain gifted vampires who could split into two equal parts.

A cry sounded in the air. The Adrien to the right withdrew his blade from his attacker's throat. Only one enemy remained and Lily wasn't surprised when Adrien reformed his body and, with unearthly speed, all but whirled around the final attacker. The man started to levitate and almost gained a quick takeoff speed, but Adrien launched above him, the chains tugging hard, cut his neck, and the vampire fell back to the roof. He would have slid off, but Adrien flew again, caught him, and finished what these men had started.

Lily rose up and gained her footing more easily than she thought she would. She glanced down and realized her feet were only partially touching the tiles: more siphoned power. She walked, or moved, or half flew in Adrien's direction.

He breathed hard, hands on knees. He met her gaze. *Sorry you had to see this.*

She looked down at the dead vampire, blood pouring from his neck.

"I'll get a cleanup crew." The Ancestral had his phone out. It struck Lily as funny that these creatures, who could create disguising waves out of nothing, who could split into two parts and do battle, would use human technology to call for cleanup.

"You're smiling?"

Lily glanced at Adrien. "I can't believe you even need phones, with everything else you can do." She put her hand to her cheek and shook her head. "I might be feeling a little hysterical right now."

"They'll be coming from the south, about two minutes out." The Ancestral, who looked to be no more than thirty, wore his hair corporate-short. He had large brown eyes, visible in Lily's continually improving sight.

He met her gaze, took in the chain, and dipped his chin once.

Adrien introduced her to Sebastien, and by the time she'd exchanged bizarre pleasantries on the roof of his home, a disposal crew had arrived.

Sebastien extended an arm, a graceful gesture in the direction of the home beneath his feet. "Shall we?"

Adrien quickly took Lily's hand. "Which room?"

"They'd just started into my study when I escaped to the roof. I believe that chamber might still be intact."

Sebastien disappeared first, sinking through the mass of the building. With his free hand, Adrien wiped sweat off his forehead. He called to the foreman of the crew, thanked him for his hard work, then the vibration began. Lily's last view of the roof involved watching one of the disposal crew, a huge pack on his back, start power-spraying the blood away.

Maybe for that reason, or because she'd just witnessed more killings, or due to the action of moving through another solid mass, the moment Lily's feet touched the soft carpet of Sebastien's study she dropped to her knees. She worked hard not to hurl all over what she could see was a finely woven Persian carpet.

She felt a hand on the back of her head. Waves of energy pulsed through her, and the nausea passed. Her head didn't even hurt. She sat back on her heels and looked up at Sebastien. "Thank you. I don't know what you did, but I feel much better."

"Good. I take it you're finding our means of travel difficult to take."

"Nearly impossible, unless I'm fully prepared and we take it really slow."

He stepped away from her suddenly. In fact, he crossed to the opposite side of the room, but she wasn't certain why.

When she rose to her feet, however, she turned to find Adrien in a state. He was growling again, his head low, his fangs bared. His flecked teal eyes had what was now becoming a familiar wild appearance.

Instinctively, Lily reached up and put her hand on his face. *Is this because he touched me?*

Adrien turned into her hand, kissed her palm, then

hauled her into his arms. His thoughts came at her in a fragmented jumble: *Kill Sebastien. Don't. Lily, my God. Hurting. Fangs. Must stop. Lily. What's happening? I could take her now.* An entire string of expletives followed.

Panicked, Lily threw her arms around his neck. *I'm here,* she said.

Lily?

I'm here.

I'm sorry.

What do you need?

He can't touch you again.

He won't. He didn't understand. I'm sure he gets it now.

She felt him take a deep breath, then another. Because she was pressed up against him, she also felt his arousal and was stunned all over again. Was it possible she'd need to give it up for Adrien, again, in a stranger's study?

She wasn't sure she had a choice. *Tell your friend to leave the room.*

No. I'll get through this. I can't keep giving in to this terrible need I have for you.

He trembled as he pulled away from her, but they were alone. Sebastien had left the room anyway, which helped.

At first Lily opened her mouth to yell at Adrien, but what she sensed through the chain stopped her. The vampire was humiliated by what had just happened.

He moved to a large desk, planted his hands on the top, and worked at his breathing. She stared at him, uncertain what to do. Her chain began to vibrate heavily against her neck as powerful emotions worked in Adrien. Humiliation, yes, but something more, something that fueled his rage.

He shook from head to toe and without warning, he lifted his head and screamed into the air.

Lily jumped back several paces at first, then moved back to him. She put a hand on his arm, wanting to calm him, but he jerked away. He paced the room in a circle and shouted. More profanity followed, reams of it.

"Adrien, what's wrong? Talk to me. Maybe I can help with this, whatever's going on with you."

"You want to *help*? You, a human. And what are you going to help with? Can you change my DNA or that this damn chain has my cock in an uproar? Or that when I catch even a whiff of you I want to bite down hard on your throat and never let go?"

She took a step away, one hand sliding up her neck. Her breath came in heaving gulps. She'd had sex with him twice and both experiences had overwhelmed her, made her crave more. Because of the chain, she could feel his need, that he meant what he said.

She stared at him, unwilling to admit just how much she responded to the call in his eyes, to the size and beauty of him, or to his primitive nature. And she hated herself for it, for desiring him like this, the feeling that not to have him would somehow destroy her life, even her soul.

She saw that he worked to control himself.

So she did the same. "We'll get past this, Adrien, both of us. We'll get the weapon and somehow get the chains off, the sooner the better, then we'll both be free of these inexplicable cravings."

He met her gaze but shook his head. "Did you have to be so beautiful?"

Lily grew very still. Tension filled the air. Silence as well. Maybe she breathed, she wasn't sure. Adrien held her gaze, his eyes dark with longing and need, now glittering in the soft dark of the room.

She heard movement near the doorway and wasn't surprised when Sebastien appeared. "Rumy called just before the fanatics showed up, demanding information about the extinction weapon. I wouldn't have survived the attack without Rumy's warning, but I've lost a good friend tonight."

"I'm sorry," Adrien said.

Sebastien nodded, his expression grim. "I've made a couple of phone calls. I think you should head north, to the Trevayne system. Alfonse is expecting you. I told him to take you to the vault."

Lily felt Adrien growing calmer by the second. Perhaps that was why the Ancestral had rejoined them, to change the subject and to give Adrien something else to focus on.

CHAPTER 6

Adrien kept his gaze fixed on Sebastien, his chest tight. It helped a lot that he'd shifted his attention away from Lily. He drew another deep breath. "What vault?"

"The one only three other Ancestrals know about, Alfonse being one of them."

Lily turned to face Sebastien as well. "What's in the vault? Is the weapon there?" Adrien could sense her sudden excitement.

Sebastien shook his head. "No, but there are documents about experiments performed here in France. I read them forty years ago. They were of a scientific nature and might have included design plans, I'm not sure. I'm asking that you secure them and take them to Gabriel. He'll know what to do with them." As a respected Ancestral, Gabriel knew a lot of trustworthy vampires. If anyone would know what to do with these documents, he would.

He glanced from one to the other. "You're in this together and you're in deep. You're both pretending that what's happening here is simple, with the chains and with each other, but it's not. Adrien, you and your brothers have served as one of our few policing forces, and you've done a great job. But our society, if we're to survive, needs more than that, from you especially. You have tremendous Ancestral power, I can sense it in you. And you've always spoken loudly about the need for an improved court system. We must have that if we're to hold maniacs like Daniel at bay. And now that he's making a power grab by using you both to get the weapon, it's even more important that you tap into your Ancestral legacy."

"But when I've spoken of this, most of the Ancestrals insist that Daniel is an anomaly among vampires, that we shouldn't build an entire system around one freak. And if we can locate the weapon at all, it's unclear what we'll do with it. We'll handle that when the time comes."

Sebastien nodded. "But Daniel's not the only one vying for control, is he? Who do you think was behind the attack here?"

"I know that Silas leads this group."

Sebastien nodded. "The long black hooded robes have become his signature."

"Yes, they have."

Lily turned to glance at Adrien over her shoulder. "Silas again. What's his main deal?"

"He keeps dozens of our young male vampires worked up about human intrusions into our world, while he profits from selling human drugs to vampire dealers in just about every system on earth. He's one of my least favorite things, a complete hypocrite."

"But I take it he wants more than just the profit from selling drugs."

"Like Daniel, he's after control."

Lily shifted her gaze back to Sebastien. "Do you agree?"

Sebastien stepped back into the room. "Absolutely." He sat down in a winged chair near tall bookshelves and settled his gaze on Adrien. "Just think about what I've said. If you embraced your Ancestral calling, you'd be able to make a difference, I know it." He lifted a hand. "I won't argue with you, not tonight. But please consider the possibility that there's something else here." He glanced from Adrien to Lily and back. "Fate has brought you to Lily and she to you."

"I don't believe in fate." Adrien flared his nostrils, slinging his hands behind his back.

"Whether you believe it or not, I'm going to tell you a truth right now that I think you won't want to hear." He gestured to the chain at Adrien's neck. "These blood-chains that you've got have very little to do with your drive toward Lily."

"You're wrong about that."

Sebastien shook his head. "My wife and I donned blood-chains once, hoping to improve our marriage. All they did was increase the hostility we felt for each other. I almost died getting rid of the chains but would have preferred death to keeping them."

"That can't be true."

"Are you calling me a liar?" But he smiled, if wearily.

Adrien backed down. "No. You always speak the truth."

Lily met Adrien's gaze. "But this can't be true. I couldn't possibly be experiencing these kinds of things on my own." She whirled back to Sebastien. "You must be mistaken."

"Sorry, the chains don't lie or mislead." He rose from his chair. "And now, I have a good friend to bury. I suggest you head north before Silas finds out about the vault."

For a long moment, Adrien couldn't move. His gaze was glued to Lily as he tried to process what Sebastien had just told him. What did his profound drive toward the human mean, then?

In the end, he made a choice to ignore Sebastien's

revelations, at least for the present. Besides, soon enough he'd come to the end of this line, then he and Lily could go their separate ways.

"You're right, we should get going. And Sebastien, I'm sorry we can't stay to help out with this."

"My people are coming. I'm not alone. Try to gather the support you need and think about what I told you. You have an extraordinary lineage. If I had half your power and even a quarter of your natural ability, Adrien—my God, what I could have accomplished on behalf of our world."

Adrien met and held his gaze, willing him to understand his thoughts. That the latent power he kept in check, those so-called natural abilities he possessed, belonged in hell and nowhere else.

He held his arm out to Lily. Accustomed to the drill, she stepped into him and slid an arm around his neck. This kind of proximity because of the way they had to travel wasn't helping his profound desire for her, but it was still the best way of traveling with altered flight.

The moment she planted her foot on top of his, he inclined his head to Sebastien and put them both in motion, gliding upward and passing easily through the house and into the night air.

He'd half expected Lily to speak to him while traveling, to contact him telepathically and discuss what Sebastien had said. Instead she remained silent.

If what Sebastien had shared was accurate, then Adrien had to face a hard fact about his desire for Lily: He'd never experienced such a powerful reaction to a woman, *any* woman, in the entire course of his four centuries.

But what did it mean? He'd known dozens of women over the decades, and had loved two or three of them, but he'd never felt a desire for a deeper commitment. He held back of course, just as his brothers did, since they each feared and mistrusted their parentage. Yet when he reviewed his loves, they seemed mild in comparison with his reactions to Lily. Even before she'd come into the cave, he'd thought, *She's here. She's mine.* And that was well before he'd worn the blood-chain.

Are we in any danger, being airborne like this?

Finally, she spoke to his mind, addressing a subject he could respond to, but she wouldn't like the answer. *Because we're traveling like slugs, yeah, we're in danger. Hopefully, though, anyone watching for us would be checking the southern routes out of Paris.*

In the direction of Lake Como and The Erotic Passage?

Yep. Rumy's business is known to be a hotbed of information, any kind you could possibly want. Most of the club's workers would have heard something about the weapon over the years.

Do you think anything in the vault will be of value?

Only one way to find out, but I need to prepare you for something else, Lily. No human has been allowed to visit the Trevayne system in a long time. I don't know if Kiernan told you this, but a large number of our cavern systems don't allow humans inside. Most interactions with your kind have ended badly for the vampire world.

You're saying I won't be welcomed.

Only an Ancestral like Sebastien could have given us access like this, so I'm asking that you be respectful despite how you feel about my kind.

Of course I will. I'm not a barbarian.

No, that you're not. I apologize if I offended you.

Apology accepted.

Lily didn't blame Adrien for not trusting her. If she'd been in his shoes she would have done and said the same kinds of things. After at least an hour of travel, and as he

dropped down to earth, she glanced around and saw a barren rise of hills amid a fertile area, except that the air looked
as it had on top of Sébastien's roof, like it moved in waves.

Another disguise.

A stream flowed nearby and a chill filled the air. She
wondered where the caves were and why vampires would
still choose to live in caves when many, like Adrien, had
apartments and homes.

She watched the stream, the trees on the opposite side.
The wind flowed along the waterway.

Adrien had grown very still but he finally said, "We
have permission to go inside."

She had no idea what he meant, but when she shifted
toward the barren land, a sight like nothing she could
possibly have expected met her eyes. A several-stories-
tall entrance, made of stone blocks, framed a massive
cave entrance on an even taller grass-covered hill. What
had appeared barren to her human eye was actually the
entrance to the Trevayne system.

The beauty of the entrance stunned her, and for a long
moment she couldn't make her feet move. The stone had
dozens of magnificent carvings, something that probably
spoke of the history of the system as well as the vampires
who'd lived here throughout the ages. But across the top
of massive columns lay an enormous curved stone, settled deep into the hill and also carved.

She felt her jaw had dropped, and there it stayed. The
cavern in the Himalayas had been an uncivilized hellhole, a perfect representation, from Lily's limited point of
view, of vampire society, violent and unclean.

But here, rising to such an incredible height, carved with
great beauty, was something else altogether. The stones,
massed together and decorated, meant civilization.

"Not what you expected?" Adrien's words held a sharp,
sarcastic edge.

"Sorry. Not even a little."

He led her up a series of steps, but each forward movement bit at her conscience. Humans weren't allowed in this place and for good reason: Her kind usually meant death and destruction, and here she was looking for the one thing that would destroy the few hundred vampires undoubtedly living here.

But as she moved deeper into the entrance, her eyes widened. She thought a five-star hotel couldn't have been any grander. The several-story theme continued, the sculpted walls rising to a massive domed ceiling with more intricate carvings. A granite mosaic of a huge oak tree decorated the entire eight-foot wall to her left. Dozens of white linen-covered round tables and tall-upholstered chairs took up the main body of the room.

Straight ahead, a vampire stood at attention, meeting neither of their gazes.

To the right, a long hotel-like desk, though unmanned, flanked the wall. From the same direction, a tall, lean vampire with large eyes and his dark hair cut businessman-short moved in her direction, his lips pinched tightly together.

"Well met, Adrien."

"And you, Alfonse. May I present Lily Haven."

Alfonse turned his piercing gaze on Lily. He didn't smile and she didn't offer her hand. "We don't usually receive humans here, madame. But you probably already know that."

"I do."

He then shifted his attention to Adrien. "Sebastien gave specific instructions that I'm to take you directly to the vault. Our people have retired, at my request. I'm not happy about this, on any level, but Sebastien indicated that a difficult situation has arisen and he trusts you. I do as well, but if you could see to your business then leave, I'd offer any favor in return that I could."

Bribing Adrien to get rid of them?

"You know about the imprisonment of me and my brothers."

Alfonse shook his head, and his frown deepened. "We're unsettled by these events and by rumors that Daniel has been stripping some of our most powerful leaders of their businesses, selling them to humans."

"I wish I could tell you differently."

"Doesn't Daniel understand that if our wealth departs, so does the ability to feed those in each system? We'll be forced out into the open. That can't be his plan."

Adrien's voice grew quieter. "I've never understood his mind."

Alfonse clapped him on the shoulder. "Of course not. No one can understand the thinking of a madman." He glanced at Lily. "I'll show you to the vault."

A woman's voice sounded to Lily's right. "Now, is that any way to treat guests that Sebastien has sent to us, my dear? I insist they receive refreshment, and if you continue to stand there like a statue and scowl at our human visitor, she will no doubt make a report that will do none of us any good."

Lily found herself swept away by the woman, who took her arm, introduced herself as Giselle, and drew her back down the way she'd come. She felt the tug on her chain, which quickly relaxed since Adrien moved to catch up.

"Giselle, we can't stay for your hospitality," Adrien said. "Time is critical."

"So I understand, but you haven't seen how my grandson has grown. You've been a favorite of his since birth and he's missed you."

Lily's astonishment grew. Grandson? Which meant children. So there were vampire children here.

Her gaze took in the walls as Giselle led her away from the entrance. They appeared to be decorated with some kind of elegant polished quartz, and went on and on, for at least an eighth of a mile, with many offshoots of more halls, or tunnels, more carvings and more crystals, more beauty and civilization.

This wasn't a cavern system, this was a palace.

After a series of descending steps, taking them deeper into the earth, the hall opened up into another vast underground cavern, also carved and gleaming with a soft light from several oil lamps. Her vision adjusted, so that once more she saw the space in a soft glow. She also felt the flow of warm air, fresh air. "You have electricity."

"Some, and as carefully hidden as possible."

Lily turned in a circle. "This is a magnificent room."

"And Alfonse works hard in his business so that we, and all the families living in our system, can maintain the necessary repairs. We're constantly battling the effects of water, and of course the moment a stalagmite appears, I'm calling in a work crew." She laughed as she spoke.

Giselle had long black hair with a straight line of bangs. Her skin was very pale. Her clothes were casual enough, but she looked stunning in a pair of black tailored pants and a soft, clinging purple top. She wore thick silver bands on her wrist and a matching piece around her neck.

She led Lily to an elevated living area on which were grouped red velvet sofas and chairs. Beneath the furniture lay an enormous carpet.

"Please, sit down. My husband is glaring at me but I insisted on inviting you to our private quarters." She had wine waiting and goblets.

When she offered, Lily accepted because to do anything else seemed wrong. But Giselle had knocked her off-stride. She'd had one opinion of vampires, and little about Adrien's powerful presence and temper had altered that.

Yet here was a woman who, in any other setting, might have become Lily's friend.

Lily took a sip and found the Cabernet flavor almost perfect. Adrien moved to stand near the chair in which Giselle sat. He held his goblet tight in his fist, his brows drawn together as he watched her. She sensed his uneasiness, but couldn't figure out the cause of it.

Then she felt it, a kind of energy emanating from Giselle. She shifted her gaze to the woman, who sat with one leg tucked beneath her. Then, leaning forward as she searched Lily's eyes, she finally murmured, "Sebastien told me you shared the bonding chains with Adrien, and I can see that you do, I can feel the bonds between you and they're powerful. In fact, I don't think I've ever felt anything like this before. When did you put them on?"

Some part of Lily didn't want to answer the question, but she felt compelled to speak anyway. "Earlier. Just after sunset when I brought Adrien out of the prison."

"I see." More of Giselle's power flowed toward Lily in soft entrancing waves. "And why did you bring him out?"

Again, Lily wanted to hold back, but the words flowed out of her as she spoke about her mission, that she had to get the extinction weapon. She even told Giselle about Kiernan and Daniel—everything, except Josh.

"I can sense that you're a tracker, that you have the locating ability. I want you to extend your powers to our system right now and focus on the weapon. What do you see?"

Lily did as she was told, closing her eyes. She reached out with her mind and focused on the weapon. She felt the familiar tendrils flow from her once more, but much stronger this time and extending in all directions. But as before nothing happened—as though she simply didn't have enough power to get the job done.

Opening her eyes, she said, "I can feel this ability at work in me, but I can't seem to locate the weapon."

Giselle glanced at Adrien. "Perhaps there isn't enough power yet for that to happen." Shifting her gaze back to Lily, she asked. "Did you agree to your mission because of money?"

She shook her head. Panic set in. By now, she knew that Giselle had some kind of power over her, but she couldn't reveal the whole truth. She couldn't. Trembling set in. "Not . . . money."

"Then what? Why do you do this thing? Are you afraid of Daniel?"

"Yes, that he'll kill me. Kiernan as well." She bit back the rest of the truth, but she broke out in a sweat.

"And what else?"

The woman's voice cajoled and coaxed Lily, the powerful vampire waves beating at her mind, compelling her.

Lily glanced up at Adrien. *Help me. I can't tell her. Please. Make her stop.*

But Adrien's gaze was hard as he responded, mind-to-mind, *We have a right to know why you're set on destroying our kind.*

I can't tell you or anyone.

But Adrien pressed her. *You're after the weapon, acquiring it on behalf of one greedy human and one maniacal vampire. We must know what's going on.*

Please, Adrien. I'm begging you. I can't give the reason. Too much is at stake.

"Lily," Giselle called out, more waves pounding on her this time.

Lily turned slowly in her direction, under the strange spell all over again. "Tell me why you must find the weapon, if not for money?"

Lily's trembling increased. Her lips formed the words.

She would try to say them, but her heart forced them back. Sweat poured from her now, streaming down her face, her back. She shook hard, resisting Giselle's power.

She couldn't betray her son. One of the terms of her arrangement was that she keep the terms confidential. If she revealed the truth, Kiernan would kill Josh.

Suddenly a new power flowed toward her, but this time possessing and strengthening her as the blood-chain vibrated heavily. Though Giselle continued to pummel her, Lily now siphoned Adrien's power. She could resist Giselle.

"Enough," Alfonse said. "Giselle, stop."

Giselle ceased suddenly and Lily weaved in her seat, but caught hold of the arm of the chair with her free hand to steady herself. That Adrien's power still flowed through her made her feel dizzy. She met his gaze once more. *Thank you.*

She set her goblet down on the table next to her then wiped the sleeve of her shirt over her face. She leaned forward and put her head in her hands.

She didn't understand why Adrien had stepped in to support her. She looked up at him once more. *Why did you do it? I think she could have broken me.*

I disagreed with the effort on principle. But I wish you would tell us, or at least tell me.

I can't.

He looked as though he wanted to say more, but a young voice called out, "Uncle Adrien. I thought that was you."

"Ah, my grandson," Giselle murmured, pride in her voice.

But what happened next stunned Lily: The warm smile that broke over Adrien's face transformed him completely as he turned to hold out his arms to a boy of maybe six or seven.

The lad half leaped, half flew into Adrien's arms. He swung him in a circle, hugging him, even levitating and whirling faster so that the child laughed, the sound bouncing around the domed, carved ceiling of the large cavern.

Because of the chain, she sensed Adrien's love for the boy. Even without the chain, though, she could see the affection on his face.

All that love. From a vampire. From Adrien.

The dizziness Lily had experienced earlier returned, but for a completely different reason.

The boy put his arms around Adrien's neck. "I've missed you. We all have."

"I've been away for a year, but now I'm back."

"The alarm sounded," the boy said, his eyes wide. "All my friends had to go into their hidden homes, did you know that?"

Adrien glanced at Alfonse. "No, I didn't."

The boy glanced at Lily, then his eyes widened further. "You're a human."

Lily nodded. "I am."

He frowned. "But you're just a girl. Why would the alarms sound because a female human came into Trevayne?" He glanced from Adrien to Lily then to his grandparents.

Giselle rose from her seat and took charge of him. "Come, Jean-Luc. You should have been in bed an hour ago." The boy stared over his shoulder at Lily as he walked away, half dragged by his grandmother who promised more information about the human once he was in bed.

Jean-Luc waved and smiled at Lily, the tips of his fangs showing.

Lily waved in return, knowing that what had happened in the past few minutes had overturned her world.

Adrien spoke quietly to Alfonse, which gave her a moment to gather her thoughts once more and to look at the vampire who had killed others of his kind in front of her, whose dark nature both made her afraid and excited her, and who had just shown a very human response to a vampire child.

She looked away from Adrien, feeling more confused than ever about this world she'd just entered. She'd had a strong opinion about vampires, which kept being confirmed over and over again. But other situations, like this one, had arisen to obliterate at least some of those preconceptions.

The one thing she knew for certain, however, was that Adrien couldn't have faked his obvious love for Jean-Luc. But even beyond this, he had interfered with Giselle's enthrallment skills, allowing Lily to keep secret the one piece of information that could keep her son alive.

Adrien called to her, "Come, Lily. Alfonse is going to take us to the vault now."

She rose, nodding, but as she met his gaze, the shift in her emotions traveled through the chain's constant stream of communication between them. Desire for Adrien, everpresent anyway, sharpened suddenly.

He narrowed his gaze. *What is it?*

She shook her head and felt another wave of heat rise up her cheeks. Damn the chains. She could hardly keep her shift in emotions secret from Adrien. *Nothing. Let's go to the vault.*

When he opened his arm, she shivered as she stepped onto his foot and slung an arm around his neck.

His gaze narrowed. *This isn't nothing. I can feel your desire.*

But she placed her free hand on his chest. *Please, Adrien, don't push me. I'm barely holding myself together.*

She half expected him to say something sarcastic. Instead, he murmured against her cheek. "No worries, Lily. Let's see what the vault says, then we'll head back to Paris to get some sleep. I can feel your fatigue, and you've been through hell tonight. We both have."

His sudden concern didn't help her response to him. Her heart swelled, tightening her chest.

Then Alfonse suddenly passed through the stone wall to her left and Adrien put them in motion. Her stomach turned once more since Adrien had to go faster than usual in order to keep up.

Lily had thought the trip would be short, but Adrien informed her that some of the cavern systems were over a hundred miles long. She was aware suddenly of just how little Kiernan had really told her about this world.

Though her head ached, and her stomach boiled, she asked, *How many vampires live in this one system?* She thought a few hundred maybe.

Over twenty-five thousand.

Lily held on tight, afraid that this new, inconceivable piece of information had also just changed her perception of the vampire world. But she wanted to know more. *And how many children?*

Not many, because we're long-lived. Only three hundred.

Three hundred vampire children, all of them loved in the same way that humans loved their children. But a new truth dawned, one closer to Adrien—that some vampire children weren't loved, but had endured hell growing up. She knew in her bones that Adrien had suffered terribly in his childhood.

She fell silent after that, struggling against the pain beating within her head, and the nausea that threatened her.

Finally Adrien began to slow, and as he passed through one last tunnel that ended in a large cavern, the pain eased. With her feet at last on solid ground, she clung to Adrien. He didn't let her go but continued to support her with his arm around her waist until the nausea subsided.

At last she opened her eyes.

"I'm sorry, Lily," Alfonse said. "Adrien tried to tell me to slow down, but I couldn't, not without giving away our location."

"Understood. It's okay. I wish I could say I'm getting used to altered flight, but it's rugged."

CHAPTER 7

Adrien let Lily go, but didn't want to. Something had changed between them, though he couldn't say what exactly. Lily's emotions came at him, her sudden strengthened desire for him that only fueled his own incomprehensible and powerful need for her. But more than that, he could feel her bewilderment, her confusion probably because of what she'd just witnessed, given her low opinion of vampires.

He didn't know exactly why he'd intervened, preventing Giselle from reaching into Lily's mind and extracting the truth from her, the real reason why she was on this mission. But some part of him wanted her to trust him enough to tell him, wanted her to feel good enough about his character that she could reveal the truth that frightened her.

"Is this the vault?" Lily joined Alfonse by a stone pillar in the center of the space. Stalagmites and their companion stalactites marred the area, a sure sign that no one had been here in a long time to do cleanup and repairs.

Alfonse put one hand on the stone and with the other shaded his eyes. Adrien sensed his concern about the contents—that he even debated turning anything over to Adrien.

He straightened his shoulders suddenly and met Adrien's gaze. "Except for Sebastien's orders, I wouldn't do this, not for you, not for anyone."

"I understand."

Alfonse drew in a deep breath. "Adrien, you've got to find a safe place to hide Lily. Giselle and I debated saying anything to you, but the underground rumors are that Silas has seen Lily in a vision destroying the vampire race, or at least that's what he's telling everyone. Which means that his followers will be after her, to kill her."

"Do you actually believe what's being said?"

"The fanatics believe Silas, just as they believe these documents are a threat to our way of life. But Sebastien and I and many others have greater faith in our ability to survive Daniel's current plan to acquire the weapon, which is why we're entrusting you with the documents."

"Why do these even exist?" Lily asked. "Why weren't they destroyed?"

Alfonse shifted in her direction, his gaze falling to Adrien's hand, the one around her waist, the one that held her and supported her. "If the weapon truly does exist, there's a good chance more than this set of designs is out there as well, maybe even more than one weapon. We need as much information on the side of good as the other side might have." He lowered his chin, once more holding Adrien's gaze. "We get that the end point for you involves Daniel, that he's behind your having been hauled into Lily's mission, that he's made use of your abilities to create a tracking pair.

"But we also believe an opportunity exists as well, something you'll be able to do to change the course of our history once you reach the end of this mission." Suddenly he switched to telepathy: *And Adrien, Sebastien is right about your connection to Lily. Something astounding is happening between you. I know how you hate humans, but even I've felt it—certainly Giselle has—that Lily has something extraordinary to give you, if you'll open yourself up to her. But you can't hold back. It might even become a matter of life and death for you to establish a deeper connection with this human, deeper than you've ever had with anyone.*

Adrien grew very still. The last thing he'd expected was Alfonse encouraging him to explore a true bonding with Lily, the kind that for Alfonse had led to marriage to Giselle. He shook his head. *What you're suggesting can't be. You know what I am.*

At that, Alfonse's lips quirked. *Yes, I know what you are. But do you?*

Lily glanced up at Adrien. "Is there something I should know?" she asked, looking from one to the other.

"No," Adrien said.

Alfonse struck the pillar with a single sideways motion of his fist, which depressed a stone lever. In turn, another part of the broad base of the pillar slid open.

Alfonse squatted and pulled out a black metal box. He set it on the floor then slid it across a flat stretch of ground that Adrien realized comprised pavers of some kind, very old. Even this deep into the Trevayne system, though perhaps millennia ago, vampires had worked the cavern.

Adrien released Lily then dropped to his knees. He opened the lid. Inside were a dozen documents or so. He flipped through them and found several engineering schematics, but unlike anything he'd seen before, as though designed with some kind of code.

He glanced up at Alfonse. "Have you looked at these before?"

"No. I never wanted to. I agreed to house them here, at Sebastien's request, over fifty years ago. I asked him why he didn't just destroy them but he said he feared that one day our world would have need of them. I guess that day's come. Just tell me that you'll do right by them."

"You know I will."

Adrien glanced at each document, written in French but also translated into English. When he finished scanning one, he'd hand it to Lily, who dropped to sit beside him on the stone floor.

As she read them, he felt her excitement as she sought the weapon's location. But as his stack grew smaller, and nothing emerged except scientific notations, experiments, and the like, that excited jolt diminished until she read the last one and examined the final schematic.

"There are references to at least two dozen countries where experiments were held," Lily said, "but nothing else, nothing of real use."

"But working from a list of twenty-four countries instead of two hundred narrows the field." Alphonse closed the metal box and put it back in the vault. Another fist on stone and the apparatus sealed up again.

Adrien gathered up all documents into a single tight stack, tucked them into his waistband, then zipped up his jacket to keep them pressed against his chest.

Lily had grown very quiet. He felt her disappointment that the discovery hadn't yielded immediately usable details. He also sensed her fatigue and that her head still ached.

He shook hands with Alfonse once more and was about to depart when Alfonse said, "Take off to the north. If you've been followed, they'll be waiting to the south. You've got a couple of hours until dawn, so you have time to take a different route back. I'd head west to the coast, if

I were you, and not return to Paris until you can enter from the east."

"That's sound advice." He held his arm out to Lily. She stepped onto his foot, but as he slid his arm around her waist and drew her close, she slumped against him. She was human, unused to altered flight travel, and the hours were all wrong for her usual sleep patterns. In her world she would have been in bed a long time before now.

He needed to get her home, back to Paris, back in his bed.

But the thought of having her there, beside him, her warm body and soft curves, sent sudden desire streaking through him all over again. He took a couple of deep breaths.

Adrien, I can feel your desire. Will you need blood again? Even telepathically her words sounded exhausted.

Just ignore that. Let's get you home. Ready?

Yes. Just . . . please try not to go too fast.

I won't.

He nodded to Alfonse then shifted to altered flight.

As he took off and passed through solid rock, aiming in a skyward direction, she asked, *What difference does it make which way we go? Why go all the way to the coast?*

Couple of reasons. This kind of slow travel leaves behind a trail. If fanatics are trying to locate us, then they probably would have found the trail to Sebastien's by now.

Which means the trail would also have led to the Trevayne cavern system.

Yes.

When nothing more returned to him, he realized Lily had fallen asleep. Just as well. He sustained his slow speed heading west to the coast of France.

* * *

Lily awoke as Adrien dropped them into his bedroom. She was surprised she'd slept but grateful even though her head throbbed.

She released Adrien, and took a moment to steady herself before crossing to the window. She could see the Eiffel Tower, lit up and misty through the rain. She was exhausted and confused about all that had happened, especially with Adrien. She put her hands on the cold glass, trailing her fingers down the rivulets.

Adrien had caught the boy up in his arms, a sign of affection, yet he was a vampire. And the system had three hundred more children, which meant families, something so *human* in design that she still had difficulty processing this new reality.

She felt Adrien behind her, very still and waiting. The chain at her neck didn't even vibrate, but lay inert. She needed to sleep, but sleeping through the flight had keyed her up.

"How's your head?" His deep resonant voice soothed her, but why should anything about Adrien soothe her?

"Much better." She glanced over her shoulder, needing to say more. He took his coat off, laying it over the bench at the foot of the bed, and set the documents on the dresser. "Thanks. I'm not even nauseated."

"Good. And I know you need your sleep. Dawn will arrive soon and I'll need to rest as well. But I'll sleep on the floor if you want."

At that she turned to face him. "Why are you being so kind to me?"

He scowled. "Am I being kind? Am I, in your opinion, even capable of that?"

She put two fingers against her forehead and rubbed. "I've always believed that you know someone by what they do, not by their past, their family, or, in this case, their species. When I learned that vampires had killed my family, I had believed that you were all made like sharks, restless killing machines that devoured anything in their path. You've proven so much to me this night and I owe you an apology."

He stepped closer to her and took her arm gently in his. But as she looked up at him, she saw the deep frown between his brows, something that seemed as much a part of him as the shade of his dark hair or his flecked teal eyes. "Lily, I want to apologize for what happened before, here, when I took blood from you. I wasn't myself and I'm sorry."

She shook her head. "I don't regret what you did but I haven't been able to make sense of why I enjoyed it so much. I feel very confused by all of this, especially by what Sebastien said earlier about the chains not lying."

He stepped closer and the chain at her neck began a new vibration as desire for him rose in a crisp, sharp wave. Was it possible this was more than just a result of the blood-chain?

His desire returned as well, flowing in waves over her body, which lit her up even more despite her fatigue.

"What about what Sebastien said?"

"About how the binding with his wife made things worse between them."

"And this hasn't been intolerable for you? You haven't hated this experience, hated being with a vampire?"

"I did at first and I've despised the situation, being forced together, but you already know the pleasure I experienced, that I . . ." She couldn't finish the thought; she was too embarrassed.

But her desire for him kept building and the chain almost shook now. She felt his need and knew that, as before, he hungered for her blood.

"Do you need to feed?" Please say yes.

He thumbed her cheek. "It's not critical, not like before. But right now, I'd give just about anything to have another taste, in every way, including your blood." He slid his hand down her neck and over her breast, caressing her.

"Adrien," she whispered. Her need had become an ache that echoed through her bones, her blood.

She shivered. Whatever fatigue she felt melted away, so that when he leaned into her and slanted his lips over hers, a soft warbling sounded in her throat.

Her hands found his arms. She stroked slowly upward, feeling the size and strength of his muscles, to shape her hands over his powerful shoulders. Adrien had a wonderful mouth, sensual, moist lips.

He cursed, drew back, and removed his Glock and harness. His shirt went next, which meant her hands got busy again as she smoothed her fingers over his thick, fleshy pecs. His muscles flexed and relaxed, which caused her to spasm low.

Was she doing this? Having a consensual experience, not just feeding Adrien out of his desperation, but agreeing to make love with him? What did it mean?

Confusion once more swirled through her mind.

Yet whatever bewilderment her head experienced, her body knew exactly what it wanted—to feel Adrien, to touch him. She'd never been with such a physically imposing man before.

His tongue played in her mouth, teasing every recess, thrusting, teasing a little more, showing her with each flick and push what he could do to other parts of her body.

Flames leaped at her now, teasing her deep within, heating her up, tightening one part, releasing another, building the tension, seeking the release.

She pulled back and stripped off her shirt, then her bra. She would have gotten rid of her pants at the same time, but he moved closer and put a palm between her breasts.

Though she wanted to touch him, she stopped and let him look at her, to stroke her breasts with his hands and his fingers, to pinch her nipples, then to lean down and swirl his tongue over each tip.

"Sit down on the edge of the bed."

His hoarse voice took out the remaining strength in her legs and she did what he wanted. He pushed her thighs apart and, dropping down to land on his knees, he got a better angle and suckled her breasts, taking turns.

She arched into his mouth and he took as much of each breast in as he could, suckling, licking, biting until she moaned heavily. She dove her fingers into his hair and used pressure on his head to force him to take more. He put a hand on her back and pushed at the same time as well. For several minutes, a sucking sound filled the room.

Her body contracted deep within, almost spasming at the erotic feel of his mouth as he nursed on her.

Without warning, he stopped and pushed her onto her back. He worked her pants off, struggling with her shoes for a few seconds. She sensed his mounting desire, and as he removed her thong she spread her legs wide.

You're bare, drifted into her mind.

I am.

Without leaving his knees, he growled, slid his arms beneath her thighs, and started to feast on her low. He used his tongue to separate the folds of her body and tease the outer recess of her sex. He grunted and drove his tongue inside her, doing what he'd said he wanted to do, to taste every part of her.

He used his mouth and his tongue, devouring her hard. His tongue moved swiftly in and out, faster and faster. She'd never experienced this kind of hard, driving speed, not with a tongue.

Her body seized and she cried out. She was close.

He went faster, gripping her hips with his fingers,

squeezing and driving until ecstasy tightened within and released in a driving flow of sensation that sent her cries up to the ceiling.

He sustained that incredible speed and sensation until the last of her whimpers filled the room and her knees grew lax.

Kissing her inner thighs, he was suddenly in her mind. *Did that please you, Lily?*

She looked down at his slow-moving head. Speaking to her telepathically, he didn't have to stop the kisses. *Yes,* she responded. *Adrien, that was amazing.*

With his lips, he plucked on the inside of her leg, then using his right hand he massaged beneath her thigh, rubbing and smoothing her skin, kneading her muscles, and working his way to the center of her body. He began licking her low again, only this time he used two fingers to penetrate her, stimulating the outer part of her with his tongue while he began to slowly tempt her once more, thrusting his fingers into her.

She was almost too sensitive, but as he worked her, pleasure mounted once more. The tip of his tongue teased her clitoris, while his fingers worked her faster and faster.

Does this please you, Lily?

You'll make me come again.

There's something I want to do.

Oh, God, Anything, Adrien.

I just need to warn you. I want to take blood from your vein, here, down low. You should be prepared.

For some reason, she hadn't considered just how many places on her body could give up the blood he sought. A shiver ran through her, increasing the pleasure of his flicking tongue and driving fingers.

May I?

And there was only one answer. *Do it.*

He shifted slightly, balancing his free arm across her

hips and moving to the skin to the side of her mons. He began to lick in long sweeps of his tongue. All the while he kept his fingers pulsing inside her.

Deep within her body, she felt her vein respond, vibrating and swelling, as though part of what he could do was call to her blood. Maybe he could.

He breathed heavily, a raspy sound as his fingers thrust into her. Pleasure began to build once more. Her abdomen rose and fell as her vein responded to him.

Ready?

Yes.

A quick sting of fangs, a withdrawal, and she felt her blood rush from her body. A new sucking sound followed as well as a pervasive sensation of pleasure in her lower abdomen like nothing she'd known before. Flames once more licked at her, this time over every part of her.

As she listened to him suck, as she heard the wetness of her body with each drive of his fingers, as pleasure rose, her back arched and she cried out. *Almost there.*

I can feel you tight in your channel. Come for me, Lily.

Something about his voice in her head brought her, only this time the sensation of ecstasy ripped through so that she screamed now, her body gripping his fingers, contracting and releasing, sensations of fire and pleasure driving through her, spreading across her abdomen, unequaled sensations.

As the climax eased, and her hips grew quiet, she heard him grunting as he sucked down her blood.

His movements grew gentle, almost sipping at her and finally he swiped his tongue over her vein. She felt a coolness enter her bloodstream. *Was that the rebuilding serum?*

Yes, something our genetics created to ensure a continuous supply of blood because we feed one another.

It feels wonderful. She was grateful for telepathy. She

breathed raggedly through her mouth and wasn't sure she could speak even if she wanted to.

Adrien rose up and removed his shoes then carefully peeled away his pants from a massive erection. She lifted up on her elbows to watch. She'd always liked looking at a man's body, at how different it was from hers, how a man's cock was designed to fit inside her.

Not surprisingly, her mouth watered. "I want a taste before you enter me."

He groaned heavily as he lay down beside her on the bed. She shifted to arrange herself, her hand gliding over his hip and caressing his buttocks.

He put his hand at the back of her head, a very controlling signal that weakened her all over again. He fed her his cock, one thick inch at a time. Her hands played with his ass and as he pushed inside her mouth, his buttocks flexed. She groaned as she licked her tongue over the crown, as she sucked and dragged her teeth lightly.

He sped up, thrusting into her mouth, still holding her head. She took him deep, as deep as she could, and let him do what he wanted. Her hands grew hungry sliding up and over his back then down his buttocks, his thighs, rubbing and feeling the strength of his muscles.

Do you want to come like this?

She looked up at him, still savoring him. He met her gaze and continued to thrust into her mouth. She sucked and licked and just stared into his eyes. How they glittered in the dark, heavy with passion.

"No," he murmured, pulling out of her mouth.

She smiled as she sat up. "You have my blood on your lips."

"Your blood tastes like nothing I've ever known before."

Adrien rose from the bed, then leaned down and picked Lily up in his arms. He'd done all this while she lay on the comforter; now he wanted her in his bed while he took her the rest of the way.

Holding her in his arms, he flipped the comforter and sheet back then settled her in the center of the bed so that he could enter her the way he wanted to, face-to-face, his hips moving into hers.

"I want to watch you come, to kiss you while I bring you again."

"Uh-huh." She nodded as she spread her legs for him once more and held out her arms to him.

The gestures were of a woman with experience, a woman who had been married and was welcoming her man. He felt moved though he shouldn't have been and he recalled once more what Sebastien had said about the chains—and what Alfonse had told him, that something extraordinary was happening between him and the human.

He planted his knees between her thighs. Her hips rocked as he positioned his cock against what was shedding her sweet-tasting fluids.

His jaw trembled at the memory. So many remembered sensations poured over him, of what his tongue had felt like moving deep inside her, how much he loved her folds and secret hidden place, the softness of her bare skin, the sense of her vein rising for him, reaching for him, the feel of his fangs piercing her and releasing her blood, then the blood hitting his tongue.

He groaned at the memory as he pushed inside Lily with his cock a rigid pole, as he rolled his hips and felt the answering undulations of her body, as she pushed her palms up his arms, then dug her fingers into his biceps and moaned.

Her head rocked back and forth.

Pleasure. So much pleasure.

He dipped low and began to kiss her as her head

moved. He caught her cheek, her chin. He wanted her to taste what he tasted.

Once seated within her, his cock thrusting steadily now and building, he crashed his mouth down on hers.

She rewarded him with a sudden cry, an arching of her body, and her nails raking down the length of this back. She suckled the tongue that had pleasured her and his balls tightened.

These past twelve hours with Lily were almost worth his year in that hellhole. He couldn't have planned this kind of all-consuming reward for his struggles.

He drew back just enough to look down at her as he drove into her. He'd never been with a woman like this, repeatedly in the space of several hours, looking at her, into her eyes, wanting to watch her come, to feel her pleasure through the shared chain.

He sped up, and that was something he could give her that a human couldn't. He had speed and strength. He hit a stride that had her lips parted, her lungs dragging in air. She looked almost panicked, almost in pain, her brow slightly furrowed as he drove her toward another powerful climax. Only this time, he would come with her, giving her all that he had to give as a man, his power enhanced by the sharing of her blood.

"Adrien. So close." Her voice was barely a breath of air.

He nodded, taking in the flush on her cheeks, the delicate sheen of perspiration on her upper lip, how her eyes were dilated. The fragrance of her sex flowed upward, making him harder.

He thrust heavily into her now, deep rolls of his hips against her, driving her to the cliff's edge, pushing her hard.

She made a sound between a grunt and a mewl.

As she began to cry out, he felt her tighten, and sensing

her low in that way, on the cusp of orgasm, triggered his release. He sped up and came, pleasure ripping through him, along all the sensitive nerves.

He heard her screaming, saw her wide-open mouth. "Look at me," he shouted.

Her gaze latched onto his and she cried out once more as pleasure flowed up his abdomen, climbing higher and higher, his skin on fire, his chest expanding. He shouted several times but kept pushing into her.

She gripped his arms. *You'll come a second time, won't you? I can feel it.*

He nodded. *Yes. God, yes.*

He pumped hard now and faster. She writhed beneath him as his balls fired up once more and another shot of pleasure, more intense this time, rushed through his cock. At the same time, he felt her grip him low as she came again, tugging on him, crying out, thrashing beneath him.

Only as she started down from the heights did his body begin to settle over hers. In stages his thrusts slowed, and her hips grew quiet until at last, panting, he lay on top of her, his body rising and falling as she struggled to breathe as well.

One hand of hers slid to the back of his neck and played with his hair, the other became tangled with his left hand, their fingers entwined.

You were so beautiful when you came.

Adrien. What is this between us? I don't understand.

Pleasure.

Understatement.

Yes. He smiled.

He didn't want to leave her body. He felt a need to say something more to her, but nothing else came to mind.

Lily lay slack against the comforter, sated. She pulled Adrien's palm to her mouth. She closed her eyes and kissed his damp skin, then licked. He tasted like heaven, like something she could devour over and over and still want more, a flavor very masculine, yet more, maybe vampire.

He stayed inside her, which suited her right now. She had missed this so much, the closeness, the pounding motion, the weight of a man.

Her husband had been six-two and worked out, but Adrien had so much muscle that his weight felt like the earth covering her and protecting her.

For this split moment in time she felt safe, like everything would be all right, that all would be well. She knew it wouldn't last, but she breathed it in and savored the taste of him as she continued to lick and kiss his palm.

She sniffed his fingers. "You smell like herbs, like something I'd put in a soup to give it a strong edge. And I'm in heaven."

He kissed her cheek gently. "Me, too. Thank you for all of this, Lily, especially your blood. You've saved my life repeatedly this night, and I owe you."

She finally shifted her head on the pillow so she could look at him. Tears welled. "I have you bound in chains, Adrien. You can't be grateful to me or owe me. You're probably going to die because of this. Kiernan and Daniel won't let you live once they've gotten their hands on the weapon."

"I'm not going to die. You should know this about me. I have a strong will to live."

"I know. I can sense it in you." She caressed his cheek. "I haven't told you everything."

"I hope you'll be able to."

Her thoughts turned to her family and to Josh, the hope that he truly was still alive. Maybe it was her fatigue or the simple reality of her situation, but the pain of her loss suddenly overwhelmed her.

Tears streamed down her face and with Adrien still buried inside her, she wrapped her arms tightly around his neck, wept, and cried out. The sounds came from so deep inside her they didn't seem to come from her at all.

Adrien held her fast in return. He let her cry and groan and shout and weep some more.

The only thing he did was occasionally thumb tears away from her cheeks.

"Lily," he murmured softly now and then. "So much pain."

His tenderness, so completely unexpected because of her opinion of his kind, kept the tears coming. She wanted to tell him the truth about Josh, but the words wouldn't come. Kiernan's orders were clear: No one must know about Josh.

"I miss my family so much."

He lifted her to a sitting position, held her close, and rocked her in his arms.

"I am ashamed of my kind right now. Your family should still be alive."

She nodded against him as she continued to weep.

Adrien petted her head, rubbed her neck. So unnecessary, these deaths.

He understood earth-based accidents like an unexpected ocean wave that took down a ship or a bolt of lightning or an earthquake that closed up a living cavern. But acts of evil, designed by men whether vampires or humans, that took the lives of the innocent were among the most abhorred in his world, in both their worlds.

He continued to rock her until she ceased crying, until her hips began to move against his, until she lifted up and suddenly her mouth was on his and her tongue teased him to firmness once more.

He lowered her carefully onto her back yet again, needing the deep connection, and rolled his hips to give her pleasure. Her soft womanly scent floated around him and made his jaw tremble. He pushed and felt her depths pull on him. She moaned and he understood her moans, her need, that her grief had turned and become a cry for connection and life and release.

For hope.

He drove into her and kissed her. He plunged his tongue deep and felt her suckle just as her depths suckled his cock and worked him to a frenzy all over again.

He didn't understand what was happening, either. What was between them was something that, if Sebastien was right, had little to do with the chains, which only enhanced what already existed.

Was this the potential, then, between Lily and him? A profound depth of understanding, of passion and desire, of need? Because that's what pummeled him as he made love to Lily, as he drove into her again: that he needed this woman, this human, who siphoned his power and behaved at times like a vampire, who responded to his body as though she'd always been with him, who wept at the loss of her family.

He'd never known a human, not like this, not a woman like Lily. He felt the sincerity of her grief, that what she'd lost had been more important to her than her own life.

Which made him wonder all over again the why of her present mission: What was Kiernan giving her, or holding over her head, that she risked her own life to go after a vampire extinction weapon?

He no longer believed that she did so for monetary gain, but something else had her hooked into the mission and his instinct told him she didn't trust him enough yet to share that information with him. Whatever her reasons, he still had to figure out a way to get his brothers out of prison before Daniel finished them off.

He took her to the edge of ecstasy once more and brought her again, releasing into her, savoring every moment.

CHAPTER 8

Half an hour later, after cleaning up, Lily lay beside the vampire, her heart now calm, her chest eased of the usual constriction, her body empty, her mind as well. She dozed off and on restlessly, worried about Josh, about the extinction weapon, and about her growing, powerful feelings for Adrien.

She would fall asleep then awaken, uneasy sensations refusing to let her sleep.

When she woke and tried to pull away, thinking she needed to get moving, needed to find her son, Adrien would grunt his disapproval and hold her close, keeping her next to him. She relented each time, relaxing against the heat of his body. The rise and fall of his chest soothed her and she slept some more.

Dawn came and went.

She remained cocooned in bed with him as each hour passed. More than once she felt a pressing need to get up, to start a new list, to make a new plan to find the weapon and to find Josh, but over and over, he pulled her against him until finally she fell into the deep void of sleep, the warmth of his skin soothing her against the cold rain that still hit the windows.

Later, much later, the faint stormy light of day disappeared, giving way to dark gray evening and finally the black of another rainy Paris night. This time when she awoke, her eyes remained open and she no longer felt the draw of lethargy.

She felt rested, an unusual state. Almost calm. Almost *normal*.

This time, when she pulled away, Adrien shifted to look at her. She sat back on her knees, aware of her nakedness yet somehow very comfortable with him. Still, she knew men, and the sight of her bare breasts would invite a different kind of interaction, so she pulled the sheet up to her neck, tucking it around her.

She touched the chain at her neck. The soft vibrations comforted her now. He stared at her, his expression almost solemn, no smile, just something close to determination.

She leaned down and kissed him. "Thank you," she said, "for so much compassion, for holding me, for letting me cry, for helping me to sleep. Though I buried my husband and daughter two years ago, my son's body was never found. I've struggled since, with all of it, hating your kind."

"I know."

She nodded several times then glanced in the direction of the window. "I tried to wake up earlier. Several times."

"That was my fault. I needed sleep and I wanted you beside me, for the comfort of it."

She shook her head. "It wasn't entirely your fault. I needed the rest as well, so I acquiesced each time."

Then he smiled, another faint curving up of his lips. "Several times? I remember pulling you back once."

At that she smiled. "Half a dozen, at least."

"I was damn tired, then, because I don't remember any of those. Just the one."

"You've been through hell," she said. She could feel the pinch between her brows as memories returned, of being in the Himalayan cave and seeing him hanging in chains. Her jaw grew tight.

He leaned forward, shifting on his elbow. She thought maybe he meant to kiss her in return. Instead, he said in a strong voice, "There's a way to change the experience of travel for you, and Alfonse alluded to it. There's a double-chain I could take on that would make my power greater, but I'm unwilling to go that far." He seemed so solemn as he continued, "I know traveling is hard on you and puts us both at greater risk, but I need you to understand that accepting a more powerful chain will do something to me that I've rejected for as long as I can remember. Unlike this chain, which could be removed, the double-chain can't. I just need you to understand that it isn't as simple as the single-chains we both wear." He lifted his blood-chain.

She met his gaze and felt his distress, even his hostility. "What exactly would accepting the double-chain mean for you that you've rejected so long?"

He shifted his gaze away from her, scowling and silent. After a moment, and still not looking at her, he said, "I'd be taking the first step to achieving Ancestral status."

"And that would increase your power?"

"More than you can imagine. The gift is rare, but my brothers and I all have that capacity. It's just that our father was a monster and none of us wants to be like him."

"Then you can't do it."

He still leaned up on his elbow, his fingers playing over her arm, his thick, dark hair rumpled from sleep.

She marveled at the tender feelings this closeness aroused in her—like she wanted to smooth away the furrow between his brows.

"Several of the Council of Ancestrals have been begging for me to step up for the last two centuries, to embrace my power."

"You seem to despise the Council."

He blinked a couple of times before adding, "I can't believe how easy it is to talk to you." He still rubbed her arm, and it felt good.

"I know," she said.

He smiled suddenly, a real, full curving of his lips. "My God, I'm almost happy. It must be you."

She laughed. Oh, my God, she laughed. When was the last time that had happened?

Her heart blossomed, a sensation that swelled and swelled.

At a moment like this, she could almost forget what he was.

And yet looking at him, his beauty, the strength of him, his tenderness with her, a spattering of gooseflesh rippled down her back and sides. She started to pull away, but he reached up, caught her lips with his, and kissed her, so of course she stayed put.

When he drew back, he added, "Don't get ahead of this, Lily. Try not to think too far into the future. You'll go crazy and I need you close right now. What we're doing right now, this is good."

Maybe he'd read the expressions on her face or maybe he'd sensed her feelings through the shared chains, but whatever it was, his words calmed her down. "Right," she whispered. And he was right. This had to be a one-step-at-a-time process.

"I was serious before. You can't become an Ancestral

just to make traveling easier on me. It would be so wrong. Once we're done, and we get these chains off, then you can pick up your life again."

She drew a deep breath, trying with all her heart to actually believe the words she'd just spoken.

While Lily showered, Adrien sat outside the bathroom door, his phone in hand. He'd ordered food from his favorite restaurant and now his stomach rumbled.

He'd spoken with the owner, a fine Parisian, a human actually, who had complained that Adrien had forsaken him. He was reminded that he'd had a life once upon a time, before his world had gone all to hell. He was also reminded that there were some humans he did value.

Now he had Lily.

And freedom.

Sort of.

He couldn't believe he was out of that prison. Despite the chains and his bondage to Lily, at least he wasn't hanging from wrought-iron chains so fat they could have dragged elephants.

He set his phone on the floor and rubbed his wrists.

He was healed up now but the memory was still there, as though the weight of the manacles lived in his mind. He thought of his brothers and it filled him with pain.

He touched the chain at his neck. Yes he was bound, but this was still much better than the cavern. He swore to himself that he would succeed in his mission with Lily so he could defeat Daniel and free them from the hell they were enduring.

"You okay?" Lily called out.

"Fine." His head lolled back and thumped the door.

He closed his eyes and breathed, bringing his focus back to the present. The chains kept them in constant communication so that even now he knew she was worried. No doubt if she tuned into the chains, she'd sense his own sadness and loss.

"I ordered dinner," he called back.

"Thank you," came muffled through the door.

He reached down and turned his phone over and over. Smartphones were good, and he kept his close at hand. Always.

His thoughts turned again to rising to Ancestral level.

God help him, he would do everything in his power to keep from taking that step. He just had to figure this out. Since Lily could siphon his power, then it was possible he could work with her, strengthen her, build her up so that she could survive the next few days until they got hold of the extinction weapon and the situation was resolved.

As for altered flight, which was his primary concern, he would have to move her slowly. It would take them considerably longer to get from place to place, but he really had no other choice given her previous reactions.

However, there was one serious problem: While flying, he and Lily would be easily visible to other vampires. In such a large world, it wouldn't normally be a problem, but he knew in his gut he was being tracked—not in an electronic sense, but through opportunistic surveillance. Needing to seek out Rumy, for instance, who knew every underworld bastard who existed, made it likely that his adversaries would stake out The Erotic Passage.

Gabriel, his longtime mentor, had also suggested he pump club patrons for information because it was a real gathering place for the dregs of vampire society. Someone was bound to know something about the weapon.

Of course the nature of the club—and the many times Adrien had taken advantage of any number of women there—set his cock in an uproar again.

Once more he leaned his head back, this time without banging on the door, and took several deep breaths.

He felt certain he'd meet up with a few assholes that needed offing, and he'd take care of business. But how the hell was he supposed to protect Lily? If she was incapacitated by the flight, or if several assailants attacked once they'd arrived, he didn't know what he would do.

But then he'd been battling a long time, for centuries, keeping an uneasy peace all around the world, so he knew a few tricks.

He supposed that would have to be enough.

Lily.

My God.

Lily.

When she emerged from the now steam-filled bathroom, his cock stood at full attention. He rose to his feet and gave her a curt nod, at which she frowned. He pushed the door wide and said. "I need a shower."

Wrapped up in a towel, she gave him space, stepping back as he all but shoved his way in. She barely had time to step outside when he closed the door perhaps more forcefully than he should have. He heard her slide down the door and sit outside to wait, just as he'd waited.

"I'll make it quick," he called out. "Dinner will be here in a few minutes."

"Okay. But, hey, did I do something? You looked mad."

He glanced down at his still-firm cock and rolled his eyes. "I'm in a hungry state," he responded, willing her to understand. When she remained quiet, he added, "And not for food."

"Oh." Then he heard her chuckle.

He smiled. Dammit, he liked her.

He shaved quickly then showered as fast as he could so that within a handful of minutes he was back in the bedroom with her, both of them getting dressed. This time he donned his battle leathers, which could house several daggers and two different lengths of fighting chains.

Lily put on jeans and a shirt and now towel-dried her hair. She wore no makeup, and her large eyes tracked his movements as he slid daggers down the sheaths sewn into the leather, five in all. In bottleneck pockets, the shiny black tabs of the chains locked into black clasps that gave way with a tug. The short battle chains could take a man's head off with enough strength. It was messy work, but sometimes necessary. The longer chains could wrap around and incapacitate an opponent, while a dagger finished the job.

When he'd donned a black tank, he turned to her. "You need to prepare yourself, Lily. I know in my gut this is going to get messy. Once we leave the safety of this apartment, there will be others." He spoke for a moment about how long he'd been fighting and that he was used to killing. "And I'm sorry for what you'll be going through as we press on."

By now, she'd folded her arms over her chest and held her lips in a tight line. She nodded several times. "I understand, Adrien. I do. After everything that's happened, I know this night won't be child's play. But thanks for warning me. I appreciate it."

He stared at her for a long moment, once more taking her measure. Though he could sense what she was feeling, it helped even more to see the look in her eye. Though she was afraid, she also had a boatload of courage.

He heard the soft buzzing of the front door. On instinct, he held a hand up to her, very flat, a strong warning, then waved her toward him.

When she drew close, he picked up the documents from Trevayne then took her hand, walking with her in the direction of the living room. He didn't head to the door but beelined to the office. "I need to check the security monitor," he said in a hushed voice. "And I want to get these into the safe before we leave."

He took care of the documents first, then went straight for his computer. He didn't like that he had to release Lily's hand, but he pulled up the security system and saw a familiar delivery boy, rocking to his music, as he readjusted his earbuds with his free hand, holding a large take-out bag in the other.

Adrien grabbed some euros and made for the door, Lily close on his heels.

He opened the door carefully and looked beyond the boy, but the hall was empty. He traded the money for the food and exchanged smiles.

When Adrien shut and locked the door, he breathed a sigh of relief. Lily took the bag from him and cooed. "I am so hungry, you have no idea."

Since she turned around and headed back to the kitchen and dining room, he followed quickly. As soon as he caught a whiff of Jean-Paul's famous roast chicken, he groaned.

Lily looked over her shoulder. "I know, right? Oh, God, let's eat."

Lily had finished the chicken dinner Adrien had brought in from a local restaurant and now made some notes on a pad and paper she'd taken from one of the kitchen drawers. "So we're headed to The Erotic Passage. Where exactly is it in Italy? Como, right?"

"Lake Como, in the north."

"It's beautiful there, lovely hills, even mountainous in places. Lots of wealth."

"And one extensive vampire cavern system dedicated just to Rumy's club."

"An entire system? As big as Trevayne?"

Adrien chuckled. "No, but big enough."

"And do you think Rumy can help?"

"Rumy knows everything. He's one of the hubs of our

world. He's connected to our extensive underground, and I'm not talking about our caves."

"You mean illegal stuff?"

"Yes and much worse as well. He's on good terms with every terrorist cell in our world."

"You're kidding."

"That's the nature of Rumy's business, that he deals with powerful criminals of all kinds. He's known for keeping secrets but if you need information, and if he can get it without acting against one of his other clients, then he'll deliver. Given his clientele, though, this trip of ours won't be a picnic."

"Does your kind deal in drugs?"

"Mostly human, imported from *your* world."

"I can't fault you there, Adrien. That's well-deserved censure. We have a terrible drug problem in the human world."

Adrien frowned suddenly, placed his hands flat on the table, and looked slowly around.

"What is it?"

He met her gaze. "No, don't be afraid. It's just that I'm remembering something, from decades ago." He turned toward the fireplace and frowned.

Lily followed the line of his sight and noticed an antique clock.

Also, for the first time, probably because she was rested and had a full stomach, she actually looked around at Adrien's apartment. The room was a strong combination of modern furniture mixed with a few antiques. The dark leather couch fit Adrien well.

"The clock must be very old," she said.

"Not when I purchased it."

And there it was again, his long-lived state. But as her gaze shifted back to the clock then once more to Adrien, she felt her chain vibrate softly. Suddenly images rushed at her, swirling at the edges as a new vision surfaced. And this time she was pretty sure the vision would involve Adrien.

Within the vision, the furniture was different and so was Adrien, but there he stood in this very room, near the fireplace, dressed in formal white silk breeches, white stockings, and a fitted black coat. He turned and looked in her direction, but she could tell that though he sensed something, he couldn't see her.

Adrien stood up from the table. "What is that? What are you doing?" He even looked toward the fireplace. "It was you," he said. "I felt something, a very long time ago, in this room, maybe two centuries ago. I was near the fireplace and you would have been right where you are now. I felt your presence. My God, Lily, it was you. I sensed your presence all the way from the past, yet you were looking at me just now."

She rose as well. "Yes and you looked amazing in white breeches and a black coat. The room was full of important people, too."

He stared at her as though amazed. "I carried that feeling around with me for days, that I was supposed to do something but couldn't place it. Now I know why, because here you are. Lily, do you know what this is called? You have revisiting visions. You're in the present and you see the past, people from the past."

"I had one in the cavern just before I saw you hanging in chains. The vision was of you two hours before, when they first tortured you."

"You saw that?"

She worked to keep the memories at bay. "Yes. All of it. It was horrible."

He shook his head. "This world of ours must be a nightmare for you, something that won't end, that keeps delivering."

"But good things, too," she said quickly. "Like making love with you. That was unexpected and wonderful."

His chest rose and fell. His gaze had locked onto hers so that the last of the present vision faded.

A look came over his face that pushed the air from her lungs. His scent followed, suffusing the air with strong herbs and what she'd come to know as Adrien. The chains set up a vibration against her skin.

Once more, she felt his desire for her. Hers rose as well, along with the strange need her body felt to offer a vein. Could her life get any stranger?

She glanced down at her list. Her list-making was one of the things in her life that had kept her sane over the past two years. This list, though, had more to do with finding a killing machine: *go to The Erotic Passage for more information, ask Adrien more about his brothers.*

She'd left off the most important thing, the one thing she couldn't write: Josh. Find him, save him, make a new life with him.

"We should go," she said, rubbing her finger back and forth over the notepad.

"Lily," he said softly, rounding the table so that he stood next to her. "I didn't mean to upset you. My need for you is fierce and I know you can feel it through our connection. I blame these damn chains, which is one more reason I want to avoid adding a new layer of power. I can't imagine what would happen with an even stronger bond."

She nodded, but she felt dumbstruck all over again by his proximity. Her knees felt weak. Her gaze fell to his lips. He leaned in and as she closed her eyes, his lips touched hers, a moist pressure that didn't help her knee-situation at all.

The kiss lingered and her heart began to set up its own demanding racket. Her hand slipped up and around his neck, beneath the long weight of his hair, then she was just in his arms, wrapped up in the cocoon of his phenomenal strength.

He could crush her and yet she knew him already, knew that he'd never hurt her. He was kind to children and respected women. She couldn't believe how much she'd grown to trust him in twenty-four hours.

We should go. Her mind reached to his, but his arms tightened around her.

He deepened the kiss. Her body weakened further as she leaned into him. She parted her lips, needing air, which of course prompted his tongue to dip inside.

She moaned against his mouth.

Yes, we should go, he said mind to mind.

But there was something so perfect about being wrapped up in his arms that she forgot the hour and her desperation. She sank into the thrill of his mouth, his lips, his powerful arms that flexed and released against her.

She shuddered. His scent, now surrounding her thickly, made mush of her thoughts. He could take her if he wanted to. She had no will but his right now.

Despite the intensity of the moment, he began to pull back, easing up on his embrace, kissing her with only his lips, then withdrawing that sweet pressure to lean his forehead against hers. "I wish to hell we had more time because I'm feeling urgent all over again."

"Me, too, and very forgetful when you touch me." She drew back and met his gaze, struck again by how beautiful his flecked teal eyes were, the shimmering depths that weren't quite human, but more, much more.

Vampire.

She looked away. She needed to remember what he was, that she wasn't like him, that once she had Josh back again, she'd be rebuilding a life with her son, a life that couldn't include Adrien.

Releasing him, she ripped the list from the notepad and slid it into the pocket of her jeans where her fingertips touched her iPhone. "If you're ready, let's go."

He nodded. He ran a hand down each side of his battle leathers, checking his weapons again, no doubt, as well as his phone.

He slid one arm around her waist, holding her against him. "I'm sorry that this process hurts."

"It doesn't matter, Adrien." She took a deep breath. With any luck they'd find the information they needed at The Erotic Passage and she'd be one step closer to Josh. "I'm ready."

The flight began and as before a sudden nausea took her over, but she fought it back. And as before, her head began to pound, but because he kept the speed slow, she could manage the pain.

Soon he'd flown them away from the city lights of Paris until the blackness of the countryside below took over, with only the occasional village lights. She closed her eyes and leaned against Adrien's chest as he took them south toward Italy.

As they went farther the clouds began to thin so that when she checked her surroundings once more, she could see stars. She smiled. Yep, much better to take it slow.

We'll be moving through the Alps soon, he said from his mind to hers. *Just wanted you to be prepared.*

How clear the words sounded in her head. *Thanks for the warning,* she returned.

When blackness engulfed her she knew she was passing through rock—that and the strange clinging sensation of solid matter.

The flight went over Italy now and the same occasional lights of villages or towns.

Another two minutes passed and his mind once more

sounded within hers. *Almost there. We're over the lake now. The club is on the eastern shore.*

She looked down; sure enough, she saw a black expanse of water. He descended toward the lake, traveling in a southeasterly direction.

In this position, his head cleared hers easily. But movement drew her attention and she shifted slightly to gain a better view. She saw that several distant figures, all robed with hoods, approached out of the northwest, something Adrien wouldn't be able to see. Fanatics.

Adrien, there are four men coming in from the northwest, wearing robes and hoods.

Shit. I have to speed up.

Do it.

She shifted to look away from the intruders so that she could see the light from the club. But the vibration grew until instinctively she looked up.

Another attacker sped toward them from above and before she had time to warn Adrien, the fifth vampire slammed into Adrien's shoulder, knocking her out of his arms. The next thing she knew she was falling toward the blackness below.

She had enough sense to take a deep breath just before she plunged into the cold lake. Down she went, her body instantly shocked and numb from the frigid water.

Her first instinct was to pull for the surface, but the chain vibrated in a way she'd never felt before, a powerful warning.

She felt the connection to Adrien, and chose to rely on his battle instincts, on all that she was in this new world. Though anxious to reach the surface, she forced her body to remain hidden below.

She adjusted her vision, siphoning the familiar power from Adrien. She could see as though a soft light cleared a path through the water and the night.

While Adrien battled four of the vampires, the fifth zigzagged over the waters hunting for her, probably waiting for her to surface. She had always had trouble floating and right now was grateful for it.

That her pursuer couldn't see her reminded her that she could siphon Adrien's power. Here was one of the differences then—that she could remain hidden while a real vampire couldn't see her through the water.

Slowly she released the air now trapped in her lungs.

As Adrien battled, first one then a second vampire fell into the lake. She could make out Adrien's quick movements as he blended his flight skills with his battling ability. Like before, he split into two parts, almost directly above her because of their perpetual proximity issue.

But her lungs had begun to hurt and the vampire hunting her was getting closer. Maybe she'd released too many air bubbles at once.

Her vision grew gray at the edges. The vampire hovered nearby now. If she surfaced she was dead. But she was running out of air.

Adrien, her mind cried. *Hurry.*

Slowly, blackness engulfed her.

CHAPTER 9

Adrien heard her last desperate telepathic cry. He had one more in the air and he saw the fifth vampire dive suddenly into the water.

The vampire he battled had lost his religious garb and now fought him with dagger and chain, battling as fiercely as he and his brothers battled. Adrien had a few cuts, nothing too serious. But he had to get to Lily. If she died, they both would because of the chains.

He allowed his second self to appear weaker, listing toward the water.

The vampire took the bait and followed. With his first self, Adrien caught him from behind in the kidneys with his dagger. The man screamed and plunged into the water.

"Lily!" he shouted.

The vampire who'd dived earlier now surfaced, jeering. "She's dead." He lifted Lily's pale hand and shook it.

Adrien could sense that she was close to death, but not yet gone. The sudden rage he felt was so raw that before he understood what he was doing, both parts of him moved at light-speed toward the vampire who now opened his eyes wide. He tried to dip below the surface, as though that would do any good.

His rage had opened his vision. He could see Lily floating now as well as the panicked, thrashing movements of the gloating vampire as he tried to escape. Adrien pierced the water, dove straight for the bastard, caught him with one self while his split-self cut his throat.

He turned in the water, grabbed Lily in all four of his hands, and took her straight into the air. He meant to get her to the club, but as he spun in a 180 he saw a dozen more hooded figures closing in.

He held Lily close to his primary self's chest, re-formed, then flew away from the lake, faster than he ever had before, faster than any of these bastards could move.

He reached one of his private cavern homes, this time in South Africa, within twenty seconds of pulling Lily from the water. He stretched her out on the stone floor of his living room and began pumping the water from her lungs, then gave her mouth-to-mouth.

The moment she coughed and spewed all that liquid, her food followed. She cried out, grabbed her head, undoubtedly in pain from the speed of the recent flight, and with one arch of her back passed out.

He sat back on his heels, knowing that his life had just changed . . . forever.

Lily had almost died.

And his stubbornness about not embracing his Ancestral power had almost gotten her killed.

Well, that had to change.

He made plans with his housekeeper about caring for Lily.

Then he called Gabriel.

Three hours later Adrien sat in a chair by his bed, where Lily now slept. A fire roared in the nearby hearth.

He sat in jeans and a T-shirt, his leathers and tank drying out. His housekeeper and one of her staff had taken care of Lily, changing her, washing the lake water off her, forcing a healing herbal tea down her throat.

The tea contained a short-term sleeping potion as well so that Lily fell into a deep sleep and no longer thrashed and cried out for Adrien, or for her family; for Josh, for Jessie, or for her husband, Robert.

Now she was quiet, though very pale.

He'd sent two of his more powerful male servants to the Himalayas to check on Lucian and Marius, to let his brothers know that as soon as he could, he'd come for them and arrange their escape. Somehow. He also sent them to Lily's Manhattan apartment to bring more of her belongings back to South Africa.

He'd done all he could for his present situation, but the hardest truth about Lily's near-drowning, and what he needed to do about it, hit him square in the chest.

From the time she'd put the chain on him and he'd flown her back to Paris at full speed, hurting her the entire way, he'd been avoiding what he needed to do.

Now he saw no real way out.

Lily had basically drowned in Lake Como tonight, and all because of his hatred for his parentage and his fear that if he embraced greater power, like his father possessed, he'd become like him: without conscience, a risk to his friends, even to his half brothers, certainly to his world.

If there was some way he could predict where and how the fanatics might attack, he could manage where he took Lily and how fast they traveled. But from the events of the past twenty-four hours, he understood they meant to stop him from getting the weapon at all costs.

He couldn't let that happen. Silas and his fanatics were no more to be trusted than Daniel.

But the truth was, the source of the attack didn't

matter—only that Lily's vulnerability and his stubbornness had brought her to the point of death. Now she had one more horror she'd have to recover from, of drowning while under attack by goddamn fanatical vampires.

Some kind of change needed to come to his world. Maybe Sebastien was right, maybe there was something he could do, especially with so many loose factions out there, ineffective courts, and not enough laws on the books to protect the innocent. The governing Council, prior to Daniel's takeover, had failed time after time to do what needed to be done. So here he was, sitting in a goddamn chair in one of his favorite caves, on the edge of despair because he'd been pushed to this point through no fucking fault of his own.

He leaned forward and shoved a hand through his hair. Sweet Buddha Christ, and all the vampire gods thrown in together, he didn't want to do this thing.

He scoffed mentally, then offered a deep disgusted grunt into the air. He knew about pain. He'd been on close terms with cuts, bruises, and suffering from the time he could remember. His father had been a sadistic brute and had taken the flesh off his bones a hundred times with his whips and razor-sharp knives.

Dear old Dad.

His sire had been a sociopath who tortured his children. Worst of all, though procreation was rare in their long-lived world, his father had been one of the few extraordinary vampires able to sire as many offspring as he liked. And his siblings had all suffered as he had.

All of them.

Yes, his pain went deep, his disgust even deeper for the governing Council who had accepted Daniel's bribes and lain down for him, one and all.

When Lily began to stir, even to stretch her arms over her head, he rose from his chair and moved to the doorway. His housekeeper, who oversaw all of his homes, sat in a comfortable chair in the opposite alcove, reading the *Vampire Quarterly*.

She lifted her gaze, then her brows. "How's she doing?"

"Starting to wake up. Is the soup ready?"

She nodded and unfolded her legs from the chair. Setting the journal aside, she headed to the kitchen.

When he turned to look at Lily from the doorway, her eyes were open. Her fingers moved uneasily over the edges of the sheet and blanket that covered her. "Where am I?" she asked.

"South Africa, a good five thousand miles from Italy. No lakes around." He tried to smile, but the panic in her eyes as she put a hand to her throat set his lips once more in a tight line.

He returned to his chair, pulling it close to the bed. He reached for her hand and held it in his. She had long fingers and beautiful nails. He lifted her fingers to his lips. A swell of emotion tightened his jaw.

"You drowned," he said. Some things need to be faced head-on.

She nodded, tight bobs of her chin. "When will this horror stop?" she murmured, not meeting his gaze.

He leaned forward and rested his forearms on the bed, folding her hand into both of his. "Hey, you're alive. Right now, that's all that matters."

She let go of a quick sigh, nodding once more.

"Think about why you're doing this."

Her gaze slid to his and she frowned. "Why do you say that?"

"Because I've decided, knowing all that I sense about your character, that you're not doing this for money, are you?"

She shook her head. "Not even a little."

He watched her eyes fill with tears.

"I wish you'd tell me." There it was again, that profound need he felt to have her trust him.

"I can't." She shook her head back and forth, her gaze looking panicked again.

He eased back on pressuring her. "It's okay. But I hope at some point you can trust me enough to tell me."

She glanced around the room. "This is really nice." Then her gaze drifted to the ceiling and her eyes widened. "Oh, my God."

Adrien looked up as well. "It's beautiful, isn't it?" This part of the cavern was on a long ridge of granite that he'd had tunneled out into various living quarters. Vampire craftsmen had then chiseled and polished the ceiling of his apartment into a variety of patterns. "This design is called 'The Brook.'"

She wrinkled her nose. "I'm not seeing it. I suppose there's sort of a flow of water."

He chuckled. "No, the design was named after the creator, Edgar Brook."

"Oh, I see. Well, I believe Mr. Brook must be a genius."

"He was. He died about three hundred years ago."

She shifted her gaze to him once more. "Are you saying that this cave, in this state, has been around that long?"

He liked that the color was returning to her face. "Yes, that long."

The housekeeper arrived with a tray bearing a small tureen of soup.

Lily moaned. "That smells like heaven."

"We're indebted to the age of electricity," she explained. "And to hydroponics. We have acres of the best vegetables in the world growing deep in this system."

Lily pushed herself to a sitting position, and the housekeeper carefully placed the tray over her lap. She said she hoped Lily enjoyed the soup then left the room. Adrien listened to the sound of her soft-soled shoes disappearing down the hall.

Lily wore a white cotton nightgown with small pleats across the bodice, which made her look youthful, even fragile. Her hair was clean and she swept it back with one hand to rest over her shoulder. As she lifted her spoon and dipped, Adrien didn't know what to make of this woman or her sudden appearance in his life.

She didn't look at him as she ate. The trip of her spoon from lips, to bowl, to broth and back, became a slow, steady progression.

He waited until she had finished the last bite, then rang the bell. The housekeeper returned to take the tray.

Adrien knew the time had come to tell Lily what needed to happen next, but she was already sliding out of bed. "We need to get to that club. What time is it? Wait, I didn't sleep through the night, did I?"

He glanced at the clock. "No. We have several hours till dawn, but Lily, we're not going there, at least not yet."

She sat on the edge of the bed, and her brows rose. "Why not? I mean, I've recovered. I feel fine. I really do." The whiteness of her complexion belied her true condition. Hell if he didn't admire her all over again.

"Gabriel will be here shortly with a new set of chains, a double set. He said it wouldn't take long to get this thing done."

"I don't understand."

Absently, Adrien touched the chain at his neck.

Her eyes widened. She reached out and grabbed his wrist, hard. "No," she cried. "No. We decided we're not doing that."

"You're not doing anything. And all I'm doing is becoming something I should have become when I first flew you to Paris."

She glared at him in response.

"Don't look at me that way. Lily, you drowned. Don't you understand? You were almost gone when I pulled you out of the lake. Once we were airborne I might have tried to fly you slowly, but another, larger group of assassins was on us. I can't risk your life again. I can't because if you die, then I'll die and Daniel will kill my brothers. I have to keep you alive, just to stay alive myself."

"But I know how much you don't want to do this thing. I can feel that it's almost unbearable to you."

"My mind's made up."

She grabbed him harder and leaned forward. "No. I won't allow it."

"At this point, you don't get a say. Or do you want to be dead? And frankly, you are too much of a liability for me not to add a new power level to my arsenal."

Adrien felt like a strong wind blew over his face. He didn't recognize the sensation right away, but he was stunned. He'd only known Lily a little over two nights, and she sat here gripping his arm, standing in his corner, battling for him. What made it more intense was knowing that *his kind* had taken the lives of her family, changing and ruining her life forever. Yet she cared about him enough, after so short a time, to want him to hold his course.

Maybe that's what settled everything in his mind: As much as he detested what he was about to do, saving Lily's life was worth it. She hadn't deserved to have her family ripped apart, or to be somehow forced onto this mission of hers. And she sure as hell didn't deserve to die because of fanatics that apparently wanted them both dead no matter what.

He covered her hand with his once more then leaned in and kissed her.

She drew back, surprised. "What was that for?"

"Thank you," he said, with emphasis. "You're a true

friend and I'll never forget that. In all my long centuries, I can count on just these two hands the people in my life who would have stood up for me as you just have. It means a lot." He drew in a deep breath, then said, "Now, here's how this is going down."

An hour later Lily was dressed in appropriate sex-club attire: a shimmery, low-cut blue halter, a short black leather skirt, and long sexy boots.

She teased up her hair and added more eye makeup than she usually wore, hoping to create a different appearance so that she wouldn't be easily recognized.

Gabriel had arrived with the more powerful bonding chains. Apparently, no more was involved than for Adrien to put on his chain and let the process work through him. She'd reap the benefits, too, in terms of taking on more vampire abilities.

Even though Adrien stood just on the other side of the wall, she felt his unease about taking this step. From all that she understood, his father had been evil and powerful. Whether he still lived, she didn't know, but the last thing Adrien wanted was to be like him. "Lily, we're ready when you are."

The room had a full-length mirror so that she could get a good hard look at her reflection. Her heeled boots finished off the look better than anything else could have, and a zing of pleasure went through her knowing that Adrien would probably like this look on her.

He'd told her to wear anything she wanted. She'd considered another pair of jeans, but this was the better choice.

"Lily? What's going on?"

She rolled her eyes. He'd probably sensed her sudden excitement. Those chains again.

She moved toward the doorway and, after taking a deep breath, crossed the threshold.

Adrien turned toward her, his mouth agape as his gaze drifted slowly down her body, rested for an eye-popping moment on the stilettos of her boots, then retraced the journey to her face. "Holy shit," he murmured.

She shrugged. "I thought I'd blend in at Rumy's."

He nodded. "Yes, you will."

He moved toward her, dazed, and took her arm. She felt his desire for her like a hot, sizzling wave that washed over her and left her tingling head to toe. "You look really nice, Lily, but then you always do."

She shifted to look up at him. He wore black leather again, more weapons no doubt, ready for anything. "Thank you. So do you." The chain at her neck vibrated heavily, and if Adrien's friend Gabriel hadn't been standing a few feet away she would have thrown her arms around Adrien's neck and kissed him.

She wondered suddenly what would happen between them once Adrien wore the new double-chain.

He nodded once more, searching her eyes. "You okay?"

"Overwhelmed."

"I know what you mean."

She turned her attention to Gabriel. Adrien made the introduction.

Gabriel had short spiked black hair and warm gray eyes. He was nearly as tall as Adrien and wore a tailored shirt and slacks as well as a fine silk tie.

"Nice to meet you." Her gaze fell to the cloth-covered board Gabriel held in his hands and to the double-chain clamped in place on top of the cloth. Then she felt the vibration of the chain even at a distance. "So this is it."

"Yes, it is." Gabriel turned slightly in Adrien's direction. "You just put them on. The chains do the work."

Lily sensed a sudden rush of anger from Adrien, and she caught his arm. "It's not too late to stop this. I'm willing to take the risk."

At that, he met her gaze once more, but the flecked teal of his eyes darkened. "I've put this off far too long. And maybe if I hadn't, I could have stopped Daniel before he got this far."

With that, Adrien closed the distance between himself and the chains, pulled the double-looped silver set out of the clamps, and without skipping a beat slid it over his head.

At the same time, he jerked the single-loop blood-chain off his neck and threw it on the floor.

Lily blinked.

A second passed, then two.

A new vibration entered her chain and a wave of dizziness hit hard. She weaved on her feet and even held her arms away from her sides to balance herself.

Then her head began to hurt all over again.

Adrien saw that the new chain had put Lily off-balance and he wanted to go to her, to steady her, but he couldn't move. The natural power, Ancestral power, that he'd felt from as early as he could remember flowed through him in a succession of almost painful waves.

Power.

The most corrupting influence in the vampire world.

The thing that had made his father a monster.

And now it filled every cell of Adrien's body.

Would he become corrupt like his father?

His muscles contracted painfully, released, contracted again, his arms, his legs, chest, and back. Sweet Buddha Christ he hurt. He sank to his knees and held his head.

The waves struck hard again, causing the double-chain to vibrate.

He didn't want this. He'd never wanted this level of power because there was nothing he feared more than becoming like the one who'd sired him.

The more he resisted, the greater the pain, yet he couldn't let go, couldn't embrace what he'd always hated so much.

He groaned and rocked on his knees, his head still in his hands, his eyes squeezed shut.

He felt a pressure on his arms, a cool touch that began to ease a new kind of soothing wave through him. His muscles stopped seizing and the throbbing in his head calmed. The new waves of power began to flow.

He let his hands fall away from his face and opened his eyes.

Lily stared back at him. *I didn't know what else to do,* she said. *But I remembered that in the cavern, when I first met you, my touch calmed you down. Remember?*

He nodded. Lily was so beautiful and so pure—pure of heart, of soul, of conscience. He saw an aura around her, a silver shining glow. He blinked several times but the glow remained.

"Are you all right?" she asked.

He touched her cheek. She had soft skin and a creamy complexion, much prettier than a vampire's usual porcelain look, healthier, more alive.

"Adrien?"

He nodded. "I'm okay now. You were right to touch me. For whatever reason, contact with you helps."

"It's the bond of the chains."

"Maybe. Probably. Who the hell knows." He rose to his feet, lifting her with him, but he was surprised how much lighter she felt. Apparently even his physical strength had been enhanced.

He turned to Gabriel. "Thanks for helping out."

"Anytime. You know that."

"Yeah, I do." He turned and clapped Gabe on the shoulder.

"You're going to feel strange for a while."

"I can tell."

"And your speed will increase during altered flight, so watch those takeoffs and landings." He smiled crookedly. "I mean it. Be careful."

"I will. And thank you for doing this."

Gabriel nodded.

Adrien shifted toward Lily. "You're anxious to get going." He touched the chain, the double loops feeling strange beneath his fingers. "I can sense you even more clearly than before, the level of concern, almost desperation that you feel." He narrowed his gaze at her. "Almost as though you believe your life depends on getting that weapon. That's how you feel, isn't it?"

But the sensation that returned to him in a ripple of emotions felt more like deception than concern. He grabbed her arm. "When are you going to tell me the truth?"

But that stubborn chin of hers rose. "Never."

"Never's a long time," he murmured.

"Yes, it is."

"Fine." He released her arm, then addressed another issue. "You're a locator, we know that. And so far, you've had little success getting a fix on the weapon. But with this change of mine, I'm hoping that you'll be able to do better. Can you give it a try?"

Lily's hazel eyes widened. "Absolutely." She closed her eyes and touched the chain at her neck.

He felt her effort, even that his increased power was assisting her, but after a moment she opened her eyes and shook her head. "The tendrils were more active, but seemed to be reaching out in every possible direction."

"That would make sense," Gabriel said. "I know that when the Council shut down the scientific experiments all those years ago, many of the documents and more than one of the actual weapons were hidden in a bunch of cavern systems."

"Then we need more information."

Lily nodded. "So, it's on to The Erotic Passage."

Adrien slid an arm around her waist and pulled her tight against him. As she had been doing, she put her left foot on the top of his right boot.

She slung an arm around his neck and for a long few seconds desire for her rose, as it always did when he got this close to her. Only this time, given that his power level had been bumped up, a wave of need poured over him like a brushfire.

He trembled—not just because of what he felt, but because his desire ignited hers. This terrible attraction between them, which shouldn't have existed, roared to life.

With every ounce of strength he possessed, however, he turned away from his need, dipped his chin at Gabriel, and took off in a streak of altered flight that stunned him, straight up through the cavern, up and up.

Lily's arm around his neck tightened.

Are you in pain? Shit, I'm sorry. I'm going too fast.

He started to slow down, a process he found incredibly difficult since he'd launched them well through the cavern system and into the night sky.

I'm fine. Her arm relaxed. *Adrien, there's no pain at all. Don't slow down. You don't need to. You were right about this; more power has changed the experience for me. I have no pain.*

He rocketed through the air, heading north back to Italy. But as he passed over the Mediterranean, then the Italian landscape, before he knew it he found himself well over the Alps, having overshot his destination.

That's never happened before.

What?

I'm having a little difficulty gauging distance.

Well, just remember what Gabriel said about landings.

Right.

He spun around, headed south once more, then promptly overshot Lake Como by about fifty miles. And he kept overshooting. Again and again.

Eventually, he made enough adjustments to finally reach the lake, but it still took three landing attempts before he finally brought Lily to Rumy's private side entrance.

The bouncer knew him well and didn't even glance at Lily as he opened the door for them. Adrien had brought lots of women to the club over the years, and Lily, in her halter, short skirt, and damn sexy boots, fit right in.

Of course he'd donned a new set of battle leathers and was armed to the teeth. He also wore a black tee made of soft cotton, which seemed to make Lily happy since she kept touching him, or maybe it was the chains, or the sex. Hell, he didn't know. Didn't care, only that she stuck close, because that's where he wanted her, which begged a new question: How had he come to care so much in just a few hours?

He heard Lily gasp.

He stopped and turned toward her. "What? What's wrong?"

But she was staring at the carvings on the wall. "These are couples *doing it,* in about every position imaginable. Oh, that one is really inventive." She tilted her head sideways.

Instead of following the direction of her gaze, he looked away from the wall. He didn't need a reminder of what he really wanted to be doing right now. "I guess I should have warned you."

"I should have known. I mean, come on, *The Erotic Passage*?" She laughed.

He took her arm and gently put her back in motion.

"Are all the walls carved like this?"

"No. Some have bigger etchings."

"Well that's not going to help anything, is it?"

"Tell me about it." Her sweet feminine scent rolled around him now, and if that wasn't bad enough the new double-chain told him the rest of the story. He could sense the level of her desire and it matched his. He took deep breaths and started doing sums in his head.

A few yards more and the tunnel branched.

He made a right and after another ten yards, he came to Rumy's office. He glanced up at the security camera, red light winking. He rapped on the arched, wooden door. Black wrought-iron hinges and a ring-pull above the latch fit the club's overall feel, very dominance-based.

A masculine voice, muffled by the heavy wood of the door, called out, "Adrien, get your fucking ass in here."

He smiled and leaned down to Lily. "Rumy's home."

"Oh, goody."

At that, he chuckled once more, depressed the latch, and pushed.

Unfortunately, he met three automatic weapons pointed straight at him, all held by men in black robes; more fucking fanatics.

Rumy stood to the side of his guests offering a shrug and a roll of his eyes. He wore the usual extra-snug black T-shirt that emphasized that he worked out. He was short, maybe five-five, his black curly hair oiled and glistening in the dim light. He wore a silver belt and tailored Italian slacks, leather tasseled shoes, his typical style.

With a wry smile, he shrugged again. "Sorry, Adrien. There's a bounty on your head and the prize is a portion in the Rio Crystal Casino. I couldn't turn it down." His gaze shifted to Lily. "Of course the bounty includes your woman here. You must be Lily Haven. Heard a lot about you."

Adrien's hand naturally dropped to Lily's waist, especially since her body had stiffened. Holding her close, he said, "I guess somebody wants us bad."

Rumy glanced at his armed guests. "And don't try any of your altered flight shit. I've been assured these boys know how to use their weapons and you'll be full of holes before you punch past even one of these walls." The points of his fangs showed as he spoke, which almost gave him a lisp. He'd taken so much Double-V in recent years that he could never fully retract his fangs. He had permanent calluses on his lips from daily use. Nothing like a black-market vampire Viagra to change things up.

His operations suite had been carved out of granite in an intricate maze of rooms, each with a curved polished ceiling, marred only by discreet black tubes carrying electrical and air-conditioning. This front room had a couple of large black leather chairs near the front door and a wide wooden desk opposite. All three armed, hooded men, as well as Rumy, stood in front of the desk.

One of the back rooms of the office suite included a central command for his extensive security staff.

New question: Where were Rumy's men?

Adrien had the beginnings of a plan, but he wanted Lily's input, so he sent a telepathic stream. *Lily, he doesn't know that I have an increase in power and my gut tells me I could fly us both out of here, without injury, but we still need information and this is the best place.*

What do you suggest?

That we ride this train to the next stop. Can you handle it?

Hell, yeah. Take them all on.

He held Rumy's gaze. "As you can imagine, I'm not crazy about the idea of turning my woman over to your friends. Got any other ideas? I have a fortune I'd happily spend to change this scenario. Care to make a trade?"

One of the fanatics started to protest, but Rumy held up his hand. "Not to worry, my fanatic friend. My course was set the moment you stepped into my office bearing your guns."

Inwardly, Adrien began to smile. Rumy, for all his shortness of stature and absurdly callused lips, didn't allow anyone to bring firearms into his club, not without repercussions at some point. The fanatics with their religious bent couldn't possibly understand the rules of an underground.

To Adrien, Rumy offered a subtle jerk of his head toward the archway at the back corner of his office, which led to the security center.

Adrien understood the signal. Rumy's men waited in place for their boss to give the word.

Good.

As he assessed the hooded men, he didn't know which he despised more, his father and the weak-willed Council of Ancestrals that he now owned, or these fanatics, who in the name of spirituality killed the innocent.

Spit gathered in his mouth.

But the faint pressure of Lily's hand on his arm reminded him why he was here, that he wasn't alone, and that these men were hopefully just a bump in the road to get where they needed to go.

Funny how just her touch reined in his all-over-the-map emotions and drives.

He covered her hand with his and gave a squeeze. He felt her try to reach him telepathically, but he blocked her, a strange event all on its own. He needed to figure this out, though, and do it quickly. The middle bastard was sweating and had his finger too close to the goddamn trigger.

"Again, don't even think about altered flight," Rumy said. "You're not fast enough."

Rumy was giving him a hint about how he wanted this to go down.

He opened up his mind to Lily and said, *I need you to stay right where you are and ignore what I'm about to do. Got it?*

Yep.

"I wouldn't think of altered flight," Adrien said.

Then he did.

He moved fast—a little too fast, shooting past the first gunman. He adjusted, gripped his gun, took the next, and just as the third asshole would have fired, he took him out of the room, carrying him straight over the water and dropped him into Lake Como.

When he flew back into the room, Rumy's security staff had the two remaining assassins on the floor. One of them was using the butt of his gun to pound the vampires in turn, over and over, although purposely avoiding the head.

The men screamed and balled themselves up.

He returned to Lily's side and tried to take her in his arms, knowing she shouldn't be watching this, but she pushed him away. "Make them stop, Adrien."

At first he thought she was distressed by what she was seeing, but the chains told a different story and he felt her determination.

"We need to know what they know," she said. "Maybe they have information about the weapon."

At these words, both Adrien and Rumy yelled at the guard to stop hurting the robed reptiles, but he got one last hit in before he stepped back.

Rumy glared at the men on the floor. "Nothing I hate

worse than fanatics. I don't even despise a rat in my organization as much as these assholes who use religion to persecute those who can't protect themselves. Fucking bastards."

Adrien chuckled. "Rumy, I knew there was something about you I liked."

"Aw, can the flattery. Just tell me how the fuck you did that altered flight shit. Usually, you glide out of here. This time you vanished. Whoa. Hold the fucking phone." He looked him over, his gaze landing on the chain at Adrien's neck. "You've bumped up your power level with a double blood-chain, and there's only one way you can do that. Well damn my ass, you finally made the leap. You're on the Ancestral path." He glanced at the chain Lily wore. "And you're all bound up with a human and now you've got more power. A lot of it, too." For half a second, panic hit Rumy's eye.

Adrien held up a hand. "Not to worry. I have no takeover plans for you or your business. Trust me, I'm not that man."

"Good. That's good." He plucked at a couple of curls above his ears then patted them flat.

The assassins had grown quiet, which meant both had dipped into vampire-healing mode and would be back at full strength in a couple of hours.

Adrien thought about killing them, and in any other circumstances that's just what he would have done. He and his brothers dealt swiftly with fanatics who murdered the innocent. So long as there was irrefutable evidence of the crime, they held a brief trial, took off the head, and burned the bastards to ashes just to make sure they couldn't come back to do more damage.

Their leader, Silas, knew what Adrien and his brothers did to fanatics proven to kill the innocent, who laid waste to some of the outlying cavern systems when average vampires refused to agree to Silas's decrees. The man and his followers were spiritual tyrants, and Adrien and his brothers had sworn to battle them to the death, if need be.

Rumy sat down on the side of his desk, one leg swinging free. "I take it the trip north didn't help much for what you're lookin' for."

"Not much, which is why we're here."

"I kind of figured."

Lily ventured, "So, what exactly do you know about the extinction weapon?"

A hush fell over the room. All the vampires stilled, which made the space a room full of statues for at least ten long seconds.

When the breathing resumed, Rumy shook his head. "I haven't got a clue. I mean, there's not been a peep about the weapon in decades, not since the nineteen fifties when everybody and their uncle was doing experiments in hidden caves all over the world. Jesus-Buddha-and-Confucius all wrapped up in a fishnet, I hate even thinking about something so powerful that it could wipe us off the face of the earth."

He huffed a sigh, his gaze fixed to Lily. "I don't know what Adrien here has told you, but our kind doesn't have big numbers—less than a million against your virus-like billions.

"Our people are spread out over every country in the world. Most of us never procreate. We're so damn long-lived that our genetics decided early on we'd better not be a fertile race. So why are you after the extinction weapon anyway?" Rumy stared hard at Lily.

Adrien nodded to her and watched her take a deep breath.

"I've been contracted to get the weapon . . . for a price."

A single oily brow rose. "That's a language I can

understand. So you'll turn it over and get paid for your troubles."

Lily nodded. Adrien watched her closely. The new chain had enhanced what passed between them but in this case what he felt from her remained the same, just a powerful level of determination.

One of the vampires on the floor moved and Adrien felt his quick sudden distress. He shifted his gaze from Lily, then shoved at the man's arm with the toe of his boot. "What do you know? And don't tell me *nothing,* or I'll let Rumy's guards start pounding on you again."

His eyes lit up suddenly, the fervent light of the devoted. "The human, Lily, is destined to destroy all vampire-kind. You must listen to me. The *great one,* Master Silas, whose visions always prove true, has seen her coming, has been able to predict where she would be with tremendous accuracy, like this moment. He said this would happen. And I've heard you say you're looking for the extinction weapon. Don't listen to her. She means harm to our race. She intends to destroy us all."

Rumy glanced at Lily. "Do you intend to destroy our race?"

Lily shook her head. "No. I'm only here for the weapon."

Rumy turned back to the fanatic and brought the butt down hard on his head. "Asshole."

CHAPTER 10

Lily didn't know which was worse, that she'd actually heard the man's skull crack or that she just didn't care. Of course, it was hard to be compassionate toward a person who wanted her in the ground, or maybe burned at the stake. Still, it bothered her that she wasn't more upset.

She might even have voiced the thought, just to get it out in the open and have a look, but at that moment the part of her born from the chain around her neck activated her revisiting power.

By now she had some command over it and knew she had a choice whether to allow the vision to come or not.

"What's going on, Lily?"

She glanced at Adrien, but switched to telepathy. *A vision, but I'm not sure what to do. I don't want to waste our time with something from the past.* She glanced at the two fanatics on the floor, then her gaze flitted to Rumy and his bodyguards.

Adrien narrowed his gaze. *A lot has happened over the years in this room, and you just heard the fanatic say*

*that you've been seen here by Silas. I think you should
give it a shot.*

Thoughts about her son, always roaming the edges of her
mind anyway, flowed to the forefront. She'd do anything to
get Josh back, including allowing a vision in a place like
this, with two beat-up vampires on the floor and more
weapons than she'd seen in the whole course of her life.

She opened herself up and the edges of the room began to spin, only faster this time than before, something
she attributed to Adrien's new set of chains and increased
power.

She held her arms wide and the scene emerged, like
watching a movie, of a vampire in a fine black suit, a pure
white silk shirt, and a gold tie.

The man towered over Rumy, the way Adrien towered
over other men. His hair was dark and slicked back and
he had a tightly trimmed black goatee. He was achingly
handsome and something about him seemed familiar,
even though she was sure she'd never seen him before.

In the vision, the vampire leaned down close to Rumy's
cheek. *"So, little man, have you found the right woman
for me yet? I've grown impatient. You know my needs."*

Rumy shook in his fine leather shoes. *"I . . . I have a
lead from Nairobi. Perfect dark skin, white teeth, and
thin sharp fangs."*

"Tell me of her breasts."

"I don't know anything yet, just that she's a beauty."

He held his hand open, palm up. *"But you know what I
like: very full, voluptuous, more than my hand or my
mouth can hold. Don't fail me, Rumy, or my appetites may
extend to this club and I'll take the whole thing over
before you can even blink."*

Lily felt Rumy's fear, then her own. This man, so elegant, so beautiful even in profile, defined malevolence—
something so evil that his dark presence, even in a

revisiting vision, had the power to reach her, to frighten her.

At that moment he leaned back, closed his eyes, and turned slowly toward her. When he opened his eyes, he looked right at her, stepping in her direction until he was only a few feet away. The vampire could see her—all the way from the past, he could see her.

He met and held her gaze, then looked her up and down. She trembled and could feel that Adrien had slipped his arm around her waist, that he held her close to his side in the present, but she couldn't tear her gaze away from what she knew to be a monster from the past.

His eyes were a strange yet beautiful color, almost a teal like Adrien's, but lighter and flecked with hints of green and gold.

His nostrils flared. "I smell a human female. Yes, definitely human. But tell me, lovely one, why are you here at The Erotic Passage?"

She felt very strange, the way she had felt with Giselle. She understood then that even from the past the vampire had enough power to enthrall her. "I'm here looking for the extinction weapon."

"How intriguing." The man smiled, showing large, even teeth. "What is your name, lovely one?"

"Lily. Lily Haven."

"Where are you from?"

"Arizona, near Phoenix. Deer Valley. But I have a place in Manhattan as well."

His smile broadened. "So you're a woman of wealth?"

"Some wealth, yes."

She began to weave on her feet, back and forth, rocking harder and harder. Her name came to her from a great distance, and suddenly the vision disappeared and Adrien was shouting at her and shaking her.

She felt herself falling backward, falling and falling, yet she never hit the floor.

Sometime later, she opened her eyes, expecting to be on the floor. Instead, Adrien held her in his arms, his brow furrowed.

As she blinked, her brain finally righted itself. "How long was I out?"

"Just a couple of minutes. Are you all right? What happened?"

"A man spoke to me."

Adrien's brows rose. "From a revisiting vision? A man spoke to you from inside a vision?" He seemed incredulous.

Lily nodded.

"What did he look like?"

Lily described him. "He scared me, Adrien."

"And his eyes were similar to mine, but lighter?"

"Yes, goldish flecks."

Adrien turned around and dropped into the large leather chair by the door. "Fuck." His scowl formed a deep furrow between his brows.

Lily had a sinking sensation in her gut. "Who was he?"

He met her gaze. "You probably already know."

But it was Rumy who enlightened her. "I guess you're screwed, because you just met our equivalent of the Prince of Darkness, Daniel the A-hole. He gives vampires a bad name, and that was long before I opened The Erotic Passage, long before an underworld, long before anything of importance, really. Some say he built the black market himself, that he keeps as many rogue vampires drugged out and in service to him as he can, and he has more sex-slave rackets going than hills have ants."

"Daniel," Adrien murmured in a low voice. He shaded his eyes with his hand.

"Okay," Lily said, moving carefully through what felt like an emotional minefield. "I've just met *the evil one*."

He grabbed the chain at his neck and shook it, his rage flowing in waves. *Daniel is the most powerful vampire on the planet, and has been living at this power level for over two thousand years, maybe longer. But Daniel*—His thoughts ceased like a wall falling down between them, as though the memories were too painful to continue.

He took a deep breath. "These problems with our world won't be solved in a day or a week. Maybe not even in a millennium. What disturbs me right now is that you told him your name and where you live."

"Yes, I did. He had control of me in that moment, the way Giselle did earlier. I can't even fathom that level of power—that he could speak to me and reach me from the past."

She staggered on her feet, and Adrien suddenly rose up and caught her as she listed. "Oh, God, Adrien, please don't tell me that in this moment Daniel discovered who I am and because of it he hunted for me until he found me and two years ago destroyed my family. Please, don't tell me it's true. Please don't tell me that I was the cause of my family's destruction?"

He drew her hard against him, holding her tight in his arms. She buried her face in his shoulder. She didn't need him to answer these questions; she felt them to be true. Somehow Daniel had reached into the future and seen this day, using it to exploit her.

He tilted his head, and compassion filled his eyes. He drew her into an embrace, holding her fast. She forced air in and out of her lungs, and choked back the tears that wanted to escape.

Lily, what happened to your family isn't your fault, because you can't protect against crazy. It's not possible. Do you hear me?

Lily nodded against his shoulder. On the deepest level, she knew he was right. She'd thought the same thing every time some madman went on a killing spree. All the details would come out in the news, and everyone would try to figure out how to prevent it from happening again.

But when people were out of their minds, they were still going to run the red light.

I'm so sorry, Lily.

And Daniel is insane, isn't he?

The worst kind of insanity.

As the seconds passed, however, something new entered her mind, her thinking, a kind of cold hatred that found in Daniel a single pertinent object.

She drew back from Adrien slowly, crossing her hand over his chest to flow down his opposite arm until she had his hand in a tight grip, right palm to right palm.

He seemed to know, to understand her meaning and her intention. They'd each been wounded by Daniel, as had the entire vampire world. "He needs to be taken from the face of the earth."

Adrien nodded. "Yes, he does."

"I'll help you. I swear it, Adrien, by all that I hold dear, I swear that I'll help you."

Rumy called out, "I'm glad you two lovebirds have gotten everything settled between you, but what do you want me to do with these assholes?" He inclined his head toward the floor.

Adrien waved a hand in their direction. "Get rid of them."

Rumy's security uttered several approving grunts, grabbed up the fanatics, and vanished with them through the walls.

"Good riddance." Rumy clapped his hand and took a deep breath. "Ah, that's much better. The air smells fresher now, cleaner somehow."

She met Rumy's gaze. "So, do you know anyone here

who might know where we should look for the weapon? As you can see, we've got a shitfest going on."

At that Rumy grinned, the tips of his fangs sliding over his lower lip. "I like you." To Adrien, "She's a keeper." Back to Lily. "Since I've basically told you all I know, which is why I sent you to that prick Hardesty, your best bet would be to ask Eve. She knows even more than I do about the underworld. If anyone has information that I don't, Eve will."

"So where do we find her? Is she working tonight?"

"She's here every night." Rumy slid off the desk, which he then rounded to flip open a laptop. He started tapping keys. "She'll probably be in her theater right now, but I'll check for you." He continued tapping the keys and after a moment a strange, rhythmic slapping sound ricocheted through the room.

"Nice. She's flog-fucking one of her subs, big motherfucker, too. Listen to the rhythm. She knows how to use a flogger like no other dom I know."

Lily felt the air in the room change.

She glanced around. All the men had become fixated on the sound and the deep moans that accompanied the slaps. There was something else, something in the background, soft and low. Not music exactly, but close.

To her surprise, she turned her ear toward the screen and with a power that only made sense because of the shared blood-chain, she stretched her hearing.

The background sound proved to be a woman chanting softly, but the words seemed to be in a different language.

"What is she saying?"

All the men glanced at her, predatory shifts of attention, and she suddenly became acutely aware how short her skirt was, how much leg she revealed, and the exact height of her boot-heels.

Yep, sex charged the air, a blatant raw sensation that plucked at her body in several places at once.

Adrien drew close, turning to face her and standing slightly in front of her, to shield her from the other men. "Eve is a dom and she's reciting Ancestral chants that affect a male vampire's desire."

"We need to talk to her now."

He searched her eyes carefully. "I don't know you very well, Lily, but Eve's theater can be hard to take if you aren't prepared."

"I don't care about that," Lily said. "It can't possibly be worse than anything else we've been through so far."

"You've got a point." He turned back to Rumy. "Is she still using The Ruby Cave?"

At that Rumy smiled, a crooked tilt to his scarred-up lips that looked lascivious and cute at the same time. "Yep."

Adrien thanked him for his help.

Rumy called out, "I'll keep my ear to the ground. If I hear anything you need to know, I'll give you a holler."

Adrien nodded, turning back when he reached the doorway. "You've been a good friend to me."

"You're all right, Adrien. You're always welcome here, you and your brothers."

He thanked him again, then took Lily by the hand.

Once in the cool hallway, she asked, "What did they do to those men?"

"I won't pull any punches here, Lily. They killed them."

"No prison time?"

"That's part of the problem. We don't have dedicated prisons and no real justice system."

"What about that cavern where you were held?"

Adrien snorted. "That's not a prison, just one of several locations Daniel uses to inflict pain, or couldn't you tell?"

"How would I even know what's true or not true about your world?"

"Another good point."

He led her back the way they'd come, crossing to the other branch of the tunnel, which led deeper into the Como system.

The tunnel widened and intersected with a broad avenue-like hallway, richly appointed with crystals in patterns over the walls and an opalescent gleam to the floor.

A number of sounds assaulted her at once. First was a low level of music that had a strong bass beat, very rhythmic, like Eve's floggers, very *sexual*. She had to keep reminding herself that this was essentially a sex club.

Adrien led her down the broad hall, which opened up into a massive cavern, definitely the biggest one she'd seen so far.

Much to Lily's surprise the music was live, performed by a band of musicians composed of beautiful men in elegant leather outfits, studded, exposing muscular arms and chests.

She watched them for a moment, and noticed that the audience listened while seated at small intimate tables, candlelight casting a soft glow throughout the space.

She opened her mind to his. *Everything is so tasteful. I thought*—But she broke off the rest of it. Maybe he was getting tired of all the slurs she cast on his kind.

Adrien smiled, however, something he didn't do much, as he glanced down at her. *You thought it would be one big orgy?* He still had hold of her hand.

She couldn't help but chuckle. *Yes, that's exactly what I thought. I mean, the flogger—*

Rumy has dozens of specialists. He runs a tight ship, everything by appointment, each theater with doors that close. His hand was on her waist and she felt the sudden tension in him as he guided her to yet another hall. "This

staircase takes us to a new level of the cavern system."
She descended what proved to be about a hundred steps
that circled down and down.

Once the music grew faint, he said quietly, "The club
extends several miles deep into the surrounding hills.
Many of the workers have homes here, including Eve.
Rumy has numerous guest suites and even has a villa
somewhere deep in the earth and hidden. I've never even
been there. Again, everything is very private. I'm going
to use altered flight to get us to The Ruby Cave where Eve
presents her Dominance Theater. Just wanted you to be
prepared."

"For what? Your new version of altered flight or Eve's
act?"

He laughed. "Both."

A moment later the flight began.

Lily had expected to arrive in a room with a red theme,
since Adrien had called it The Ruby Cave. But she hadn't
expected the entire theater, except for a black onyx ceiling, to be a rich scarlet. Although *ruby* was the right word,
as though the walls had been covered in the precious gem.

What's this made of? she asked, mind to mind, her gaze
fixed to the glittering walls.

But nothing returned to her.

Adrien's lack of response sharpened her attention. Piv-
oting toward him, she saw that he stared hard at the scene
on the stage below, of a tall woman, her blond hair in a
long ponytail that hung past her buttocks, slowly rubbing
with one hand the thighs and backside of a large, powerful,
and very naked man chained facedown on a table.

The theater was unusual in its layout. Those nearest
the stage sat in a small cluster, but almost everyone else
stood in loose pairs and groups throughout the angled
room.

Lily felt her cheeks heat up. The air here, as in the

office earlier, was charged with sex. The man's face was turned toward the audience. His eyes were closed, his face squeezed up as though he was in pain. But she knew it was much more than that.

The soft chanting once more filled the air as Eve lifted her flogger and once more began a rhythmic beating of the man's back, thighs, and ass. She kept up her indistinguishable, singsong words.

Lily thought the woman's voice mesmerizing.

The next moment, however, Adrien tugged on her hand and pulled her out of the room the way they'd come.

The hall was cool, and for that she was grateful. She took a deep breath and was about to express her gratitude that Adrien had brought her back out here when she realized something was wrong. He was turned away from her, one hand on the smooth wall of more polished granite, this time in flecks of brown and black, the candle sconces in bronze.

Her chain vibrated strongly once more and she opened to Adrien, to what he was feeling and experiencing.

What returned to her was a level of arousal that astonished her.

He was close. That was why he leaned against the wall, his forehead pressed to his wrist.

Bondage? Chains? Flogging?

And yet what flew through her mind was a fantasy of seeing him chained up like that, held immobile and worked over. She touched the chains on her neck. Was this his fantasy or hers?

Her breathing hitched as she felt the depth of his need. Maybe she didn't understand why Eve's theater had affected him like this, taking him to the edge so fast, but the scent he exuded, so masculine and full of erotic herbs, had given her a new idea.

"Adrien," she said softly. She laid a hand on his back and he arched at her touch then groaned. "Take me. Now."

Adrien felt Lily's hand like a hot coal against his back. He hadn't expected to become aroused like this. He didn't even understand what had triggered the intensity of sensation this time. He'd seen dominance shows before, but not with Lily so close, not with the chains vibrating against his neck and chest, not with his increased power.

Within seconds he'd become fully aroused, and though he tried to calm himself down, he couldn't.

Of course he was in a near-constant state of arousal around Lily as it was, but her clubbing clothes didn't help. How many times had his gaze taken in her naked back, half hidden by the waterfall of her exquisite hair. He'd wanted his lips on her back and lower, over her ass, then lower still, parting her legs from behind, God help him.

Now she was offering herself, and he didn't deserve her right now. Shame ripped through him at the source of his desire—that he wanted Lily binding him and taking him, maybe even hurting him like he'd been hurt repeatedly throughout his life.

Her hand floated up and down his back and her scent thickened through the air. He could sense her desire as well and smell it, so he knew he wasn't alone in his need.

I'd like to have you chained on that table.

Oh, God, had she really just pressed those erotic words into his mind? *Lily, this isn't right.*

Fuck what's right, came straight back at him. *I need you. And I don't care the why of it. Adrien, fuck me now. I'm aching for you and I'm all yours.*

He turned into her and dragged her roughly into his arms, slanting a kiss over her lips.

Can we do this here? In the hallway?

Holy fuck, even her voice in his head did something to him. The vibration of the chain seemed to enhance his ability to feel what she felt. He could tell that her need had sharpened to match his.

What had she asked him? Could they do this here?

Rumy had several rules about the where of an encounter. Hallways were forbidden, but Adrien knew his way around this labyrinth of a club. The cavern had three significant layers, miles of tunnels, and at least a dozen secret niches, all of which he'd used at one time or another.

I have to fly you to a private place. You sure you want to do this?

God, yes.

She panted against him as he set them in motion. Though he wanted to kiss her while he flew, the new level of his power demanded that he be careful right now.

He only overshot the location once, but he finally made it, landing on the last scrap of tile laid out at the end point of the system. He took a quick glance around. The space was as he remembered: a crevice in the mountain, still undeveloped and very private.

The problem with caves, though, was how well noise traveled. "No sounds," he said.

Got it. Just do me, Adrien. Oh, my God, your need is flowing over me in waves. It must be the chains but it feels so damn good.

Your scent. You don't know what you smell like to me, all female and ready. I could come just breathing along your neck.

With one hand supporting her around her waist, he unbuttoned and unzipped his leathers, shoving them down his hips and thighs. She pulled her short skirt up, blessing the polished walls behind her because he needed leverage right now.

He lifted her leg, tucked his hips, and thrust, easily pushing past her thong.

She slung an arm around his neck and held on. She got her mouth close to his ear. "Adrien, fuck me."

The words, her scent, the feel of her wetness that allowed him to glide as he thrust hard, sent him into a frenzy. Her arm became a vise around his neck. He could feel she was close and when her body jerked and she pressed her open mouth to his cheek, her breath came out in a harsh agonized whisper of "Oh, God, oh, God, oh, God."

As she came, her well was a fist around his cock. An image flashed through his mind, maybe a kind of knowing, he wasn't sure, but he saw himself chained to a table, her mouth surrounding his cock.

That heady image was all it took. He came hard, seeing himself chained up, thrusting into her mouth—her pussy—her mouth, the future vision and the present sensations trading places at light-speed so that he felt as though he released down her throat while at the same time he spent himself inside her.

He was breathing hard as the last pleasurable pulse jerked through his cock. He felt her gasping for breath as well.

But as he came back to himself, she kissed his cheek then dipped lower to his mouth. *That was exquisite,* she said within his mind as her tongue circled his lips.

Gratitude flowed through him as he kissed her in return, dipping his tongue inside. *Thank you. Lily, you're one of the most generous women I've ever known. You didn't have to do this, but I'm so glad you did. You have every reason to hate me for what I am. Instead, you've offered yourself to me repeatedly.*

To his surprise, she chuckled and with her hands encircled the back of his neck, tugging at him playfully. "I could say the same thing to you. I've never felt so needy before. I guess it's the chains."

"Not just because I'm pretty?" The words sounded stupid to his ears, but he felt such a powerful well of emotion flowing toward her that nothing else would do.

But she smiled and with one hand petted his cheek. "You're damn gorgeous and you know it. Worse, I like you. I admire you. That goes a long way to making me this willing to give in to all these sensations. But I have to admit, it didn't help to see that man *enjoying* what was happening to him."

His heart skipped a beat. "You weren't disgusted?" He needed to know the answer.

She searched his eyes and squeezed the back of his neck. "Truth? I thought it was hot as hell because of how he felt. And how you felt watching him. I think that turned me on more than anything."

He almost felt compelled to tell her of his fantasy of the table and the chains, her mouth and his cock. But something held him back, that sick feeling that the whole thing was wrapped up with the shit of his past.

"And now, my good vampire, I have a little problem. I didn't think we'd be doing this or I would have come prepared, but you can imagine my present difficulty." She rolled her hips against his.

He thumbed her cheek and kissed her. He dipped down and tugged at his pants, dragging them up his thighs one-handed as he stayed connected to her. He reached into his back pocket and pulled out several folded tissues. He showed her then reached between them and wiped his cock as he withdrew from her. He then pressed the tissues against her opening. He didn't remove his hand, though. He pressed now and again and felt the tissues grow damper. He knew the drill, especially since he'd left a lot of himself inside her.

She released a sigh. "Thank you. I just didn't think. Hey, does your kind use condoms much?"

He smiled and shook his head. "Not much. Disease doesn't affect us and as Rumy explained, children are rare."

"Right."

After a moment, he removed the tissues. "How's that feel?"

"Good." She adjusted her thong then her skirt.

He then pulled up his pants and slid the used-up tissues into his pocket.

"I'm liking your battle leathers more and more," she said. "You're a man who's ready for anything."

"Hell, yeah." But for a moment, he was caught by the light in her eyes, the warmth, the humanness that he'd come to value, her grace, her willingness to take care of him, and that she wasn't embarrassed by the mess that sex could make.

But then she'd been married and she'd given birth. A woman with children was used to a lot of things.

On impulse, he leaned in and kissed her, wrapping his arms around her fully, willing her to understand that he valued her, all that she was in this moment, all that she'd done for him, the sharing of her body and her blood, the sacrifice of binding herself to him.

She held him tightly in response and he felt her intensity, almost her desperation. "Oh, Adrien," she whispered against his neck. "What's happening here, between us?"

"I don't know." His heart was swelling with emotions that didn't make sense, not with a human, not with someone he'd met a little over a day ago.

After a long moment, he drew back. "Eve's performance is probably over. You ready?"

She nodded. "Yes. Let's get on with this."

CHAPTER 11

Eve was a great beauty with large breasts that overflowed a tight black leather bustier. Her height put her at Amazon status. In her stilettos, she had at least two inches on Adrien.

Lily's gaze ended up at collarbone level, which meant she had a good view of the sweat beaded in the valley of the woman's cleavage.

She wore leather wrist guards studded with ruby-red crystals, about a dozen silver rings, a barely there thong, and what she could only describe as western leather chaps so that a lot of her inner thigh and outer buttocks showed.

She wiped a hand over her forehead. "Adrien, my love, when are you going to relent and let me put you on my table? I'm very good at this. I can take you to the edge about a dozen times and then let you fly in such a way that you'll shout for a century."

A strange knife-like sensation pierced Lily's sternum and started cutting her up. Instead of pain, however, all she felt were streamers of blood-red rage flowing through her chest and into her muscles, even down her arms until her hands were balled into fists.

Adrien glanced at Lily and slid his arm, as he often did, around her waist. Only this time, he pulled her in a powerful jerk against his body so that she stilled. "We're chain-bound, Eve. You can see that, so stop with this shit right now. It's been a rough night."

Eve turned ice-blue cat eyes on Lily. She didn't smile, just gave a long, slow look up and down.

"Does the kitty play?" she asked, her voice soft, low, seductive.

Lily's nostrils flared.

A small smile curved Eve's lips. Then she sidestepped toward Adrien, sidling close.

That did it. With lightning speed, Lily slipped in front of Adrien, planted her hands on the Amazon's arms, and shoved her.

But the woman was a vampire, worked out, and it was like pushing against a granite wall. "Leave Adrien alone." Her voice echoed up and down the corridor.

Eve's eyelids dropped. She dragged a hiss of air between pursed lips that was more sensual than hostile. "The kitty has claws. Me like. I could do you both, have you both chained to my table."

When Eve reached for Adrien's arm, Lily blocked her hand, slapping it away. Eve tried again and again, half-heartedly, chuckling each time.

This wasn't working and the female vampire was too damn strong so Lily began pushing backward at Adrien. That her buttocks connected with his arousal sent fury washing through her veins. She whirled in his arms. "What the hell?"

But his eyes fell to half-mast. *It's you, Lily, taking on a vampire, keeping her away from me. I'm hot for you. Eve has always left me cold, and damn, if you and I hadn't just fucked I'd take you right now.*

She dialed down her rage and planted a hand on his soft tee. "You'd better be telling me the truth, because I've got a lava flow of rage in my veins right now."

"I know." He held her arms and to Eve said, "Stop the nonsense. You've got my woman ready to go volcano. Can you give the act a rest? You know I'm never going to sleep with you and I'll definitely never lay myself out on your table."

Eve glanced from one to the other. "But you might let her do it."

"I might," he said. "Now, where can we talk that doesn't have a table or a bed or a closet full of your gadgets? I'm serious and if you don't oblige me, I'll tell Rumy you've been hitting on me again." Rumy had made it clear that Adrien and his brothers were off-limits to Eve.

At that, Eve straightened her shoulders. "Fine." She whirled around and shifted to altered flight, disappearing through the opposite wall.

Lily was flying with Adrien before she knew he'd started them after Eve. But it only took a couple of mind-and-eye-jarring seconds to catch up, even to get used to passing through walls of stone, through furniture and groups of people, mostly without flinching.

She kept her eye on the red glitter effect that flowed behind Eve as she flew, her ponytail swaying from side to side. The color suited her and seemed to sparkle. *How is she doing that? Or do all vampires have a kind of signature when they fly?*

It's all for show, something Eve concocted.

I don't like her very much.

She's not so bad. You'll see. Again, it's all for show.

Adrien began to slow and the shimmering red glitter bunched up suddenly then disappeared.

Passing through one last wall, Lily landed with Adrien in what looked like a nicely furnished home.

"I always wondered how you lived," Adrien said. "And thank you for bringing us here."

"Aw, hell, if I'm not going to get any action, I'd rather be comfortable. Give me two secs to clean up and change. Then I'll tell you what I know." The woman seemed almost normal as she disappeared down a side hall.

Lily's heart lurched. Maybe she'd finally get the information she needed.

The sound of water running, or rather flowing in sheets, drew her attention. As she turned around, her brows rose: She was looking at a waterfall not thirty feet away. She wended a path through some elegant modern black leather furniture, past a long rectangular dining table, to an elegant creation of rock, water, and lighting.

She wondered where the pump was, then looking up realized she was seeing the real deal, a waterfall inside the cave system.

Vampires and caves. Why not waterfalls? It all made sense, and everywhere she went in this strange new world, she saw that the caves, the sculpted walls and floors, the tunnels through hard rock, had all been around for a long time. Behind the flow of water, she could see that granite had been carved and polished so that it appeared as though light glittered through the flow of water.

When she heard Eve call out offering her guests wine, which Adrien accepted, she returned to him. A servant appeared, a much shorter woman in a crisp white, tunic-like apron over a maroon gown, and took Adrien's request for two Cabernet Sauvignons.

After taking the first sip, Adrien suggested they sit down in the chairs opposite the couch. Lily sank into the soft leather and gave herself to savoring the wine and trying to let go of some of her tension about where she was, that she kept having some really outrageous sex with a vampire, and that a sex-club dom was now changing in the other room.

She eased back and closed her eyes, a mental list popping into her head: Category, The Erotic Passage, item one, get information from Eve about the weapon; item two, get Josh back.

As always happened when she thought about her son, her stomach tightened, but she forced back the tension and sipped her wine. She had to relax through this process, through these soul-shattering experiences that kept turning her world upside down. The more relaxed she was, the better her decisions would be—but much easier said than done.

"You okay?"

She opened her eyes and shifted to meet Adrien's beautiful flecked teal gaze. She nodded. "I'm surviving."

His lips quirked. "Sometimes that's all that matters." He lifted his glass to her. "For what you've been through, you're doing great."

His voice soothed her; that was what she understood, the deep resonance, the kindness. Maybe it was that quality that surprised her most of all, just how kind Adrien was.

Guilt pierced her suddenly, about why she was here, that she was using Adrien, and that she would go to any lengths to get her son back. "I don't want to hurt you," she whispered. "But how can this end well, any of it?"

"Lily, what's going on? Tell me." He tilted his head and frowned.

She wanted to tell him about Josh, she really did, but how wise would that be? She'd agreed to the terms of the mission. Was her need to tell Adrien the truth worth putting her son's life on danger?

She touched the chain at her neck. On the other hand,

this wasn't a normal situation and the bond she shared with Adrien had already told her so much, had made her care for him. She almost opened her mouth to speak—but at that moment a very different Eve returned to the living room.

She was barefoot, she'd lost the makeup, and her long blond hair, only partially dry, hung about her shoulders. "I hope you enjoyed the wine." She met Lily's gaze and all the flirtation was gone. "I have an import business, and of course Italy is exactly the right place for it. So how are you liking our world?" She sat down on the couch, spreading her arms along the back of the cushions.

Lily glanced briefly at Adrien then back to Eve. "It's not what I expected, not on any level." Thoughts of Adrien catching the vampire child up in his arms in the Trevayne system raced through her mind, stealing her breath away all over again.

"We're not all bad," Eve said. "Or at least, not all the time, and for the sake of my friendship with Adrien I apologize for my earlier misdeeds."

Oh, great. Now Eve was proving her character as well, which made the whole situation one big nerve itch. Good vampires. Bad ones. A world lacking a system of justice. A world of the individual. She liked too much of what she saw.

"Apology accepted."

Eve nodded, offering a half smile. "So once I showered, I had a little chat with Rumy and he tells me that the shared chains have brought on a revisiting power—that you actually saw Daniel in Rumy's office."

"That's true. I did."

Eve narrowed her gaze at Lily. "Daniel's one good-looking bastard, isn't he?"

Lily nodded. "And very charismatic. It's no wonder he's caused all sorts of problems. He also seemed familiar to me, though I know I'd never seen him before."

Eve glanced at Adrien and smiled. When her gaze returned to Lily she still wore a smile. "He might seem familiar because he's fathered any number of children, all sons."

"Really? But I thought they were rare?"

"In our world, you mean, yes, children are rare, but Daniel has great power and he doesn't mind playing around with science. No doubt you've already seen one of his sons in passing."

Lily shuddered.

Adrien cleared his throat. "And as fascinating as Daniel's progeny might be, Eve, how about you tell us what we need to know. I take it Rumy already told you what we're after."

"Yes." She wrinkled up her nose. "But the extinction weapon? What a nightmare."

"Then you know something about it?" Lily searched her face, her heart rate climbing.

"Of course I do. And from the information I've received over the past several decades, a weapon like this could be used to take out an entire cavern system at once."

Adrien leaned forward, his arms on his thighs, his hands clasped tightly together. "How the hell do you know this?"

Eve chuckled. "Because, darling Adrien, I sleep with a lot of men who tend to become talkative at certain times and I have a variety of skills that can keep them talking."

She called for a glass of Silver Patrón. When the tumbler arrived, she took a long drink, savoring. She leaned into the couch again and released a deep sigh. "God, I love tequila, one of the human race's finest achievements." She chuckled softly. "You both look so tense."

"Eve—" Adrien chided. "More details."

"Fine. So here it is: In the nineteen fifties, just like in the human world, scientists in our major Paris university went mad with experimenting, especially with sound waves and bats, which have super-sensitive hearing, just like vampires.

"At certain decibels, the bats died, and so did a number of scientists." She then spoke of what Lily had heard before—the Council of Ancestrals ending all experiments. "The Paris laboratory was destroyed, filled in with rubble, but word has it that the actual data and weapon, and the key to operating it, were hidden away, probably behind powerful Ancestral disguises. I've also heard that the same thing happened with other labs, other weapons, so there might be more than one.

"But of everything that I recall, the place I'd suggest to start is the group of crystal caves in Mexico. I know that a significant, secret, and highly illegal research facility was located there and operated against Council law, over the next decade well into the sixties, until a tragedy occurred, namely that a large number of scientists were killed."

Lily settled her elbow on the arm of her chair and let her head rest in her palm for a moment. Her heart now thumped in her chest. The moment Eve had said "Mexico," Lily felt the location click with her tracking ability.

Adrien reached a hand toward her and touched her arm. "You're feeling it, aren't you?"

She nodded. "Mexico will give us some answers." Then she looked down at her halter, skirt, and boots. "But I need to get changed before we head out."

Adrien flew Lily back to his Paris apartment, the unofficial hub of their operations, and watched her lose her short skirt. Though her jeans were much more practical, the leather skirt revealed a lot of skin so he had mixed feelings about the switch-up. When a pair of blue running shoes replaced her boots, he repressed a sigh. What was it about heeled boots on a woman that got a man going?

Her body had become like air to him in this short time of being bound, but as he watched her brush out her hair, he seriously started questioning if what he felt was just about the chains.

His experience with Lily had begun ass-backward, and yet what he felt toward her, the tenderness, the compulsion to stick close and protect her, the off-the-charts need to get her beneath him, seemed completely disproportionate to the time spent or even to the bonds of the chains.

So what the hell was going on here?

It didn't help that the chains vibrated almost constantly, metal against skin, informing him of Lily's emotions at all times, if not her thoughts. But those he could guess at.

The situation freaked her out and why wouldn't it? Shit, if he'd been in her shoes, he'd be going nuts right now. Vampires and a world she hadn't known existed until a couple of months ago? He'd always been acutely aware of the human world, something all vampires avoided except in matters of business, like Eve's wine-import company.

When Lily turned to face him, rubbing her earlobe where a single flash of amethyst could be seen through her thumb and forefinger, his heart lurched.

He was so damn attracted to her, plain and simple, as though every gene in his body reached for her. It had been this way from the moment he'd laid eyes on her in the Himalayan cavern. And he hadn't worn a binding chain then, yet he'd struggled to get to her, overcome by a hurricane of need not just to get her on her back, but to hold her close by his side, to protect her, *to be with her*.

He felt the same way now as she gave a tug on the hem of her purple tank top. "I like that the new chains give us a greater reach. What would you say it is? Twenty feet? Thirty?" She frowned slightly. "What's the matter? You're kind of, I don't know, all over the place."

He shook his head and forced himself to breathe. He even liked the tenor of her voice. She had a certain resonance that spoke to him, that spoke of a deep sense of confidence she had in herself even in the face of her current nightmare.

"I'm proud of you," he said, without thinking, his feet in motion as well. "You're one of the most courageous people I know."

He could feel her confusion, her surprise, and beneath those emotions, a texture of having been pleased. He took her in his arms. "Whatever happens, Lily, from this point forward, I want you to know that I value who you are."

"You do?" she asked, frowning.

"I do."

She searched his eyes and drew in a ragged breath. "Thank you." Her large hazel eyes were bright. "I don't know what to say."

She needed the moment to pass, that's what the chains told him. So he let it go. "It's okay. We need to focus on Mexico. Can you access your tracking ability? Now that we have a lead, I'd like to know if my Ancestral power can help with that."

"Good idea." She blinked a couple of times then met his gaze. "That was so strange. I thought about Mexico and suddenly those weird searching tendrils zoomed there and I saw a cavern of white crystals. There were also three tunnels, and I had the sense that the weapon was down one of them."

"Was this easier now, because of the new chain?"

"Absolutely. Night and day, like altered flight."

He held her gaze, realizing that they'd become the very thing Daniel had been working toward: a tracking pair that could locate whatever needed to be found. Which meant that though he could celebrate having accomplished something with Lily, essentially he was still doing Daniel's bidding.

"What do you know about the crystal caves?" she asked.

"A system of great beauty, filled with white crystals of all sizes, some massive, some very small, and a full range between. Mostly abandoned these days after one of the tunnel systems collapsed and killed nearly a thousand inhabitants. But given what Eve told us, maybe there was another reason the system was shut down."

"Because of the extinction weapon."

He nodded.

Lily drew in a deep breath, and her gaze skated away from his. "Do you think we'll have company?"

"Yeah, I do, so let me ask you this: Are you sure you want to continue?"

"Yes." He felt her despair and wished he knew the truth.

She glanced down at his leathers and to the new weapon he now wore in a large sheath attached to his belt. "That's the biggest blade yet. More than a dagger, I take it."

He nodded.

"Any particular reason for it?"

"Instinct."

Her lips curved just so. "I can get behind that."

He smiled as well. "We're for Mexico then. We'll fly straight through but I'll slow it up at the end, once we're inside the system, to have a look. I'll only stop if I think it's safe."

"Good. That sounds good."

When he opened his arms, she stepped into him. He closed the circle, the chains vibrating heavily against his neck. The new double-chain enhanced everything, including his reactions to her. Proximity sent a thrill straight down his chest, all the way down to make his cock twitch and his balls tighten. More ragged breathing. The smallest touch and he was ready for her.

He oriented himself, focusing on his internal directional awareness. He pivoted in an easterly direction, toward the night, always east, always flying away from the sun just in case. Paris to Mexico would have been shorter heading west, but what was a few seconds to keep the larger portion of night close at hand while he flew.

Some lessons were learned early and learned hard.

Dropping out of a altered flight in sunlight just *hurt*.

Besides, his new power made the journey as smooth as glass. Passing through anything solid like trees or mountains, even water, was like swiping a hand through fog.

As he neared Mexico, he began to slow.

The cavern drew him like a beacon, his flight true, the altered flight a dream.

Passing through the outer shell of solid rock, he slowed even more. Once he arrived in the cave's massive central cavern, at least two hundred feet into the earth, he flew in a slow circle, but the space appeared to be deserted. Unfortunately, while still moving in the altered state, he wouldn't be able to extend his senses to determine if other vampires or humans were present.

He'd have to stop for that. But not just yet.

Parts of the original cavern, full of sculptured masses of crystals, had been left intact, but the rest had been chiseled away over the millennia to create a vast polished floor, walls, and a tall intricately carved ceiling. Adrien had only been here a couple of times over the course of his life. He didn't like this place—too cold, almost unfriendly in atmosphere.

He took his time and entered the three large shafts that led off from different points of the compass, but the tunnels appeared to be empty as well.

He took Lily back to the center of the original cavern floor, keeping his arm around her in a tight hold. Time to find out what was what.

But the moment he brought the altered flight to a close, he felt the presence of another vampire, an Ancestral, accompanied by the sounds of booted feet running in their direction from all three tunnels.

"We're outta here," he said. Gripping Lily hard around her waist, he started to fly, but he couldn't sustain altered flight. Something had hold of him and he fell forward, rolling so that Lily landed on top of him. His head struck a crystal; his mind spun.

"What happened?" she asked. "What's going on?"

"I just got hit by something only a few vampires can do; a vampire of power stopped my altered flight. Shit, I don't even think Daniel can do that."

"I didn't know that was possible." Lily clutched his arm.

He sat up, helping her to do the same, then lifted her to her feet.

Fanatics, all in black robes, surged into the space until at least thirty male vampires surrounded them.

Strolling in and wearing a long silk black robe, embroidered in silver thread down the front, the Ancestral appeared.

Silas.

The great one.

Tall and lean, he had thick, fiery red hair, smoothed into a loop at the back of his head. His light blue eyes glowed with a fanatic's fervor.

What Adrien had never quite known, however, was whether Silas truly believed what he taught or whether he used his teachings to control those around him, to keep reaching for greater ambitions involving more control.

Probably a little of both.

"Well met, Adrien," he said, his voice strong and steady, a deep baritone in the cavern.

"Silas. I've not seen you in a year, not since that sham of a sentencing that put me and my brothers in prison."

The Ancestral's lips curved and his shoulders lowered slowly. "That was a lovely day. I'd been waiting a long time to see the three of you locked up. Gabriel was understandably upset. You spit at me, as I recall."

"Come close. I'll spit again." He could feel Lily grow tense beside him, but there was no help for it. They were in trouble now. "I have to admit, I never thought you'd align yourself with Daniel."

"I saw the opportunity to break the Council's control over our world and I took it. We've needed a change for a long time, and Daniel offered something I couldn't resist."

"You mean, he made it possible for you and your boys to take over all the temples, to start demanding that our world do your bidding. How many temples are under your command now?"

Silas's smile blossomed. "Eighty percent. I would suggest you get used to things being different, but I have no intention of letting you leave this cave alive. This was Daniel's gift to me for aligning with him against the Council. Then he and I both got what we wanted: Daniel has the Council and I have every temple priest, from here to Paris to Mumbai to Beijing, under my command. We'll have order, Adrien."

"But you do know that it's Daniel who has sent Lily and me, as a blood-chained tracking pair, after the extinction weapon."

"Yes, of course. I've seen it in several visions, including Daniel's part as well as his human servant, Kiernan."

"He won't remain unopposed to what you're doing, if for no other reason than that you'll gain too much power. Daniel will turn against you."

Silas shrugged. "My agreement with Daniel only went

so far as support in taking over the Council. Of course, if I'd foreseen that the signing of your incarceration papers gave Daniel this power over you, to bind you to a human through the blood-chain and force you to hunt for the one thing that could give him absolute control, I might have refused. You realize of course that if you fail and die, he'll use both Lucian and Marius to the same end."

"That thought has crossed my mind. He seems determined to get the weapon."

"And I'm determined that he shouldn't."

"And if you got hold of the weapon instead?"

Silas's grim expression softened and a kind of ecstasy entered his blue eyes, a glitter that told Adrien all he needed to know. "As to that," Silas said, "I would at least have righteousness on my side."

Adrien's jaw hardened. "You are no different from Daniel. You can claim the worthiness of your cause, but I see what you are—as does any sensible vampire in our world."

"I never could persuade you differently, but at least after this night, you won't be able to incite the rabble against me and my followers ever again."

Adrien felt the weight of Silas's millennia, an oppressive sensation that he'd despised from the time he could remember. Daniel had a similar feel to his bones. And now Adrien was headed down that path irrevocably as well, becoming one of a rare group of powerful vampires in his world, an Ancestral.

Sweat broke out on his forehead. Would he become like his own father and find the level of his power so intoxicating that he had to rule the world instead of serve?

Without warning, Silas turned his power toward Lily, focusing all his attention on her. And because of the bonding chains, Adrien could feel Lily's response, a sudden impulse to go to Silas.

Adrien placed his arm in front of her, a physical act that preceded a mental one, as he drove his thoughts into hers and created a shield over her mind.

He almost had me, Lily's appalled telepathic voice returned to him.

I know. Ancestrals have tremendous power, especially ones like Silas who are very old. Trying to control you is a massive perversion of his power.

Silas shifted his gaze slowly, methodically to Adrien. "So you've finally taken your first infant step in *our* direction. Interesting. I suppose this human prompted the move, am I right?"

"Call it self-preservation."

Silas narrowed his gaze at Adrien. "You care about her. You've been with her just a couple of nights and you care, very deeply."

"Doesn't matter. You can't have her, Silas. Not today. Not ever."

"I've had several visions that this one—" He gestured with an elegant wave of his hand toward Lily, the sleeve of his gown flapping "—destroys our race. I think it an appropriate exchange: one million vampire souls for one human, don't you?"

"I think the moment we start trading lives one for another, no matter the number, that's the day we deserve to disappear from the face of the earth."

He clucked his tongue. "Four hundred years old and still so naive. Have it as you will." He began to back up slowly. As he did his minions, bearing chains and daggers, advanced on them.

Adrien turned in a circle, holding Lily against him. How the hell was he supposed to fight thirty vampires?

He knew the men in front of him lacked battle experience by the way they moved, the way they held their blades and battle chains. Several began to spin the long six-foot chains, hoping to catch either him or Lily about the neck and end things quickly. The long chains also had razor-sharp points at the tips, as many as six at one end, which could do a tremendous amount of damage.

He spoke into Lily's mind. *In order to keep you safe, I have to get a wall behind us. I'm going to swing you up onto my back. Wrap your arms around my neck, your legs around my waist, and pin yourself to me like a monkey.*

A monkey? How inelegant, she responded. But she made him smile.

Ready?

Do it.

Using his left arm, he reached for her left arm, dipped, and with a swift, smooth jerk flipped her into the air, turning her at the same time, until she slid down his back. She locked her arms around his neck, her legs around his hips. With two of his own chains spinning and with speed just short of altered flight, he moved backward, past the nearest fanatics. He heard the cries of those men who got cut by his whirring chains.

Lily's arms and legs clung to him like a vise. He dropped his chains and drew two blades. "Slide down my back and make yourself small. I have some deviants to off."

He felt her drop to the smooth crystal floor at his feet. He moved with lightning speed, so that those who reached him first had little chance against his trained reflexes. He caught the first of the long chains, above the whirling points, gave a jerk and brought the assailant to him. He drove his dagger into the back of his neck so fast that as he let the man go, the last word the vampire muttered was, "What?"

Before the first man hit the crystal floor, Adrien sank the blade in and out of the throat of the closest vampire to his left, then his right, grabbed another chain, jerked, sank another blade into yet another neck. The fanatics fell, grabbing at their throats and moaning.

But the bastards kept coming, stepping over the dying bodies so that Adrien was forced to inch backward, closer and closer to Lily. As fast as he killed, two more launched at him. He shunted one body aside, then another.

His speed made the kills a simple matter, but at some point, either he'd be overwhelmed by sheer numbers, or someone would get behind him and slay Lily.

CHAPTER 12

The thump of Lily's heartbeat drowned out the sounds of the moans all around her, one small mercy. She met the gaze of the nearest fallen vampire, blood oozing from his mouth as he blinked. His eyes seemed to clear for a moment as he met her gaze and said, "Sorry. Not my fault." Then he was gone.

Not his fault? He'd come here to kill her but it wasn't his fault?

Lily knew she had maybe thirty seconds left to live. Adrien fought cleanly and efficiently, but where the wall curved to each side of her, several fanatics were moving in close, stealing in behind Adrien.

She had to do something, but what?

On instinct, she put her hand over her chain, and despite the desperate nature of the moment, her revisiting power called to her. She let it come, the edges of the horror-filled room beginning to swirl so that an entirely different image of the same space opened.

She felt the time sequence: one hour earlier. She saw

the same vampires sitting in easy groups around the crystal floor, chatting, some playing cards, rolling dice, a friendly scene, in fact, not *fanatical* at all.

Then Silas entered the vaulted cavern from the middle tunnel and with strange, stiff movements, one by one, the men rose to their feet and stood at attention. But there was nothing normal about what they were doing as they packed up their dice and cards and donned the robes that Silas passed out to them.

Their lethargy helped Lily to understand that these vampires weren't acting on their own.

Not my fault rang in her head.

Then she got it and everything made sense.

Adrien, she said forcefully, mind to mind. *Silas enthralled these vampires, all of them. I've just seen it in a revisiting vision. They didn't know they'd come here to fight.*

Fuck, came back to her.

Blood now pooled in too many places over the beautiful crystal floor. Adrien was about to slice open another throat when he stopped suddenly and held his arms wide. The vampires closest to him launched then seemed to be repelled away from him at the exact same moment.

Even the vampires sneaking in from the right stopped moving and looked around, horrified at the fallen near Adrien.

"My God, what's going on here?" one of them said.

"You've been tricked." Lily waved a hand in Silas's direction, "By that man."

She watched the vampires struggle, shake their heads, take a step toward her as Silas tried to regain control of them.

But Adrien battled only Silas right now, his body rigid, all his attention focused on the Ancestral.

Lily felt the need to support him, so she rose up from

the floor, moved in behind Adrien, and surrounded him with her arms. The chains began to shake against her body this time, responding to Adrien's concentration. She could feel him battling Silas for control of the men.

She relaxed and let her thoughts flow with his, binding her mind to his. The moment she did, she felt the boost in power—but the experience hurt her, that rush of energy like molten lava through her mind. She wanted to pull away because of the pain, but she knew Adrien needed her.

She held fast. Though she could see little of the cavern, she sensed that the vampires began to fall back then fly out of the cavern using altered flight.

The moment broke suddenly, the pain in her mind flashing bright then winking out. Adrien relaxed and she released him. He had won the battle with Silas.

Of the living and uninjured, only Silas remained; the rest of the vampires had escaped. The ones on the floor were dead or dying.

"It would seem you've won the contest, for now, but only because of the support of the woman." His light blue gaze shifted to Lily. She felt him try to pull her in, but once more Adrien's mind slipped into hers and blocked him.

Silas shrugged, and in a blink of an eye he was gone again. But just as fast Adrien moved to stand beside her, two blades drawn, his flecked teal eyes fierce and almost glowing.

"You think he's still here?" Lily settled a hand on his arm.

"Just want to be sure."

Lily, however, could feel that the Ancestral was gone for good, so she wasn't surprised when Adrien, breathing hard, slid his arm around her and walked her to the curved wall, pulling her down to sit beside him. "So many unnecessary deaths. How I hate that man, that he would hide behind religion and cause this disaster." His gaze moved slowly over the slain, now in an arc in front of them.

Lily avoided looking at the number of dead, but turned toward Adrien to focus, if for just this moment, on him. His sweat had a metallic smell, yet underneath was that rich scent that she loved. "Thank you for saving my life. Again."

He shifted to look at her, leaning his head against the smooth, polished crystal wall. "I'll say the same thing because that boost of power made it possible for me to defeat Silas. I honestly don't know how long I could have held him off, then you were suddenly there, and in my mind as well." He put his hand on her knee. "But I felt your pain when you helped me. I'd do anything if you didn't have to feel that kind of pain."

Lily stared into his eyes, startled yet again by who he was, his compassion for her. He just wasn't what she'd expected from a vampire. She drew in a ragged breath. "Hey. We're both here right now. That was a small price to pay."

He nodded. "I take it your revisiting power came online again?"

"He'd enthralled all of them." She told him what one of the vampires had said just before he died, as well as his sudden awareness of where he was, what he'd done. "The men weren't fanatics, Adrien. They'd been playing cards and rolling dice. I think they'd been led here under false pretenses."

"That makes sense. I knew most of them weren't fighters, but until right now I thought they were devoted to Silas, to his religious cause."

Her gaze flitted around the floor, which caused her to turn into Adrien once more. "This was a tragedy," she whispered.

"Yes, it was."

"How can a man profess religion of any kind then create and encourage this kind of slaughter?"

"I don't know." He pulled his phone from his battle leathers and made a call similar to the one he'd made in Paris after killing the assassin.

A few moments later at least a dozen vampires arrived bearing stretchers. Two corpses at a time, the bodies were taken away.

Much to Lily's relief, Adrien remained where he was, sitting beside her. The cleanup crew had given him a towel, and he kept wiping sweat off his face, neck, and arms.

With the last of the debris and stains dealt with, the crew left. The emptiness of the cavern, the sterile quality of the air, surprised Lily, as though nothing had ever happened there.

Adrien had grown very still, but she sensed something from him that caused the chain around her neck to vibrate softly. She felt his deep respect for the men who had died here today, even a kind of love for them as someone who had spent his life serving as his society's protector. And maybe under that respect was grief.

She looked up at him, surprised all over again by his depths, by his kindness despite his warmaking, by his careful respect for others, though he could have easily bulldozed his way in any situation and taken what he wanted, with all the strength and power he carried in his bones.

She inched closer and looped her hand beneath his bare bicep, still damp from battle-sweat, and gave a squeeze.

As he turned to look at her, his head no longer against the wall, she offered a small dip of her chin, wanting him to know that she understood. He smiled and leaned down to place a kiss on her lips.

Thank you, came from his mind to hers.

Her heart squeezed up tight.

This was not simple between them, not on any level.

Was it just the blood-chains that had brought up such a powerful level of understanding, or was it Adrien? Would she ever know the difference?

The questions were unanswerable, so she turned her attention to the cavern and her mission. She opened up her tracker senses and focused on the extinction weapon, on what she'd been told about the Paris experiments on bats, on the sensitive hearing of vampires generally.

The tendrils of her power, made real because of Adrien, traveled swiftly away from her, deep into the cavern system, miles from where she now sat.

"What is it, Lily? My chain is vibrating heavily."

"I'm getting a call from the branch on the right." She gestured to the far end of the vaulted chamber.

"How far?"

She shook her head. "Miles. Whatever relates to the extinction weapon is a long way away."

Adrien rose to his feet, then extended his hand to her. She took it, and because of his increased Ancestral strength, when he pulled she flew upward a couple of feet then flopped into him.

He laughed, gave her a quick squeeze. "Sorry 'bout that. Still learning."

Smiling as she slid down his body, she almost kissed him, but stopped herself. What was she thinking? That she'd have a long-term relationship with a vampire, with someone no doubt slated for death by Daniel once he got his hands on the weapon? She had to start being sensible where Adrien was concerned.

He led her to the tunnel on the right, but given her sense of where they were headed she suggested they use altered flight and communicate telepathically.

"I'm all for shaving time off this mission. I'll just pause at each branch and you can tell me which way to go."

"Done." How simple this all seemed.

She turned into him and he slid his arm around her waist. But instead of pulling her against him, chest to chest, he held her to his side so that she was facing forward.

Her feet dangled as he started the altered flight.

Once he started to fly, the miles dissipated quickly. At each juncture, she made her decisions quickly because she knew the route as though it had been imprinted on her DNA. Of course, it was just the chains, and the power she siphoned from Adrien, but she never wavered as she communicated each shift in course telepathically.

We're getting close. I can feel it now.

The tunnel had narrowed badly and finally reached what looked like a dead end, a wall of jagged rock. Adrien brought them to a complete halt, a jarring movement that rocked her against him a couple of times. She stared at the wall that wasn't a wall, sensing that something critical lay beyond.

"I've seen this before," he said. "An Ancestral has infused this wall of rock with a nearly impenetrable disguise. No wonder this has never been found before."

"You mean a disguise like the ones used to prevent humans from finding your world?"

He nodded, putting his hand on the wall. "Yes, feel the vibration. Can you sense the power?"

She reached out and even before her fingers connected with the stone, she felt the disguising field. "Someone with great power created this."

He moved his hand over the stone. "An Ancestral. I can almost get a reading on who the vampire was, but not quite." He drew his hand back. "I suppose it really doesn't matter. Just tell me, is this the place?"

"Yes," Lily said "Absolutely."

And yet, he hesitated.

"What's wrong?" Lily asked.

He shook his head. "I don't know. Something doesn't feel right."

But she chuckled softly. "Whatever is beyond these walls can't be worse than what we just left behind, can it?" She shuddered slightly at the memory of so much blood.

"I don't know," he said. "Maybe. You sure you want to do this?"

"Yes. Please take us through."

He nodded and swallowed hard. "Okay. Let's see what we've got on the other side of this wall."

The altered flight took only a split second, as Adrien took her through the dense rock, setting her on her feet in yet another vast internal cavern.

What she saw, however, forced her to grow very still. "Oh, my God."

"Shit," Adrien said, his voice a mere whisper.

Scattered around what looked like an old-fashioned laboratory were long-decayed corpses, mere skeletons now, all crumpled piles of bones still covered in clothing, often with fingers pressed to skulls as though the people here had died in exactly the position they fell, all in terrible pain, holding their heads.

The air, however, was fresh, as most of the caves she'd been in were.

She glanced around. "How many do you think there are?" She moved slightly to the right, to look down another row of tables and cupboards. Sure enough, several more people lay curled up, hands to heads.

Adrien took hold of her hand and drew her close. "Looks like about fifty. At least."

"Do you think this was the result of the weapon we're looking for?"

"Maybe. Hell, by the looks of it, probably. I still can't believe something like this exists."

At that moment her revisiting power came alive, but with it a terrible sense of foreboding. For an instant she debated pulling back. She let go of Adrien's hand, but turned into him and reached for him.

Because he no doubt sensed her fear, he slid his arm around her waist and pulled her close. "I've got you. Another vision?"

She inclined her head. "This is gonna be bad."

As the revisiting vision came alive, time moved, a deep funneling motion accompanied by shifting waves that began to swirl around the edges of the cavern, creating an almost tornado-like impression at both sides of her vision.

A past view of the current environment emerged, as individuals swarmed through the facility, many running as though something was happening. Each scurried, gathering up papers, turning off equipment. All wore crisp white lab coats. Very 1950s.

When a sound began to pulse within the room, there was a moment when everyone paused to look around, eyes wide. The sound continued to release in a steady rhythm.

She felt the sudden horror of the group.

"This shouldn't be happening?" someone called out. "Who fired up the weapon?"

Then, "Run!"

At the far end, several of the scientists headed into the tunnel, which was located opposite where she and Adrien now stood. They were running and calling back for others to leave as well.

A few escaped, but the pulsing sound grew louder and suddenly so shrill that even Lily's ears began to hurt. Amplified by the shared chains, her hearing sharpened, so that as the sound escalated into higher and higher frequencies, she began to tremble.

Suddenly everyone dropped to the floor, holding their

hands over their ears and screaming, blood pouring from mouths, nostrils, and ears.

Just as suddenly, the screaming stopped.

And the vision ended.

Lily looked down, and she knew the people she'd seen were the present-day skeletons. The places where they'd died were the same, hands to skulls, the blood having long since dried up and disintegrated.

Suddenly she felt the presence of others in the space and gripped Adrien harder.

Three vampires arrived at the mouth of the opposing tunnel, Daniel and two others, equally tall and powerful in build, like Adrien.

Daniel wore another fine suit but with a scarlet tie this time. His hair, slicked back and oiled, as well as his goatee, looked exactly the same as the previous vision. Only this wasn't a vision.

"So, we meet again, Lily Haven." Then he smiled, an expression both charismatic and seductive. He even bowed as though carrying forward for effect the affectations of earlier centuries.

She drew closer to Adrien. It was one thing to have heard tales about the monster or even to have spoken with him in a revisiting vision. But right now, in this moment, the serpent slithered through the room.

Adrien stared at Daniel, now standing on the opposite side of the room. The monster who now ruled the Council and who held Adrien's brothers in the Himalayan prison stood flanked by his two oldest sons, Quill and Lev. Daniel, of all vampires, didn't deserve to have even one child, never mind the several he had sired.

All male vampires, brought into the world and raised during the first years of life by human mothers.

He'd hurt all his children.

And killed off their mothers.

Adrien stared at Daniel, and his two lackeys, the sight of him clamping around Adrien's heart like a vise. "What are you doing here?"

Daniel looked at Adrien, still smiling. "Protecting my investment, of course." He glanced around the room. "I never could find this place. All those decades of searching, but this one remained hidden to me. Naturally, I'd heard rumors. After all, it was my friend Charles who had run this laboratory illegally for at least a decade after the Council had shut everything down. Too bad he died when he did. Other rumors said he'd built a weapon and hidden it."

"You've been following us."

"I've kept tabs." He levitated and started moving slowly, above the corpses but between tables and cupboards in a distant row. His minions trailed him, matching his flow. Dread seized Adrien's heart, an old familiar sensation from childhood. How much pain would Daniel inflict this time?

He couldn't breathe. Lily's hand, normally comforting, felt like fire on his back.

Her voice pierced his chaotic thoughts. *Daniel is more to you than just an evil in your world, isn't he? I can feel through the chains that you fear him like no one else we've encountered. Who is he to you, Adrien? Who is he?*

He turned to Lily but he couldn't tell her, he couldn't speak the words. "Stay close. No matter what happens, stay close to me. Do you understand?"

Her hazel eyes looked huge as she stared back at him, nodding once very slowly. *He hurt you before, didn't he? I can feel it now. A long time ago. Centuries ago.*

Yes, Adrien responded slowly, remembered pain flashing through his body. *He hurt all of us, me and my brothers, even the two with him right now. He hurt us all.*

She blinked once. He watched her mind open to the truth, the one he hated to speak. "Oh, my God. Adrien, he's your father, isn't he? Daniel is your father?"

Adrien nodded. "The one who sired me, yes. Lucian helped us escape but others found us and protected us, Gabriel among them. But Daniel is my father. I carry his genes, and I'm never to be trusted." He grabbed her arm and squeezed. He stared hard into her face. "Do you hear me, Lily? Never to be trusted."

Again she nodded, in that way that seemed to almost draw time to a standstill.

Daniel still glided slowly, milking his approach, one of the few who could sustain altered flight in such a perfect, slow-drifting manner. All part of his performance, to remind Adrien how powerful he was.

At the top of the row and now hovering fifteen feet away from Adrien, he turned and surveyed the room, his gaze raking across the various counters and tables, the skeletons on the floor, silence in the space suddenly deafening.

Lily once more entered his head but very quietly, as though afraid Daniel could hear her telepathy. *He's looking for the weapon.*

Of course he is. Adrien's gaze never left Daniel. He knew how fast the bastard could move.

But Daniel's gaze, after making a careful sweep of the large, vaulted space, finally landed on Lily. "The weapon isn't here, is it?"

Adrien shifted so that he could look at her. She frowned, and he felt her focus her tracking abilities on the weapon once more. He felt the truth as she shook her head. "No, it was removed. This is the remnant, this laboratory and these corpses."

Daniel began to move slowly once more, but this time Adrien saw that his father had focused his energy on Lily.

"I created this," he said, now ten feet away. He swept his hand to encompass Adrien and Lily. "I created this bond because I knew that with her tracking ability and your power, you'd form a formidable tracking pair, something I couldn't do on my own, something I tried a hundred times to achieve. Every tracker I tried to bind myself to died immediately. My power was too immense for them. When I discovered Lily, one of the strongest trackers I'd found, I couldn't risk losing her like all the others, so I brought in another vampire whose power isn't as great as mine. Now I expect results, Lily. Kiernan must have told you that, must have told you carefully everything that was at stake, all that precious flesh and blood."

"He did."

"Lily, what's he talking about?" Adrien felt dizzy suddenly, sick deep in his gut, as though his body knew exactly what Daniel had used to force Lily on this journey. He swallowed hard as Daniel closed the last few feet to stand a yard away from them.

He heard her breath hitch in her throat, but she said nothing.

"So you kept your word and you didn't tell him?" Daniel chuckled and smiled, that broad, charismatic, beckoning smile of his.

"I told him nothing. I followed Kiernan's instructions."

Adrien felt panic rising in Lily, a wave of sensation that vibrated the double-chain at his neck.

Daniel shifted his gaze to Adrien. "And you didn't tell her who I was. What an interesting pair you are. Well, I won't give up Lily's little secret, either; Kiernan wouldn't like it."

His cold light teal eyes shifted to Lily.

Adrien felt her trembling now, fear washing through her, then rage, then fear, then rage hot again, her skin flushing and burning Adrien. He held her pressed against his side, the relative position that tended to keep them both safe now.

But what would happen next, he couldn't guess, except for one great truth: Pain would follow. When Daniel entered a room, pain always followed.

Try not to listen to him. Adrien needed Lily to be as strong as possible right now. He could sense what was coming and he needed her with him, aware and focused.

"You haven't exactly fulfilled your promise to find the weapon, Lily, and I'm very disappointed. But use your power right now, the tracking ability you have, and focus on the weapon. Tell me where you sense it coming from. Do it now!"

Lily jerked at these last words and the force behind them. She obeyed and turned slightly to face the far wall, where the tunnel had allowed a few of the scientists to escape. Adrien felt her siphon his power and he let it flow as she reached out over the earth. "I don't know," she said. "The tendrils go to a hundred places at once, nothing specific. I've since learned that there was more than one weapon and that many of the separate parts were hidden away in over twenty cavern systems."

"Yes, a plot to confuse even a tracker. The Council at that time didn't lack for intelligence." Daniel's gaze shifted away from Lily as he once more surveyed the laboratory. "So there's nothing here, just evidence that the weapon works and how it works, how it kills—very effectively, I see."

He grew very still, the kind of stillness that broadened the pain in Adrien's gut.

Daniel turned toward Adrien, his gaze fierce and controlling. He smiled. "At least you've taken a step to becoming an Ancestral like me, like your brothers here." He turned his shoulders first one way then the other, slight movements that indicated Quill and Lev.

Adrien felt their Ancestral status. As Daniel's devoted followers, they would have taken on the Ancestral mantle long ago. And yet, because of his new power, he could feel their inherent weakness, that neither would become as strong as Daniel. Had Daniel created them to be less than him? Or was it just the result of genetics, the luck of the draw?

Daniel's eyes took on a fiery fervor. "You have such potential if you would just open yourself up to the true possibilities of your nature, that part of you deeply vampire. I was wrong to have created you from a human female because you've been polluted, you and your younger brothers. Yet strangely, the potential in you astounds me. You could almost be as powerful as me, if you'd just try." He took a step closer, lowering his chin, holding Adrien's gaze in his tight grip. "That's why I'd treated you so harshly in the past, you and your brothers. It was to strengthen you and prepare you for your inheritance, what I've given you because of who I am as an Ancestral."

"I'll never do that," Adrien returned, also lowering his chin, battling Daniel's hypnotic abilities. "I took on the chain to keep Lily safe so she could fly without hurting. The rest, the potential you value so highly, revolts me. I have no intention of opening myself up to the kind of power that has devoured you."

Daniel laughed. "You're so naive, so much like Gabriel. I can see his handprint on your life. But who rules the Council now and is likely to rule for centuries, if not millennia, to come? Answer me that?"

Adrien remained silent.

"My son, you always lacked something indefinable, a certain finesse, or courage, perhaps, or confidence. I was never quite sure what defect it was that kept you from being a real man. You're weak, not in power, but in those attributes that define a man, a willingness to set his eye on an object and take it merely because he wants it. Without that drive, a man is nothing but a whimpering shell, a child weeping at his mother's knee because life is too hard. Poor Adrien. You'll always be nothing, a little maggot of a vampire."

The taunts piled up, one after the other, so familiar, a clanging bell from a torturous childhood, until Adrien's brain seized, right in the middle where a sharp pain split his hemispheres in half. He breathed hard through his nose. He blinked and tried to pull his thoughts back into some kind of order, but couldn't.

He wished like hell that he could believe Daniel was using some kind of thrall on him, but he wasn't. No, what he felt, this kind of numbing pain and disorientation, always happened because at the core of Adrien's being, when he confronted Daniel, was rage, a knife of rage that severed his soul and his mind into two dysfunctional parts. He couldn't even speak. All he could feel was a profound need to slay the man now hovering in his fine Italian shoes a few inches above the ground.

He wanted to strike, but he didn't have the power and Daniel knew it.

"Well, what an asshole you are."

The words came from beside him, from Lily, the weak human, the one that Daniel could crush with a thought.

Adrien didn't know what to do because suddenly, as Daniel shifted his gaze to Lily, turning all that evil on her, Adrien knew he would do her harm, and that he'd enjoy doing it because Lily now meant something to Adrien.

His sudden concern for Lily had at least one good effect: His rage dissipated enough to allow his thoughts to come back to him, for his brain to re-form and start functioning again.

He watched Daniel sweep his hand in a killing arc toward Lily. He knew the gesture and what it meant, and just how much pain Daniel would deliver in that one blow, *pain to the edge of death.* Or maybe with Lily, in this one strike, it would take her the entire distance and she would be dead.

A few hours ago Adrien could have done nothing about it, but he was no longer just a vampire; he had the beginnings of his Ancestral-based power that would one day make him as strong as the man in front of him. He swept in front of the blow and took it hard across his face, chest, and left arm, so that he fell prone to the floor at Daniel's feet, his skin, all over his body, burned from the sheer preternatural power the man wielded. He was bruised as well from the force behind the blow.

But he knew his father, that one strike wouldn't be enough to satisfy his rage at Lily's slur. Adrien rose up swiftly as Daniel struck again, this one worse, and this blow would have reduced Lily to ash. Once more, he fell to the floor, dizzy, battered, and burned.

As Adrien recovered, his head spinning, he looked up at Daniel and watched as his father stared at Lily, his eyes wild with his mania, preparing for a third strike.

But something inside Adrien rebelled. He tapped into his growing Ancestral power and a new kind of energy flooded his body so that when the blow fell, Adrien flew up and into it, meeting all of Daniel's power with an answering power of his own, a release of burning energy that caused Daniel and his sons to fly backward.

Daniel returned swiftly, his gold-flecked teal eyes glowing with a fierce light as once more he caught Adrien's gaze, his intention to cow Adrien again, to fold him in half mentally, to break his will once more.

But something had shifted deep inside Adrien. This time Daniel couldn't get in, couldn't tap into the deep wounds he'd inflicted throughout Adrien's childhood, couldn't make him tremble in fear.

Adrien's need to help his brothers survive, his fierce intention to keep the extinction weapon out of Daniel's hands, and his mounting drive to keep Lily safe, built a cement foundation beneath his battling abilities. Power flowed like it had never flowed before, as Adrien stood up to his father for the first time in his life.

Sweat dripped from his forehead and chest. The energy he exerted coupled with the pain of the wounds taxed his strength. He stared hard at Daniel and let him feel how much he despised his father, hated him for the vampire he was, for the pain he'd inflicted on him and his brothers from the time he could remember, but mostly for the deaths of all three human mothers.

Yes, he hated Daniel.

And he wanted him dead.

With that desire, he opened up another fraction of his Ancestral power and let it flow. A jolt of energy fell on Daniel and he jerked backward as though punched in the face. A shot of surprise passed through his light teal eyes, then pleasure as he battled back. "That's it, Adrien, keep reaching for your power. It's intoxicating, isn't it? There's more, so much more. The fullness of your Ancestral power will be like nothing you've ever known."

Adrien reached for his power, deep within his mind and his soul. He saw the open door and a beckoning of bright light and heat. He saw how easy it would be to just take it all in, drawing the power through his body, but he couldn't for no other reason than doing it would be what Daniel wanted. Beyond that, would walking through that door turn him into a monster?

He had to do something, however. He couldn't stand against Daniel forever. He knew his limitations.

Lily, I'm getting us out of here. Be ready.

I am. Do what you need to do. I can sense your intentions from one second to the next.

He'll strike and I'll fall. Latch onto my back like before.

Do it.

As Adrien drew back his power, Daniel completed the third blow. Just as it struck Adrien and as Lily latched onto his back, he took her simultaneously out of the cavern, engaging in altered flight, straight through the opposing wall of rock. He was right. Daniel didn't have Silas's ability to stop him from flight.

The repeated blows, however, had done something to Adrien, and he saw spots in front of his eyes. But he flew fast and hard as Lily clung to him, her arms and legs wrapped tight around him.

Yet as he flew, the wounds he'd sustained caused more spots to float before his eyes. His disorientation increased.

Adrien, you're heading deep into the earth. Can you shift course? Adrien?

Was Lily speaking to him? Where was he? *I need to stop.*

But he couldn't do that. If he stopped in the middle of rock they'd both die and he didn't have a sense of where he was. *I can't see or think. Lily, I can't do this, can't get us out of here.*

He felt pressure on his neck. *Yes you can.* More pressure. *Just keep moving and relax. You're doing fine.* More small bits of pressure. Then he realized Lily was kissing his neck.

For some reason that made him smile. His mind cleared at least enough to allow him to feel the heat of what he knew was the earth's magma.

He turned, heading back toward the surface.

Much better. I must be siphoning more and more of your power because travel is easier on me now. Her thoughts reached into his mind and eased him. *Adrien, is it possible to get a magma burn? I might have blisters on my ass. What were you thinking, vampire?*

Adrien smiled a little more and he sped up. Flying through the last of the rock, he took them into the air toward the stars. He could finally breathe.

Oh, thank God.

You okay?

Fine. Just a blistered butt. How about you? Dear old Dad gave you a beating, one of many in the course of your life, I take it.

He didn't like that you called him an asshole. He would have killed you.

He felt her draw in a long deep breath. She hugged him hard. *I think I might owe you one. Again.* She fell silent, then after a moment said, *I'd be dead right now, wouldn't I?*

Yep.

What a prick, but damn if you aren't traveling fast. You took on a new piece of power, didn't you?

Had to.

Where are we headed?

Rumy's. We'll be safe there.

He wanted to say more, but the spots began to return. Daniel could never get deep inside The Erotic Passage.

We're almost to the lake. Hold on. I'm not feeling one hundred percent yet.

I'm good.

He slipped around to Rumy's private entrance and slowed. His brain was still shifting about so he had to attempt his landing twice. Even then, he ended up on his hands and knees.

Lily slipped off his back as the door opened.

He looked up and Rumy smiled. "On your hands and knees, I see. Looks like Lily's got you trained. Glad someone finally did."

As Adrien stood up, his brain refused to function and

he listed to the left. He would have gone straight over the low balustrade and into the lake, but Lily caught his arm and pulled him back.

"Hey," she said. "Where you going?" Then, "Rumy, I need some help here. That bastard Daniel tried to fry him in Mexico."

Rumy called out and the next thing Adrien knew, he was being lifted up by several pairs of hands. This time the black spots grew to the size of potatoes, and that was the last he knew.

CHAPTER 13

Lily sat at Adrien's bedside.

He looked really bad. His face was both seriously burned as well as black and blue. Because she'd removed his shirt and leathers to bathe him while he healed himself, she saw how almost half his body had either serious red welts or massive bruising from Daniel's preternatural bludgeoning.

He lay on his back on a bed in one of Rumy's guest suites. The curly-haired owner of the expansive nightclub had immediately provided shelter, just as Adrien had said he would.

Now Lily was alone with Adrien, sitting at his bedside, touching him, wishing he would heal faster, wanting him to wake up to talk to her yet knowing he needed rest more than anything.

Earlier, when Adrien was settled in bed, she'd talked things over with Rumy, needing to be reassured that Daniel wouldn't be able to reach them here. But Rumy was adamant that his security surpassed everything else out there and that even the über-powerful Daniel Briggs couldn't get through the layers of disguising shields he had in place throughout his cavern system.

She also got a message to Gabriel about Adrien's condition since by now she understood that he was like family to Adrien. Gabriel had eventually called her and set up events for the following evening. Apparently, the Ancestrals were having their annual Gala at the Black Caverns Beijing Resort, a place known as a high-end playground for rich vampires and rumored to have extensive human sex-slave trafficking. Adrien, having advanced to Ancestral level, would now be allowed to attend the gala with Lily as his guest.

Lily at first refused since they needed to keep searching for the weapon, and not waste their time attending a black-tie affair. But Gabriel then informed her that the Beijing system had numerous associations with the extinction weapon. With Lily's tracking ability, if the weapon, or some part of it, was there, she'd probably sense it immediately. So she'd agreed to set up the event on behalf of herself and Adrien.

When she told Rumy what the plans were, he offered to arrange to have evening wear secured from their respective Paris and Manhattan homes and delivered to the guest suite.

So there was nothing to do now but to get Adrien healed up, to sleep through the day if he could, then to attend the gala that night at nine o'clock Paris time.

For now, however, she stayed by Adrien's bed for a long time, just tending to him. When he moved restlessly, dealing with his pain, she would touch him and he would calm down. She watched the bruises grow lighter, the welts diminish, the burns fade. The restless episodes grew fewer and farther between.

Still she waited in the chair, turning everything over

and over in her mind: the weapon, her son, the stress of the hunt, all the time pressures, the attacks, and of course Adrien, and all the tenderness she felt toward him.

And then the terrible truth that Adrien was Daniel's son.

My God, what Adrien must have endured.

Adrien slept with his eyes squeezed shut as though even unconscious he lived with a certain level of tension. And why wouldn't he?

Daniel was his father and had probably done terrible things to him for who knew how long.

Adrien moaned and, after a long moment, opened his eyes. He rolled his head to look at her. He tried to sit up but flopped back down on the pillow. "Lily."

She leaned over him. "We're safe at Rumy's. Just concentrate on healing yourself."

His eyes were closed as he nodded. He turned away from her to rest on his right side, the sheet sliding down to his waist, exposing his back. She put her hand lightly on a healed portion of his shoulder and rubbed gently. Adrien sighed and seemed to relax, if just a little.

She loved how he looked but would feel much better when the redness and bruises went away for good.

But as she looked, she saw a thin, silver line that ran from the top of his back, four inches from the base of his neck, straight down his spine. The line continued, so she pushed the sheet away and saw that it ended almost at his tailbone.

She didn't understand what she was seeing. Vampires always healed . . . unless . . . the wound occurred repeatedly. This was one thing Kiernan had told her.

Her fingers trembled above the scar. The edges of the room began to spin.

"No," she whispered. She didn't want the vision to come. She didn't want to see anything that related to the long silver line. And so long as her fingers hovered, the vision remained just out of reach.

She didn't want to see.

And yet in some inexplicable way, she felt obligated to know the truth, to understand what Daniel had done to his boys.

She summoned her courage, took a deep breath, and pressed her fingers against the scar. Once more, the edges of the room spun, going faster and faster until the vision opened and she saw Adrien as a child, chained facedown to a table, trembling.

Daniel held a thin, sharp blade in his hand. "This will make you a man. The more pain you can tolerate, the stronger you will be. My father taught me and now I'm teaching you."

He set the blade four inches from the base of the boy's neck and began to cut, a deep cut that flayed the skin, splitting it into two parts that folded back as he progressed down the spine.

Lily heard Adrien's screams, watched his legs thumping, his arms thrashing though bound, his body held flat by one of Daniel's hands as he continued to cut, down and down.

She couldn't bear watching another second. She moved her hand away from Adrien and the vision ceased, dissolving into thin air. She swiped at her now wet face, then sat back in her chair and wept as quietly as she could. She wept for Adrien and for herself, for Josh and for all her neighbors who had perished, for Lucian and Marius bound by chains in prison, for so much pain and suffering.

When her tears slowed and finally stopped, when she'd blown her nose and no longer felt as though her heart were being ripped from her chest, she marveled at the vampire recovering in front of her.

He'd survived a horrendous childhood, enduring unimaginable pain and suffering, and had become exactly what Daniel had predicted, *a real man,* at least by her own definition. A vampire, yes, but one who understood loyalty and service, who cared more about others than for his own safety, who could have fallen into rage and bitterness after leaving his childhood behind but instead served his world with relentless dedication. And he was the man who had swung Jean-Luc in a circle, giving evidence that he knew how to love despite the deprivations of his youth.

Her heart swelled at the memory of being with Adrien at the Trevayne system, at all the memories of Adrien.

Another truth surfaced: In this short but very intense time with Adrien, she'd grown to respect him and to care deeply about him. She might even be falling in love with him.

But as she stared at his back, her thoughts took a hard turn as she recalled Adrien's reaction to the man in The Ruby Cave, chained to the table, the one Eve had used her floggers and chants on. Eve had told her she should put Adrien on the table, that he could benefit from it. Was this why? Did Eve know what Adrien had endured at Daniel's hands when he was just a boy, what it would mean for Adrien to be chained to a table?

Her heart rate picked up as new thoughts tripped through her mind, one sensual image after the other, of having Adrien chained and under her control the way Eve had suggested, what it could mean to him but uncertain what it would mean for her.

She stood up from the chair, her gaze still fixed on Adrien's perfect back and the thin silver line that told the tale of his life. She owed Adrien a lot, even her life. She wanted to repay him, at least in a way that made sense to her. Yes, this she could do for him, especially since everything in her heart told her it was exactly what he needed.

Her chain vibrated heavily now and she left the room,

closing the door behind her, grateful that Adrien's double-chain gave her the extra distance. She withdrew her phone from the pocket of her jeans and called Eve and told her what she wanted to do.

To her surprise, Eve wasn't flippant with her, nor did she make a sexy joke. Instead, she praised Lily for having the courage to do what needed to be done.

There would be plenty of time before the gala to explore a journey into the darker side of sexual experience. Eve made several suggestions on how to go about it.

After making the arrangements, Lily showered, slipped into a cotton nightgown, and stretched out beside Adrien. His body, tense until she pressed herself up close to him, relaxed into her.

"Lily?" he murmured, his voice thick with sleep.

"I'm here."

"Good. You need your rest."

A tear escaped her eye. Why did he have to say that, to be thinking about what she needed when he was still raw from his wounds and still purple from so many bruises?

The tenderness that she knew to be at the heart of Adrien's soul confirmed that she was doing the right thing to take him to Eve's apartment in Rome, to chain him down on the dominance table, and maybe lay some of his ghosts to rest.

The heat from his body covered her in a drowsy warmth, a very welcome sensation. She had so much to think about, but the night's adventure had taken a toll. Before she knew it, she joined him in a dreamless abyss.

Adrien awoke to darkness, his back really warm, his chest cool.

Ah, Lily was curled up behind him.

He reached for her, found her arm then her hip. She

snuggled tighter, murmuring something unintelligible against his shoulder.

In the dark, he took a deep breath. She knew the truth about him now, the terrible truth about his genetics and his parentage, something he could never undo. What would she think of him now? Probably the worst, and he wouldn't blame her.

He released a heavy sigh, but despite his distress, he fell asleep again.

When he awoke later, he was alone, although he heard the shower running.

He recognized one of Rumy's guest suites, this one very private, in the lowest level of the Como cave system, extremely secure. Rumy had given them shelter.

He could always rely on Rumy.

He stretched his hearing beyond the walls of the suite but could hear nothing. Of course, some of the guest suites were miles away from the club and it was probably still daytime, the hour when all good vampires slept.

He sat up wondering what the hell to do next. This whole thing had to be getting to Lily. That's when he heard the softest muffled sounds through the noise of the shower. He extended his hearing and realized she was crying.

The last time she'd wept, he'd been making love to her and her grief had overwhelmed her. Was she thinking about her lost family? Probably. Or maybe just the hell his kind was still putting her through.

He flopped back down on the bed and clasped his hands behind his head. He hated to hear a woman cry, but he also knew that tears were a release. He wished he could help, make it better, make this whole damn infuriating, impossible situation just go away.

But he couldn't. He was as stuck as Lily and no closer

to getting back to his brothers, to releasing them from prison, than he was to finding the extinction weapon.

He reviewed all that had happened in the crystal cave with Silas and his enthralled killers. Those unfortunate men had probably thought they'd been hired to do some general cave maintenance, check for damp, remove stalagmites in living areas, relocate young colonies of bats to human-based caves.

Instead, Silas had used them as a weapon.

Here was one more prime example of the abuse that Ancestrals imposed on regular vampires, using basic enthrallment skills that had cost how many men their lives. Vampire law was basic and ineffective: If you held the knife, you were guilty. Never mind that an Ancestral could exert mind-control over lesser vampires and use them to commit murder.

One more reason he despised that he'd added the more powerful bonding chain and taken the first step toward joining the ranks of the Ancestrals. But at least his brush with Daniel had told him he'd made the right choice: Both he and Lily would be dead right now if he hadn't added the double-chain.

He lifted his arm and flexed. The bruises, welts, and burns were gone, not even a twinge of pain, one more sign of his increased power, since even his self-healing abilities had improved.

His thoughts turned to the extinction weapon. One thing he knew for sure right now was that Daniel intended to get hold of that weapon any way he could. If he had to create other tracking pairs by making use of Lucian and Marius, then he would do that. If Adrien didn't deliver or didn't join him like Quill and Lev had, then Daniel would probably kill Adrien, as simple as that, which of course meant that Lily would perish as well.

He didn't want her to. He wanted her to live.

He also wanted her to trust him, but she still kept her secret. Not that he blamed her. If he'd been in her shoes, having lost her family to a vampire attack, would he have trusted a vampire?

He snorted. Not even a little. In fact, if humans had killed his family, those he loved, he was pretty sure he would have gone on a killing rampage of his own and never looked back.

But here Lily was, bound to him, sleeping with him, donating her blood, saving his life repeatedly, and not just for the secret she kept. He'd come to know her in these past two, now three nights. He valued who she was, who the blood-chains told him she was, how much she'd loved the family she'd lost, how she'd slept close to him last night, stayed with him, comforted him. No one could fake that kind of character and if he didn't know better, he'd almost say he loved her, which of course seemed impossible.

He wasn't a vampire who could ever really love, not with Daniel as his sire. Always at the edge of his consciousness was the knowledge that he could become like Daniel, as vile, as self-focused, as cruel. He struggled against that darkness every day of his life.

But there was the other part of him, born of his mother who'd died. He had memories of her when he was young, of her singing and holding him, teaching him, and, yes, of weeping as Lily wept now.

His mother had been a good woman, a fine human woman, and Daniel had killed her.

Sometimes Adrien could barely breathe for the rage he felt against Daniel, for the deaths notched into his belt.

He closed his eyes and forced himself to take deep breaths, to press down all that rage, that hatred.

He left the bed, slid into his battle leathers, and moved into the expansive living room. He'd never been in this suite before, but Rumy did everything right; fine wood and leather furniture and blue crystals that formed a wave-like pattern above a stone fireplace. A smaller waterfall to the left, similar to Eve's, filled the space with welcome humidity.

His thoughts turned once more to Lily and he wondered yet again what secret she kept from him.

Leaving the shower, Lily dried off and blew her nose. Mourning her husband and daughter from time to time was as necessary as breathing and had been for the past two years. Her separation from Josh and living with her fears about what might have happened to him over the last two years brought on a similar round of grieving.

Was he truly alive?

Had he been hurt?

Would he even know her or be able to forgive her for not protecting him?

And should all things work out, should she actually find the extinction weapon and get him back, would he blame her for not having found him sooner?

Two more tears rolled down her cheeks.

She swiped at them and forced herself to breathe deep, to take healing air into her lungs, to try to move on.

Kiernan had told her that he'd had a caregiver in charge of Josh all this time, a human woman. Lily had asked who she was and had even questioned Kiernan about her qualifications, but Kiernan just laughed at her and said, "Suffice it to say she's in my employ permanently. I could even say she loves the kid."

These were her only consolations, that Josh might have been well looked after.

She forced herself to rein in her emotions, at least for now. She focused instead on Adrien and the night ahead.

She'd heard him leave the bed and get dressed, the results of finely tuned vampire hearing, so it was time to get moving and to let Adrien know about the two big events soon to come.

But just as she would have risen from the floor, a very different kind of thought streaked to the surface of her mind. *Can I communicate with Josh?*

Leaning against the side of the white porcelain bathtub, she suddenly sat up straighter. She'd been siphoning power from Adrien from the time she'd put on her chain, and now her power was even stronger because Adrien had reached the first level of Ancestral status. Though it was a long shot, she closed her eyes and took in a slow deep breath. She relaxed her shoulders and let her mind go loose. She focused on only one thing: her son.

The strangest sensation intruded, like movement, like she wanted to float in what must be a northeasterly direction, maybe toward Russia, as once more her tracking ability surfaced. She stayed as relaxed as she could and sent her thoughts in that direction so that pretty soon she could feel a flow of thought moving at light-speed until it encountered . . . *Josh.*

Stunned, she held herself, her mind, her thoughts completely still. Was she imagining this or was it real?

She wanted to scream with excitement, but she needed other things first. She touched the object, which felt warm to her thoughts. Yes, she felt her son and he was very much alive.

Alive. Josh really was alive!

Taking another deep breath, she formed one word and reached into his mind. *Josh.*

A kind of movement returned, but cloudy and ill formed, a child's mind.

I'm here, Josh. I can sense your presence. Mother is here.

She felt the warmth of his mind relax in much the

same way that Adrien had relaxed beside her while he slept. *Mom?*

She trembled now. *Yes, I'm here. Are you okay? Tell me you're all right!*

I'm fine. Claire is here. She's taken care of me. Mom, I miss you.

I miss you, too. So much it hurts. She couldn't believe the amount of energy she was expending to sustain the conversation. *Listen, honey, I'm doing everything I can to get back to you, but there are some things that have to be done first.*

I know. Mr. Kiernan told us.

Good. That's good. Pain swelled inside her head. She couldn't hold this much longer. *That's what I need to know.* She felt the power fade. *I'll do everything I can to bring us back together. I have to go.* The power began to fade. *I'll find you, Josh. I love you.*

Okay . . . Mom? . . .

Then nothing. Her telepathy returned to her, however, in an almost rubber-band snap of pain. She put her hand to her head, wincing. But she didn't care that she hurt. She'd talked with her son. Josh really was alive and a woman named Claire had taken care of him. At least Kiernan hadn't lied about that.

She didn't know what she felt for a long, long moment. Not relief exactly, though that was there. Then she felt it: *joy.* Josh was alive. She'd kept that thought in the forefront of her mind from the time Kiernan had first contacted her, but she'd never quite believed it. Now she could. Her son was alive. She'd felt him, talked with him.

Her son was alive.

She realized she was smiling. She was sitting on the bathroom floor and smiling. Her son was alive. *Alive.*

And there was one person she wanted badly to share that news with.

The door opened and Adrien, dressed in only his black leather pants, stepped into the room. "I could feel you speaking to someone telepathically. What's going on?"

Her heart began to race. She wanted to tell Adrien so badly.

"I feel your distress and your excitement. Tell me."

Slowly, she rose to her feet. "Please don't ask. I want to tell you but it's a condition of my part in the hunt for the extinction weapon. If I reveal this secret, I don't know what will happen."

Adrien stared at her and nodded.

She slipped back into telepathy. *You're disappointed that I won't tell you, that I won't trust you.*

His smile was crooked. *It's unreasonable, but yes, I am. I want your trust more than anything.*

I do trust you and I wish I could tell you. You've become so important to me. I . . .

She'd almost said the most impossible words of all, that she loved him. She emitted a kind of gagging sound, then turned in a circle as though she could run from the thought. "What's wrong with me? These damn chains. I feel what you're feeling and now—"

"I know." His hands were on her once more, her back to him, but she relaxed and let him touch her.

"The nightmare that wouldn't end," she said.

He didn't say anything but surrounded her in a warm embrace. He was so kind, so loving. He was a vampire— and yet he was so much more than that. She whirled in his arms and hugged him hard, her head resting against his shoulder.

After a moment, he drew a deep breath. "I suppose I should call Rumy, ask if there was any activity after we returned."

She pulled away to look up at him then told him the plan, first that she had a surprise for him then the gala.

"A surprise? What kind of surprise?"

After she answered or chose not to answer all his questions, she suggested dinner first, after which she would take him someplace unexpected.

By the time Adrien had finished grilling a pair of steaks, he knew something was up. His chains now hummed against his neck and chest and he could feel Lily's excitement.

As he cut a bite of rib eye, he asked, "What's going on in that head of yours?"

She met his gaze. "Just decided to take the advice of a friend."

He might have argued or at least made an attempt to ply the information out of her, but a new scent rose above the aroma of his meal, which made him pause mid-bite and stare hard at Lily. She wasn't just excited, she was *excited*. Her sweet feminine scent floated in streamers of sensation and her desire fueled his.

He shifted in his seat. They'd have some time before the gala and Lily had even gotten their clothes here, which meant they'd have a couple of hours or more to be together.

He brought his fork to his lips, paused, then shoved another bite of steak in. He chewed, maybe a bit harder than he should have, but the thought of taking Lily back to bed had become a quick fluttering of erotic images through his mind.

He also felt a familiar tingling near his heart that told him he'd need blood soon. But Lily was willing and by the scent of her, she'd be more than happy to donate. Over the decades, he'd served the blood needs of many aroused female vampires so he knew what it was for the donor, how stimulating the slice of the fangs and the ensuing suckling could be.

He couldn't believe how far they'd come down this road. He thought of her as belonging to him, a regular donor now, his lover, even a good friend. Yes, he thought of her as his friend, someone he could count on in the way he could count on his brothers. Was it just the bonding effects of the chains or was there more here, much more than he had ever thought or dreamed possible?

He stole a glance at her as she speared a bite of steak. She had thick lashes, a beautiful complexion, a lovely human.

When she met his gaze, she asked, "What?"

He leaned into her and kissed her on the mouth then searched her face. "Would you believe me if I said I've fallen in love with you?"

Her breath hitched. "I don't know. We're under the spell of the chains, right?"

He shrugged. "Do you remember when you first came to me in the cave, before you bound me with the chain? I felt something even then, a drive toward you that I still can't explain." He felt a deep tenderness emanating from her, almost throbbing in soft waves.

"Me, too. Almost from the first."

He kissed her again, only this time he let the kiss linger.

When he drew back, she took a deep breath and swore she trembled. "Keep eating," she commanded. "You're going to need your strength."

Because of the chains, he sensed the deep sexual nature of her intention toward him, which caused him to list in his seat. But he obeyed her and focused all his attention on downing his food.

When at last he settled his fork and knife on his plate and she'd eaten the last of her meal, she turned to him and slid her hand along his thigh. "I've had something prepared for you, Adrien, and I hope you'll like it. Also, I can feel that you need my blood and I'm ready to give it up for you again."

Since she followed up this bold statement by kissing him, his need for her spiked. He slid off his stool and she came with him, a flow of movement that felt just right as she landed in his arms. He kissed her again, this time piercing her mouth with his tongue, which made her whimper and her hips press against his.

He swiveled his hips just enough to let her feel that he was ready for her, which drew her hand gliding down his back and pressing his buttocks as she arched her hips into him. He needed to take her to bed and was about to suggest the bedroom when she pulled back, her hazel eyes glittering with passion.

She lifted her chin just a little. A dare? "I asked Eve if we could use her Rome apartment for a couple of hours and she said yes. I want to take you there. Will you come with me?" Her scent enveloped him.

Adrien's heart rate climbed. He'd never been to Eve's apartment though she'd invited him hundreds of times over the past two centuries, from the time she'd bought and refurbished it.

She'd even described in detail some of the specialty equipment she'd installed in one of the rooms.

He swallowed hard. "You don't want to just stay here?"

"I have something specific in mind, Adrien. Will you let me have my way right now? It will mean you'll have to trust me."

"What's going on?"

He felt both reluctant and ready. Maybe it was the eagerness in her face or the glitter in her eyes, or that right now she had a hand on each of his butt cheeks and was caressing him, but like any man in his right mind, he said, "Let's go."

Since they were already in Italy, the flight took about eight seconds.

When they arrived, dozens of candles had been lit and not a single electric bulb burned.

He released her and turned in a circle. Lily had already moved away from him, following what turned out to be a path of small votives on the floor. His heart began to pound.

Eve was all about dominance.

So what had Lily arranged?

And why here?

Lily walked down a long hall, where more candles showed the way. At the end of the hall was a set of double doors, slightly ajar. When she slipped inside, he would have followed, but she stopped him with a hand on his chest. "Give me a sec. There's something I need to do first."

He nodded, mouth dry.

When the door closed, he put his head on the smooth carved wood. His heart was now banging around in his chest. If it beat any faster, it would come loose from its moorings.

He'd never been harder.

He scratched softly on the door and whispered, "Lily. What are you doing to me?"

He didn't expect an answer, but one came, straight into his head. *Do you trust me?*

Yes. Sweat beaded on his brow. And strangely, that was the truth. He trusted this woman, this human.

You have a choice, Adrien. If you come in, you must do as I say, do you understand? If you choose not to come in, we'll go back to Rumy's guest apartment and you can fuck my brains out, but here, you are mine to command. Do you understand?

Yes.

Now choose.

He wanted to ask what she was wearing, but he suspected Eve had left her something special to put on.

He waited, trying to think, trying to order his thoughts. He already sensed what it was she wanted to do.

May I see you first before I decide, because if you've gone down a certain path, I'm not sure I can take it.

I'll let you see my hand.

The door opened slightly and her hand appeared. The wrist was wrapped in silver-studded leather. Hanging from each stud were several thin chains, each of which draped to encompass her fingers. If she used her hand on him, he would feel the chains.

She would hurt him, yet not hurt him.

He could feel his heart pulsing behind his eyes.

Adrien, do you trust me?

After two deep breaths, he sent, *I'm yours.*

Good.

He pushed the door open then stilled.

She stood across the room, next to Eve's table, an ancient wooden thing polished to a gleam through the years.

She was a vision in leather and wore a feathered headdress that was also a half mask. He could see the glitter of her eyes. Her lips were dark red, bloodred.

She wore a costume of black leather straps that covered only strips of her skin around her breasts and down her thighs, then broadened to encompass her knees and ended in loops of leather beneath her feet. She wore stilettos that put her just shy of his height. Her breasts and her bare peach were on display.

If he'd been hard before, now he was in pain. She'd taken sex into the realm of dark fantasy and it worked for him.

Oh, God, how it worked for him. And he knew it wasn't just about Lily and her costume or sex, but about his life and what had been done to him when he was young.

She turned her back to him and planted a hand on a long table, then bent over just enough so that he could see the bareness of her bottom. She was fully exposed and swollen.

When she turned back, she moved to the end of the thick wood table.

She put her palm flat on the table, the chains making a soft clinking sound. "Take your clothes off and get up here. On your back."

When his vision cleared of all his lust, he saw that heavy chains and manacles dangled off the sides of the table; two more chains lay taut across the top and bottom. In addition, he sensed the preternatural quality of the chains, that something very vampire would bind him in place, like the manacles Daniel used in the Himalayan prison.

He'd already made his choice. He wanted this. Hell, he'd been wanting it far longer than he could admit even now. But his heart pounded in his chest.

He stripped off his clothes then climbed up on the table and laid himself flat. He stared up at the mirror-covered ceiling and saw himself lying there, naked, and very erect. He kept looking at himself, his tight eyes, the vein thumping in his throat, his cock straight up and ready for something that scared the shit out of him.

Lily worked quietly and went from one ankle to the other, setting the heavy manacles with pins only she could remove. His legs were now spread far apart.

When she got to his wrists, he realized the air was thick with her feminine scent. He finally looked at her and saw that her nipples were peaked and that sweat lay in a sheen over her skin. Her bare labia were swollen with need. Whatever he felt, her desire matched his.

I can feel your need, Adrien. You've worked me up as well.

I want to suck your breasts and then eat you. Blatant words.

All in due course. Right now, you're mine to do with as I please.

When the last pin fell into place, Adrien pulled on the chains. That's when the panic set in. He felt the familiar power, the one that told him he was now a prisoner, trapped.

He couldn't breathe.

"Let me go," he said.

But Lily leaned over him. "No. Can't do that, Adrien. You agreed. You can beg me a hundred times, a thousand times. Not gonna happen. You have to trust me."

"I'm serious Lily. This isn't going to work. I can't do this. These manacles have power."

"I know. I requested them, otherwise you could break free."

He took a deep breath.

She glanced down at his erection and chuckled. "And something tells me you're gonna be just fine."

He hated this truth: that while he could protest, his cock loved what was happening. His hips arched and his balls were two nests of fire ready to explode.

She climbed onto the table. He was about to protest one last time, but she straddled one of his thighs, on her knees, and her hand began a slow descent of her body, from the navel, kneading her skin, all the way down to her labia. She closed her eyes and fondled herself, arching her neck. "These bonding chains are extraordinary. I can feel you shift from your fear to your desire. Do you like what I'm doing to myself?"

His mouth watered. His eyes moved from her erect nipples to her fingers massaging her clitoris and back. Using her free hand, she began to play with a nipple. He needed to get to her, to touch what she was touching.

He jerked the manacles at his wrists, trying to pull away. He wanted parts of her in his mouth, his cock buried inside her, his body thrusting.

Lily. My God, Lily.

I've never been so close. Her voice sounded rich and full of desire.

Let me see your finger go inside you.

She arched her hips forward and met his gaze. She held her lower lips apart with the hand that bore the chains, and with her free hand she slid a finger slowly down her clitoris, letting him watch, until she pierced her own body.

He groaned, wanting his fist around his cock. "I need you." Shit, his voice had dropped an octave.

She withdrew her finger and slowly reached for his lips. "Open your mouth, Adrien. Do it."

He obeyed, panting now, the chains on the table jangling because his body couldn't keep still, his hips slammed up and down trying to reach her. His arms flexed and released, pulling on the manacles.

She slid her wet finger inside his mouth and the flavor of her, ripe with excited female and her feminine scent, made him crazy. He had to get to her but couldn't.

He sucked hard on her finger, his tongue swirling over her. He couldn't get enough.

She removed her finger, then shifted suddenly so that she knelt beside him.

He froze as she bent her lips in the direction of his cock. He cried out, "Do it."

Damn but he needed to come.

He looked up at the mirror and saw the straps of her costume giving way to her buttocks, now two white mounds that he wanted his hands on, his mouth, his tongue, his teeth.

Then he felt her tongue on the head of his cock, a gentle swipe, then another.

His back arched. If she just took him and sucked he could release.

You're torturing me.

She chuckled. *I'm enjoying you.*

She drew back and looked at him. "Let me know how this feels." He glanced down at his cock, and watched her hand, draped with chains, close around his thick stalk.

He froze again, fearing, hoping.

She began slowly, up and down. She leaned over and tongued him at the same time so that the chains grew slick. It was both uncomfortable and hot as hell, though he didn't understand why.

Chains had bound him from the time he could remember.

Now she stroked him with a handful of chains. She kept moistening the chains and didn't move too fast or put too much pressure on.

I can feel your pleasure, Adrien. I can sense how much you're savoring what I'm doing to you. I love having command of you like this, taking charge of your flesh and doing whatever the hell I want.

She pumped faster now and it hurt but it felt so good.

She sustained the pace and he could feel himself ready to release, then all the pressure was just gone.

He shouted his frustration.

"Not yet," she said softly.

He groaned.

She turned to straddle his waist this time. She used the same chain-laden hand to rub deep between her legs, to gather her moisture. She put the same hand over his mouth. "Lick the chains."

He obeyed her without question. Her arousal was a

thick, perfumed cloud all around him. The chains were loose against her palm, so he drew them past his lips and sucked on them, taking the flavor of her down his throat.

His cock throbbed where the chains had rolled over his skin. He ached for her and something more, something so deep inside his soul that he had a sense all his rage at what had been done to him was about to be released.

He sucked harder on the chains. She leaned close and drifted a breast near her hand and his sucking lips. When she removed her fingers and slid her breast closer, he took all that he could in his mouth and sucked hard, muffled cries emanating from his throat. He couldn't get enough.

Her hands stroked up both of his arms at once, her fingernails digging into his biceps. Her body rolled while he suckled her nipple. Her lashes rested on her cheeks; a pinch of pleasure had formed between her brows.

You smell like heaven, came from her mind to his.

I want to fuck you.

I'd like that. Her eyes opened and her breast came away from between his lips. She met his gaze. *But you're trapped and can't. You can't do anything right now.*

The words burned like fire through his mind and his soul. She had spoken the reality of his childhood as well as the past year.

She slid down just enough so that his rigid cock touched her ass. He couldn't quite define the sensations that split him wide. Rage and lust maybe. He wanted her.

What is it, Adrien? Do you want something? Need something? What could it be?

Oh, God, she lifted up her hips. He could see her clitoris through her spread legs and now he could see his cock. He struggled against the chains as he watched her lower her body onto him. He thrust his hips upward, forging a warm wet pilgrimage into her depths.

His neck arched, his eyes rolled back in his head.

She began to move up and down, slowly at first then faster. Her voice once more penetrated his mind: *What are you going to do about it, Adrien? I have you now and you can't touch me, you can't do anything except feel this pleasure.*

But he wasn't that child anymore, and he wasn't just a vampire.

He was an Ancestral.

He had the power now to create the kinds of manacles that now imprisoned him. Understanding flashed through him.

He knew what he could do.

Did she know what he intended?

Somehow he didn't give a fuck. He summoned his Ancestral power, drawing energy into his legs and arms, wrists and ankles. The table began to shake.

She didn't seem to care. She planted a hand on his shoulders and moved faster.

What are you going to do about it, Adrien? Are you still afraid? Still chained to this table? Still trapped?

The words ripped through his mind.

Power surged.

The chains exploded off his body.

He caught her at her waist and kept her anchored to him. He spun her midair so that he landed on top of her, holding himself back just enough so that he didn't crush her as he forced her onto the table beneath him.

He took control, shoving himself into her as he ripped the feathered mask off her head. Through the chains, he sensed the depth of her pleasure, nothing but heady passionate sensation.

She panted in heavy chuffs as he drove into her, pummeling hard. She moaned and cried out as she wrapped her legs around his hips, her arms around his neck. He thrust hard and fast.

The release came like an explosion, not just from his balls but somewhere deep in his body, rushing through and streaking along his cock so that he arched and shouted.

Fuck, left his mouth repeatedly, loud, brutal, harsh.

"Oh, God, Adrien, so much pleasure."

He looked down at her as he thrust, feeling himself moving in and out of her body, watching her head thrash back and forth, her eyes squeezed shut, the orgasm finishing its ride until finally she lay slack and his hips grew quiet.

Her eyes were still shut as he looked down at her, then past her head to the broken shackles hanging open on the old wood. He'd done this. He'd ended something here tonight, some deep wound that had festered for four centuries. Power flowed through him in waves, the extraordinary ability of an Ancestral being born here, in this place that began as one thing and ended as another.

He'd just opened up a new layer of his Ancestral power—maybe not his entire potential, but enough to challenge the suffering of his youth.

"Lily," he whispered. "Thank you for this."

She nodded but her eyes remained closed.

As he lay on top of her, satiated, having overpowered his captor, something deep inside Adrien shifted, moved around, expanded, and changed.

Other chains that had held him captive in the past, were broken in this moment, obliterated forever.

CHAPTER 14

Lily was mired in pleasure. She could think of it in no other way. Her body lay trapped beneath Adrien's, a puddle of sensation, of satisfaction, of contentment.

There had been a frightening moment when the chains had come apart and he'd flipped her. She'd wondered if she would survive what was about to happen.

But as soon as she landed, and she felt that he'd somehow protected her landing, she knew she was completely safe with him. She'd barely registered the impact except for a slight loss of breath. Other than that, the fierce pounding he gave her had been just the right note.

She'd screamed, or she remembered screaming. Pleasure had flowed like an ocean finding a new dip of land to fill. A sense of well-being eased through her veins, relaxing every muscle.

Deeper still was a strange kind of release she hadn't expected, as though she'd walked from the desert, a long desert of two years, and suddenly stumbled on green plants, sea air, and a ton of welcome humidity. This strange, dominance-based experience had released something and she'd bet all her future happiness that Adrien had gone through something similar.

"Lily, did I hurt you?" He lifted up slightly and met her gaze. She was finally able to open her eyes. "Please tell me I didn't."

She stroked his cheek with her thumb. "No, not even a little. You protected me. In fact, I want to do this again and again. There were things I didn't get to do that I want to experience while you're bound in chains."

He leaned down and kissed her. "Like what?"

"I want to finish you off with my mouth for one."

She felt him shudder and deep inside her, his cock twitched. Nice.

"I want to have my hips pressed up close to your face."

"I'd tongue you."

"I'd count on that." She reached up and kissed him. "But do you know what I really want to do?"

He shook his head. His hips swiveled, and she could feel that he was growing hard again. She responded by giving her pelvis a quick upward jerk. He groaned. "What do you really want to do?" he asked.

"I want to explore every part of your body, especially the muscles of your arms, your thighs, your ass. I want to use my lips, my tongue, my breasts, my fingers and savor all that you are."

He began to move into her once more. She moved with him. She kept talking about his body, his chest, pecs, and abs, how she would suck on him and use her hand at the same time. She talked about biting his feet then each butt cheek in turn. She kept it up until he was pounding once more, hard and fast, and she was shouting into his face, "Fuck me, Adrien. Fuck me."

With her flesh made tender by the first orgasm, the second was like a skyrocket shooting through her body. She clung to him and screamed and savored the pleasure that streaked along every sensitive nerve and that kept streaking as long as he slammed into her.

His hips continued to pound her and then she felt it, like a tingling through her abdomen that ended at the vein of her neck.

She touched his face and eased back his upper lip.

His fangs glistened.

"Lily." His deep voice filled the air.

She rolled her head.

He struck quickly, a flash of pain that disappeared in a funnel of sucking pleasure as he began to drink from her. Her back arched as desire flooded her body. What was it about the giving of her lifeblood that heightened the ecstasy rising once more?

He groaned as he drank, his hips thrusting into her heavily again, his hands holding her shoulders to keep her seated against his mouth.

The well of her took strong pulls on what was so beautifully hard, and the spasming started all over again. More cries and moans left her mouth.

When his release came, she rode yet another wave of ecstasy to the point that she grew hoarse and her arms ached from holding on to him so hard.

When the last of the pleasure drifted away, she struggled to catch her breath. Her body leaked perspiration. She wiped a stream from his forehead as well and said, "Can you fly us straight back to the shower in Rumy's suite? Just like this?"

He chuckled. "In a minute, when I can breathe again."

She laughed and hugged him. She sighed and this time took air deep into her lungs, a place she was sure her body hadn't received air in a long, long time.

* * *

An hour later, Adrien stood by the mantel of the fireplace in Rumy's guest suite, staring at nothing in particular, sobered by what had happened at Eve's apartment.

He felt different, yet more himself than he'd ever been.

He wore his Brioni tux, ready for the gala, but what would he find there in Beijing? Daniel would attend. He never missed a social event of this magnitude in which at least a hundred Ancestrals would be present as well as the Council.

And now Adrien had the right to attend because he'd embraced his genetics and his future.

Daniel's machinations had forced the issue, of course. If Daniel hadn't taken over the Council, if he hadn't somehow forced Lily's hand to create a blood-chain bond with Adrien, if Daniel hadn't wanted the extinction weapon as though his life depended on it, Adrien wouldn't have gone down this path.

He'd still be a regular fighting vampire, working on behalf of the his world to keep peace and to sustain secrecy.

Now he was on the Ancestral track and he could never return to the old ways.

He stared at his ruby cuff links, frowning. He liked his new level of power, and what he experienced was just the beginning.

Everything felt new and different to him, as though even his vision had changed.

"Adrien, I'm ready."

He pushed away from the stone mantelpiece and turned, but what met his sight wasn't Lily, but the vision of her that he'd had not so long ago, before he'd even met her, the woman in the burgundy gown with gold crystals embroidered along the deep V cut of the bodice. The gown fit snugly to her waist and hips, flaring around her shoes just enough to allow for walking. Otherwise it fit her like a second skin.

"You look beautiful." He started moving in her direction, drawn to her, the chains resting beneath his shirt vibrating softly when he was this close, and yes, feeling this much.

He took both her hands in his and kissed the backs of her fingers. She wore lip gloss, which meant he needed to let her keep it on, so he dipped low and kissed down her exquisite line of cleavage. Maybe he would never have chosen this path for himself, but sharing the blood-chains with Lily had become a surprisingly tender and moving experience.

The soft moan that left her lips, combined with the rush of her sweet, feminine scent, helped him to know that she was as engaged as he.

When he lifted his head, tearing himself away from her soft breasts, he drew her carefully into his arms. "Is this love?" he asked.

She shook her head and shrugged. "I don't know, but it's damn close." Her eyes glistened.

"Aw to hell with it." He kissed her full on the lips, ruining the gloss she'd applied so carefully.

Lily slung her arm around Adrien's neck and kissed him back. From the moment she'd seen him by the fireplace, her desire for him, her need for him, had risen all over again. That he looked magnificent in black and white didn't help matters at all.

But it was more than just his appearance, which always tended to weaken her knees anyway. He had a different air, a different feeling about him, something the chains helped her to feel, of course, but even his posture was different, a little straighter, his chin higher.

She understood that feeling because she shared it—a kind of brazen confidence born from overcoming a few things, like being able to dominate a vampire on a sex table, or tracking a weapon through miles of extended caves, or even being able to siphon Adrien's power and finally communicate with her son.

Yes, she understood what Adrien was feeling extremely well because on the coattails was that elusive thing called hope. Maybe now, after accomplishing so much together, they could succeed at what needed doing, at finding the weapon and rescuing Josh because of it, so that Lily could at last bring him home.

As she drew back, she wondered if she should tell Adrien about her son. Hadn't he earned the right to know the truth despite Kiernan's warning to keep it a secret? Didn't her hard-won relationship with Adrien demand the truth?

She wanted to tell him. Desperately.

She planted a hand on his chest.

"What is it?" His brow furrowed, a familiar look for him.

She made the decision and the dam within her broke. "Adrien, my son isn't dead. He's alive. Kiernan has him. He's had him for two years, since the attack on my neighborhood. He's kept him all this time, without my knowledge, when I thought Josh was dead, so that when Daniel wanted to use him to get to me, to create this"—she touched the chain at her neck—"he'd have the tool he needed, the only thing that would have ever persuaded me down this road with you."

Adrien blinked a couple of times. His head jerked as he processed what she'd just told him. His lips parted; he might even have murmured something. He finally said, "I imagined so many things, this secret that you'd kept from me, but not this. Oh, dear God." He stepped sideways, releasing her. He seemed to have trouble breathing. He pressed a fist to his forehead.

She needed to tell him everything. "I've been through

hell since I learned he was alive. And I can't imagine what my son has gone through. I contacted him earlier, before Rome. I made telepathic contact. He's alive. I truly didn't know for sure until just then that he really is alive. I mean Kiernan let me talk to him once, but these men have such resources at their command I thought maybe he'd faked the whole thing. But I spoke to Josh this evening. He has a caregiver, a woman named Claire. A human."

She seemed to run out of words and speaking them aloud somehow made it worse, the truth of what she'd been through, what her son had suffered. A strange strangled sound came out of her throat. But Adrien caught her and drew her into his arms. Her eyes burned but she couldn't cry. The horror of her son's situation and of her own held her in mute paralysis.

But Adrien's arms soothed her and helped dissipate all that rising horror and emotion. "It's okay, it's okay. It'll be all right. We'll get him, we'll find him. Somehow we'll bring your son home."

"How?"

And then the real question surfaced, the one she'd been ignoring from almost the beginning, pretending she didn't care because she hated all vampires: how could she and Adrien ever turn over the extinction weapon to Daniel? How could she ever trade Josh's life, though precious beyond words, for a weapon that would be given to a monster who wouldn't think twice about obliterating entire cavern systems of vampires on a whim if it suited him?

He pulled back from her but he took hold of her arms, staring hard at her. "Lily, listen to me. We'll take this, as we have from the start, one step at a time. Now that I know what's really going on here, what has motivated every step of your journey, it changes the game."

"There's no way out." Her words came out hushed.

"There's always a way out. We just can't see it yet, and

right now we have a gala to get to. Maybe something will surface in Beijing that we can use. Have you tried tracking the weapon by focusing on China?"

She shook her head. "My thoughts have all been about Josh."

"Of course they have." He shook his head. "Your son is alive. How old is he?"

"Ten. He was eight when he was taken. Two years ago. Oh, God."

He nodded several times in a row. "All right. Beijing. We need to go there now, get things rolling again."

Lily forced herself to breathe once more and turned her tracking ability to China. She thought of nothing else but the weapon and Beijing. Adrien rubbed her arms slowly and she closed her eyes. His power flowed through her, the tremendous power she siphoned from him continuously.

The pull began like a gentle tug on her body to a place she could only define as very dark, but quickly became a grip of need: She had to get to China. *Adrien, what is the name of the Beijing resort?*

The Black Cavern.

I have a fix on it, and the pull of the weapon is strong, really strong. Her tracking ability roared to life as it never had before, she felt the location rushing toward her.

Good.

She drew in a sharp breath as another sensation arrived. *The weapon is there. I can feel it. The weapon is in Beijing.* But this was followed by another pull as she cried out. "Oh, my God, Josh is there as well. I can feel him. Josh is at the Black Caverns."

"Has he been there all along?"

Lily shook her head. "No. When I used telepathy earlier, it just didn't feel as far as China. Does that make sense?"

"Yes, it does. Well then, we'd better go."

She nodded. He pulled her tight against him and the flight began. The entire distance, Lily's heart ached as she thought about her son, yet she feared that the whole situation couldn't possibly lead to a happy outcome.

She wondered, too, why Kiernan would have brought Josh to Beijing—or maybe it was Daniel's doing. Did he know something that she didn't, about the Black Caverns and the extinction weapon? Did he know, for instance, that both she and Adrien, as a bonded tracking team would be there, at this particular gala?

A dark sensation moved through her as Adrien brought her closer to Beijing. Daniel would want to hurt them both because of what had happened in Mexico. She felt naive suddenly, that her previous and very brief spurt of confidence hadn't taken into account that once Daniel had tested Adrien in Mexico, he'd now turn up the heat. And what better way to remind her of the pact she had with Kiernan than to bring Josh to the Black Caverns.

But she strove to calm herself as Adrien flew them east. She needed her wits about her, to hold Daniel at bay, if possible, while she sought the weapon, maybe even to get to Josh and take him away before Daniel could stop her.

The flight lasted less than a minute, a huge change from her first night with Adrien.

He took them to the far edge of what turned out to be a landing field for those just now flying in.

Adrien chose a spot and brought them down gently, using the experience of four centuries to avoid other couples.

Lily held his arm tight as she walked beside him through a grand but very dark hotel entrance, a dozen chandeliers illuminating what turned out to be walls of glimmering obsidian detailed with white crystals in small, scattered diamond-pattern designs.

She reached out for Josh, and maybe it was her mother's heart or maybe her tracking ability, but she knew exactly where he was, even though at least two miles of rock separated her from her son. *I know where Josh is.*

We'll get to him, Lily, as soon as we can. But first the weapon. I've been thinking maybe we could destroy it before Daniel got to it.

If only we could.

Too many ifs and maybes in this equation.

She wanted to reach out to Josh telepathically, to let him know she was nearby, but she feared alerting Daniel. What if he could discern her telepathic communications with Josh? She just didn't want to take the chance.

One step at a time.

With such a large gathering of Ancestrals, even the air felt different, humming with power as she descended a wide, carved staircase into the Beijing resort.

Moving down a large hall, she used her tracking ability and focused on the weapon. What came back to her was a massive machine not far from where Josh was being held, and the pull from this machine was enormous.

The extinction weapon.

She truly had found the weapon, or at least one significant version of it.

She shared the news with Adrien, who stiffened.

Another frightening thought intruded. *Do you think Daniel already knows where it is?*

Adrien shifted to meet her gaze, shaking his head. *I sincerely doubt it, but he may have had reason to guess it might be here.*

You're probably right. If he knew where it was, he wouldn't have gone to this much trouble.

When she entered the banquet room, she climbed three steps, grateful because of her heels to have Adrien's support. The tables were laid out on a raised portion of stone and carpeted with thick, plush burgundy-and-black carpet.

At the far end was a dais beside which Daniel, his two subservient sons, and other elegantly garbed Ancestrals chatted together.

She had to admit, though, that of all the male Ancestrals present, Daniel exceeded them all in basic charisma. He had a champagne glass in hand and smiled, always his smile. He wore a finely tailored tux, like Adrien's, his black hair oiled and combed straight back.

"He seems to enjoy his role," she whispered to Adrien.

"That he does."

Daniel stood smiling, his gaze roving the guests, of whom there had to be at least three hundred present. Since there were only about five hundred Ancestrals in the vampire culture, the number here tonight was significant.

Every race was present, so that it would seem the vampire world truly did share basic human genetics. But somewhere a couple of genes had taken a hard turn that had to do with the ability to grow and release fangs, increase bodily strength, and develop a severe reaction to sunlight. The rest, even Daniel's behavior, was very human. In her opinion, he was a contented psychopath who had somehow maneuvered his way into a position of power, reveled in his rule, and intended to do whatever he needed to keep it, including acquiring, and probably using, a weapon that could wipe out his species.

As she glanced around, and saw that many vampires were staring at her, she sensed a kind of group curiosity and amazement, especially since the chain she wore drew a lot of attention. Adrien's chains were less evident, hidden as they were beneath his shirt. But as she let her own gaze wander, she noticed that a lot of women present wore chains similar to hers, though enhanced with other jewelry. There were even women with multiple chains.

From a nearby group, Gabriel joined them. She greeted him with a kiss on each cheek, something the Ancestrals tended to do. He seemed grateful that she was there, but especially Adrien, whom he clapped on the shoulder a couple of times. "Rumy has kept me informed," he said quietly.

Adrien merely nodded, then patted Lily's hand. She still clutched his arm, her heart pounding in her chest, thoughts bouncing rapidly from Josh, to the weapon, to Daniel and back again, over and over.

Gabriel drew a small, silk-wrapped packet from the inner pocket of his coat. He offered it to Lily. "I brought you a gift."

She met his gaze. "You did?" She'd never been more surprised.

"With all that you've been through, I thought you needed this, a small gesture. No, don't open it now."

Lily felt the air around her waver slightly. At first, she thought she was having another revisiting vision, but the blue silk of the present, cool beneath her fingers, had begun to vibrate.

She looked down at it frowning, then back to Gabriel.

The wave-like feel of the air suddenly made sense, especially when Gabriel's voice pierced the center of her brain. *I've created a brief disguise and we have only a few seconds to speak, but by now you know what you're holding; the companion chain to Adrien's. Lily, it would be permanent but it would geometrically increase his power for every ability he possesses. Keep that in mind. You'll have a choice to make soon. Follow your instincts and trust in Adrien's goodness above all things.*

The air warmed up, the disguise dissipated, and Gabriel

turned to greet someone else. She slipped the gift into her velvet purse, her heart pounding once more.

Adrien had also turned away, perhaps because of Gabriel's disguising skill, and she no longer held his arm. She took deep breaths and let the moment unfold.

She had with her now the companion double-chain to Adrien's, one that would bind her to him forever. She could never escape him or this world.

But she could increase his power.

Josh, the weapon, Daniel, escape.

Double-chain, no escape. Ever.

Her gaze moved to Adrien, who turned and introduced her to a handsome couple, but she couldn't register their names. Her ears felt full of fog.

She shook hands and Adrien passed her a glass of champagne. She smiled and nodded.

Double-chains.

She looked up at Adrien, seeing him in his element, as a man of confidence and ease among vampires, now his peers because of his rise to Ancestral status. He was already four hundred years old and would live to be much, much older.

What had Gabriel been thinking to have given her the companion double-chain?

She had a choice to make.

But her decision had long since been made the moment she gave birth to Josh. *He* was her priority. Her mother's heart demanded it. She would do anything to make sure he lived.

Her gaze drifted to the dais. Daniel watched her from over the rim of his glass. He was forty feet away, at least, yet she felt as though he stood next to her.

The air began to spin.

Another revisiting vision.

She wasn't surprised to see Daniel in the same space,

but the tables were gone and he stood with another vampire. Silas.

From the past, Silas frowned. "And you think the weapon is here, in the Black Caverns?"

"There are more rumors about this place than any other site on the planet."

"What do you want from me?"

Daniel snorted. "To help me find the damn thing."

"Watch your blasphemy." Silas tweaked the cuff of his robe.

A smile spread over Daniel's face. "And you, my friend, should watch your hypocrisy."

"But you know if I find it, I won't let you have it."

"And yet you just might since I can make it worth your while. You know I can."

Silas grew very still and, after a few seconds, nodded slowly.

But at that moment Daniel turned toward Lily from within the vision and met her gaze dead-on. "Hello, Lily." He looked around. "What is this? Ah, the annual gala." He peered past her. "Here, at the Black Caverns. I'll be seeing you then. I take this as a good sign. You have two children, right?"

Lily nodded.

Daniel laughed, waved his arm, and the vision vanished.

When the room came back into view, she realized two things: that Adrien had his arm around her and was asking her if she was all right, and that Daniel had raised his glass to her from across the maze of Ancestrals.

Are you all right?

Lily couldn't answer the telepathic question. Though Daniel had shifted his attention to a beautiful African female vampire who clung to him, a hand draped high over his shoulder, she still stared at him.

The monster who had inflicted unimaginable pain on his children.

The vampire who owned sex-slave clubs specializing in human females.

The ruler determined, at all costs, to get his hands on the extinction weapon in order to control everything.

And closer to home, the man who had seen into the future, during her revisiting visions, discovered her identity and orchestrated the slaughter of her husband and daughter and the kidnapping of her son.

Lily, what's wrong? I can feel that you're distressed, but not like before. What's going on?

She turned to him, aware that the other Ancestral couple looked concerned as well. But she couldn't worry about them right now, or anyone else, only the terrible truth of her current situation and the events she would soon set into motion.

She blinked once then twice, and in the space of those few seconds, her life and purpose shifted entirely. She turned to Adrien, meeting his gaze. *I've come to a decision. I can't, I won't do this anymore. I won't be used to hunt for the extinction weapon and I sure as hell won't turn the location over to Daniel, not now, not ever. I'll die first.*

Adrien's arm tightened around her waist. *But Lily, Daniel will kill Josh.*

A lump formed in her throat and her eyes filled with tears. *I'll find him, So long as I live and breathe, I'll travel to the ends of the earth to get him back. Now that I have a telepathic link with him, somehow I'll find him and save him. But I'll no longer be enslaved to Daniel, who would use the weapon to kill so many.*

CHAPTER 15

Adrien fell back into his old self. That was the only way he could describe what happened to him once he understood the level of Lily's determination to end the hunt for the weapon and find her son on her own.

But why should she have to do that? Why was she even here? How could his world have devolved so badly that a vampire like Daniel would have control over any human's life?

Then the other half of the equation surfaced as well: Daniel still had control over Lucian and Marius. If Lily refused to go farther, would Daniel kill Adrien's half brothers in retaliation?

When he thought of his brothers, his heart seized. After this night, would he ever see them again? He shook his head. After this night, would he even be alive?

Adrien shifted slightly to stare hard at his father. As soon as Daniel met his gaze, Adrien telepathed, *You're not getting the weapon. Not tonight. Not ever. Not so long as I have breath.*

Daniel offered a half smile. *Then you're a fool, my son.*

The air all around the room began to flow in strange visible waves. As Adrien glanced around, it was as though the room fell into stasis: glasses raised to lips but unmoving, gestures halted midair, bodies frozen in gala poses.

He blinked and shifted to look down at Lily.

She turned toward him. *What's happening?*

Adrien released a long breath. *Daniel. I challenged him, told him he wasn't getting the weapon.*

Then we're in for it.

I need you to know that I agree with you wholeheartedly. This is the right thing to do.

She nodded, but pain flashed through her hazel eyes and his chains vibrated heavily. He knew she was terrified at severing the link to her son, but he also felt her determination to get him back. And this was a place to begin, to stand up to the monster wherever that might lead.

He watched Daniel levitate above the silent, immobile crowd of Ancestrals, floating in his powerful way.

When he arrived, he stood in front of them both but addressed Adrien. "You don't possess a tenth of my power, which means you're going to put your woman here through a world of hurt before the night is out. Are you ready for that?"

"We can't let you have the weapon." Lily's voice sounded strong and sure.

Daniel shifted his gaze to her. "So you found it."

She said nothing. When he tried to enthrall her, Adrien again blocked him with a thought, which brought Daniel's gaze back to Adrien in a quick flash.

Daniel snorted. "Too bad Lily didn't take on a double-chain. Then this might even be a challenge." He lifted his right arm and snapped his fingers.

The wavy lines dissipated and movement and chatter

began again abruptly, as though nothing had ever happened.

Adrien tried to put Lily into flight, but he couldn't move; Daniel's power now surrounded him. At the same time, from all four corners of the room, Daniel's hired thugs—dressed in black—poured onto the raised stone platform, streaming through the guests who started to cry out, some in protest, some in surprise and fear.

Before Adrien could do anything, manacles, radiating with Daniel's power, appeared in his father's hands. A split second later Adrien wore them and now he was paralyzed, just as he had been as a boy, unable to move.

But he was no longer a child. He recalled the powerful manacles that Lily had used on him while in Rome, so Adrien summoned that same power. He could feel an effect and as his gaze shifted to Daniel, again, he watched a dart of surprise pass through the monster's eyes.

Soon enough Daniel's confidence returned as he exerted his energy toward the manacles.

Adrien felt them clamp down hard. This time nothing he could do moved them. His only consolation was that sweat beaded on Daniel's forehead so Adrien knew the amount of effort he expended to strengthen the Ancestral power he'd infused the wrought iron with.

Satisfied, Daniel turned on his heel while ordering his men to bring them to the dais.

A deep half circle had formed, creating a large space in front of the dais where Daniel left Adrien and Lily.

As gasps filled the room, Daniel levitated slowly, the showman that he was, to hold himself above everyone, his men spreading out to either side of him, battle chains hanging down with the threatening blades slack at the bottom.

He moved forward just a few feet so that Adrien could see him.

Daniel waved an arm to encompass his captives. "I fear, my most beloved compatriots, that I have discovered a sinister plot in our midst coming from my son Adrien. As many of you know, he recently achieved Ancestral status, something I had hoped to celebrate this evening with all of you. Instead, what I have learned is that Adrien has bound himself to this human in order to form the outlawed tracking bond, and has been searching for the extinction weapon for the past three nights. He even embraced his Ancestral status in order to gain enough power to accomplish his goal."

The crowd hissed at these words.

Daniel's performance went on and on as he detailed each step of their journey, more proof that he'd been following them from the beginning. Adrien felt the hard stares of his peers.

Many, like Gabriel, knew what Daniel was up to, but a great majority believed, or *chose* to believe, Daniel's lies.

Lily's voice entered Adrien's mind. *They believe him, but how can they?*

For many, this is about survival. From the moment Daniel took over the Council of Ancestrals, he's been harassing and blackmailing the weakest. I don't blame them. And Lily, I'm so sorry.

She might have said something in response, but Adrien had fixed his mind on the immediate future, on trying to figure a way out of this mess. He didn't want to die, and he especially didn't want Lily to perish—or her son.

But what could he do? If Daniel incarcerated him again, that would be one thing, but his father's dark side reigned in this moment, and Adrien had the sense that Daniel intended to make an example of him, maybe for Lucian and Marius's benefit.

The next moment Daniel's voice rang out stronger than before. "Justice must be served tonight, both swift and sure. I hereby pronounce judgment on my son and the woman to whom he so unwisely bound himself, the human who led him onto this wayward path of destruction. I, Daniel, despite my love for Adrien, must order an execution, this very night, for both these traitors to our kind."

Daniel turned and met Adrien's gaze. An unholy light had entered the monster's eye, something Adrien had never seen before. For the first time in his life, Adrien knew he would die at Daniel's hand. Every time before, he sensed that his father had intended only to inflict as much suffering as he could, but not now, not this time.

"What do you say, my fellow Ancestrals? Do these traitors deserve to die?"

Shouting filled the banquet room as well as scattered calls that Adrien and Lily should be taken to the Pit.

"The Pit, the Pit," became a horrendous chant within the obsidian cavern.

Adrien? Lily's voice pierced his mind, a soft query against the harsh calls for their deaths.

He turned to look at her, full suddenly of all that he felt for her, his respect and admiration, his trust in her, his belief in her essential goodness, her rightness of character. And in this moment, he understood that he loved her, something he'd never before truly believed himself capable.

I love you, came from his mind.

She blinked, and her eyes filled with tears. *I love you, too.* A soft smile, full of affection followed, then, *With all my heart, Adrien; with all my heart.*

Daniel's voice, louder than all the shouting combined, echoed through the cavern, "To the Pit!"

Lily felt disconnected from her body, as though the path she walked right now led straight into hell. Her heart beat like a mallet against a drum, so hard that the thumping resounded painfully in her ears.

Worse, she could feel Josh now and knew that with every step she took, she drew closer to him, which meant Daniel already had him at the place of execution.

How convenient that the Pit should be located in the Black Caverns.

She wanted to reach out to her son telepathically, but to do what, to tell him that they were vastly outnumbered by a mob bent on their execution?

She took another breath.

The path that apparently led to the Pit had a downward slope now and Ancestrals poured into the space from every direction, all coming straight from the banquet to watch the execution.

Was this really happening?

She still carried her purse, the one that contained the double-chain that Gabriel had given her. If she put it on now, would it do any good? And if she did, and somehow she survived, she'd be bound to a vampire forever. She'd never be able to leave Adrien, she'd never have the choice.

She drew the silk package out of her purse, letting the purse slip to the floor from her hands. As she walked, she opened the small packet and pulled the double-chain out.

Immediately she felt a vibration flow through her body. *Lily, what is that?*

She opened her palm and showed him. Adrien pressed his lips together and shook his head. *Won't do a damn bit of good and if we're able to survive, I'd hate that you were bound to me like this. You'd never be able to leave my world. Don't even think about it.*

She sighed and nodded, then wrapped the chain around and around her wrist, wearing it like a bracelet. The vibration remained, but she sensed no particular bond was being forged.

Still, she thumbed the chain with her opposing hand, wondering if there was some possible way out of this mess, something she hadn't seen either about Daniel or the situation, or even her own abilities.

Though her heart still thumped in her ears, she focused her attention on her surroundings, on the nature of the Pit into which she was descending, on the love she had for Adrien.

She felt his rage now rising within him, that familiar terrible ire that had defined him from the moment she had first placed the binding chain around his neck.

Yes, rage had defined Adrien, rage birthed in his childhood and continuing as he watched his society's inequities unfold.

She knew that tonight had become for him the culmination of his life experiences. He was a man who battled to keep his world in order while his father, always besieging good vampires and humans on the opposite side of justice, kept the secret world in a state of chaos.

The tunnel opened up into a huge cavern, an arena-like space, all black as the name of the resort promised, the walls in polished obsidian with intricate diamond etchings in an array of patterns. Soft light from dozens of sconces lit the space in a dim glow.

Looking up, she saw that even the ceiling had been worked well, this time in a dome of polished rock that overlooked the rows and rows of seats, all in a circle above the place of execution below.

From other hallways, Ancestrals poured into the arena filling up the seats. Lily drew in a sharp breath realizing that they'd come to watch her die. Historically, crowds often watched public executions, but in more modern times, in her human world, justice-ordered deaths occurred behind closed doors.

She wasn't used to this on any level, including the horrifying spectator aspect of the event.

Adrien's voice pierced her mind. *I'm disgusted as well.*

She moved forward and grabbed his manacled hand. He squeezed her fingers in response.

But that was the last contact she had. Quill emerged from a nearby tunnel, which caused Adrien to stiffen, drop her hand, and turn in his direction.

"Happy, brother?"Adrien spat.

Quill smiled. "More than you'll ever know. I've wanted you dead for a long time, punished for your disrespect toward our father. Now let's go." He snapped his finger in Lily's direction. "And bring the woman."

The guards hefted Adrien, picking him up beneath his arms, pulling him off-balance so that he fell forward. They dragged him toward a set of stairs that led downward to the place of execution, his body thumping down the stairs the entire distance.

She cried out, "Stop it. What are you doing? He's done nothing wrong. Daniel did this. It's always been Daniel."

But the crowd above shouted her down this time, calling her a liar and a traitor. Of course the closest seats were taken by Daniel's men, so that was no surprise.

She moved quickly down the same set of stairs that led to the base of the Pit. But that's when everything shut down for her because standing opposite, past two tables made of slabs of black granite, Josh stood staring at her, manacled at his wrists as well, a dark heavy chain looped between them.

Daniel waited beside him, his arm resting over the back of Josh's young shoulders.

And Daniel smiled.

She stopped in her tracks, staring at the child she hadn't seen in two years. "Josh," she whispered.

A thrashing began deep within her soul, a need to get to him, to hold him, to protect him, to beg him to forgive her for being unable to help him.

But looking into his eyes, his expression now old beyond his years, all such maternal thoughts ceased. She grew very still as she met his gaze. Instead, she opened herself to her siphoned ability to sense what others were feeling and directed that power toward her son.

The first thing she felt was the depth of his fear, which he'd been living with for two years, fear of his situation, of the guards around him, of the arm resting across his shoulders. So much fear, which prompted another resurgence of her mother-guilt and a second internal flailing.

But again, the serenity in Josh's eyes stopped what was useless in this situation.

What she felt next, however, was a determination so similar to what Adrien exuded, her heart finally began to settle.

"I love you," she called out.

He didn't speak, but nodded slowly and never lost eye contact. So restrained, so grown-up, long before he should have been, all the heinous signs that he'd been through a severe trauma.

Josh was taller now at ten and came to Daniel's shoulder. His hair was slicked back and his cheekbones looked sharp, as if he hadn't been fed as well as he should have, or maybe he'd been unable to eat. He wore a black T-shirt and black jeans, and he was barefoot. Even from here she could see that his feet were filthy. But a child without shoes was a child who couldn't run away.

Maybe more than any other thing the sight of his feet did her in. Something inside her began to scream. She arched her neck and let the sound pour out of her. She screamed until her lungs ached and her vocal cords could take no more.

When she stopped, she was staring up at the tall domed ceiling at least five stories up.

And the crowd was finally silent.

When she looked back at Josh, it was Daniel who

caught her eye. His gaze had a foggy appearance and his lips were slack. No doubt he was euphoric because she'd just given him exactly what he craved the most: the suffering of others, the pain of others.

When she glanced at Josh again, his eyes were tight and he mouthed something. It took her several seconds before she understood he was saying, simply, *Mom.* She nodded and using her telepathy said, *I'm okay now. I love you, Josh. I'm so sorry. I'm so sorry.*

He didn't say anything in response, but held his lips together tightly, two white lines.

So here she was, Lily Haven of Deer Valley, Arizona, and of Manhattan, soon to be executed, standing halfway between her kidnapped son and the man she loved, with no way out.

The sounds of Lily screaming her anguish at the sight of her son had quieted Adrien, had brought him out of his rage and into the present moment. His senses sharpened as the emotions of the now silent spectators hummed through his veins.

The guards grabbed him once more. Though he resisted, he was quickly overpowered, picked up, and thrown onto a hard slab of granite, one of two altar-like tables in the Pit. More chains were wrapped around him, securing him, chains that held Daniel's powerful signature and kept him immobile.

He stared up at the tall, curved black ceiling, his mind rolling backward to being a child. How many times had he been in this position, chained to a table and subjected to knife cuts, delivered close-up so that Daniel could watch him suffer? How many times? A hundred? A thousand?

And how much Lily's screams had fed the beast that lived inside Daniel, the one that needed the pain of others to thrive and to be satisfied.

He didn't want his father to win so Adrien lay very still, gathering his thoughts. He had to figure this out. He'd gained Ancestral status. Surely there was some way to access his power and overcome the chains.

The guards moved Lily in the direction of the second table. Surprisingly, mother and son didn't speak, but then what could be said? He'd watched Josh's reaction to his mother's screams, he even remembered what that was like. How young he had been when his own mother had screamed her pain, her anguish.

But he wouldn't bring those memories to this table.

This table belonged to *now* and not to the past. This table was about creating a new set of memories.

He glanced at his father, who smiled. Of course.

Join me, Adrien. Daniel's voice pierced his mind. *And all this will end. I will even spare the human's life and her son's. Just say you will serve me and I will end this suffering.*

For a split second he considered agreeing to it, if for no other reason than to spare Lily and Josh, but reason returned.

He also knew that Daniel wouldn't keep his word. He'd never let Lily and Josh go.

Adrien responded with a single word: *Never.*

How unfortunate, but have it as you will.

Lily stood beside the granite slab, a guard on each side of her, as she waited to be chained to her place of execution. She didn't look at Josh again. How could she without falling into another round of screaming anguish.

Quill's voice, loud and strong, sounded through the arena as he stated again the reason for the execution, the illegal hunt for the extinction weapon.

The crowd responded with shouts and condemnation.

Her eyes began to burn. Once more she looked up at

the gleaming black dome of the ceiling. She had heard that in a spiritual sense *obsidian* meant "truth."

What was the truth of this situation? Why was she here? What had gotten her here? Why was she trapped in a way that prevented her from helping either her son or the man she loved?

From the time of her husband's and daughter's deaths, grief had dominated her life, a pain so deep that for a long time, until she'd been contacted with news that Josh was alive, she'd felt nothing but a numbing pain without end. She had lived that pain and it had ridden her hard, for months turned to years.

Meeting Adrien had been like setting a lit match to a gasoline-soaked bonfire of sexual and emotional need. Her relationship with him had simply exploded until now that bonfire burned in her heart.

She loved him, a new love born out of this impossible situation.

Grief was still with her and she knew, in her heart of hearts, that she would grieve for those she'd lost until she drew her last breath.

But the chains had birthed something new in her. She'd come alive in the course of the past few nights, alive in ways never before imagined, bursting with strength and passion, and the awareness that she was bound to a vampire in a way that gave her unexpected powers and the ability to live in a secret vampire world.

In a sudden revelation, she understood the lesson of the chains, of her bondage to Adrien, of what they'd become over the past three nights: Their real power came from working together, back and forth, functioning as a team.

But in what way could she work with him now?

She glanced down at the double-chain wrapped around her wrist and began to loosen and unfurl it until it hung in a long loop from her hand. Time seemed to slow. The double-chain, once she put it on, would mean a final commitment to Adrien, to being with him forever, inseparable. There would be no way to remove this chain, to leave Adrien behind, and she'd never be able to return to the human world in any normal sense.

Yet as she stared at the chain and heard the crowd as through a fog calling for her death, she knew this was where she wanted to be, with Adrien, nothing held back. From her right, she saw a manacle lifted in her direction as the guard prepared to bind her and secure her to the granite table.

In a swift move she flipped the double-chain over her head and felt it fall around her neck, as the guard seized her wrist and secured her with the heavy wrought iron.

Immediately the chain began to vibrate. Power swirled around her.

"Lily, what have you done?"

She met Adrien's gaze and smiled. *What I should have done the moment Gabriel gave me the chain.*

But you'll be bound to me permanently.

She smiled. *I don't want to be anywhere else.*

In that moment she opened her heart to Adrien as she never had before. She let all her grief go as she focused her thoughts on him, letting her love flow in his direction, letting him know that she loved him more than life itself.

All this she sent through the chains that bound them.

Adrien shifted as best he could so that he could see Lily, to watch her as the double-chain came to life between them, a sealing of their fates together, now and forever.

But mostly he felt her love, her eyes glowing with emotion, with all that she felt for him. It meant more to him than words could ever express that she would have donned a chain that bound her to him. Even if this was to be the last moment of his life, and hers, that she had done this thing filled his heart with joy.

"I love you," she called to him. "And I always will."

"I love you, too."

"Silence," Daniel shouted.

Adrien felt the weight of the chains on his body, chains he had known ever since he could remember, maybe even since birth. Yes, he'd been born in chains and lived chained up, whether mentally or more recently chained in a cavern and tortured with whips and clubs.

Now he felt the chains again, so heavy that they pressed into his soul and mired him in the moment, sank him deep. He couldn't believe he was here again, knowing not only that he would die soon, but that the woman he had come to love over the past several days would also die— along with the boy she'd given birth to ten years ago, her beloved son, the remnant of her family.

Adrien turned to look at his sire, at the man who had spawned him, who had given him life, standing in his arrogance beside the boy.

Daniel looked back, his eyes glittering, his desire to inflict pain rising once more.

Adrien knew that look well.

Pain always followed.

He closed his eyes, unwilling to let Daniel feed off his suffering and pain. Instead, he focused on Lily and her love, and on the chains vibrating powerfully at his neck. He opened himself to experiencing what she felt right now. What came to him was her love, that she found him worthy and noble, that in this moment nothing else mattered. He felt her strength as well, that despite the horror of the Pit she could reach out to him, willing him to know that she loved him, though she would soon die.

That love, which she gave so easily, which was just

who she was, began to move through his soul like a healing river.

For the first time in his life, he let his rage go, all that horrible anger that had lived in him like a festering wound.

He allowed other feelings in, the better ones, the ones he'd learned from those vampires who lived in close-knit communities, like Alfonse and Giselle, and more recently from Lily, about love, about forgiveness, about opening his heart to another person and trusting that good things would follow.

Rage was all he had ever really known, a profound rage born at his birth and built with the fuel of every evil deed Daniel had committed against him and against his brothers.

Yes, he let that go, all of it, let it drain out of his body like the poison it was. He saw it sinking deeper and deeper into the granite altar he was chained to, deeper and deeper. He let love wash through him, a cleansing force that built a new strength in his body, fired his muscles as it cleansed his mind and soul.

The part of him that was now an Ancestral vampire responded, adding a new layer of power and intention. Light shone in his mind, another purifying force that wiped the slate clean, that took all his hatred, all his anger, and transformed it into . . . *purpose*.

That was what he felt, an intense, searing purpose.

And his purpose in this moment was simple: to save the one he loved and the one she loved.

Power flowed into his muscles, new power, Ancestral power. But there was something more, and this was Lily's gift to him as the added power of her double-chain ripped through him. The base of the granite table began to vibrate—then the whole structure started to rise into the air.

"What the hell is this?" Daniel cried out. "You there! Guards! Secure that table."

Guards surrounded Adrien, hands on the table, forcing it back to the stone floor.

"Let the executions commence," Daniel shouted. "And begin with Adrien, the one who betrayed me repeatedly, his own flesh and blood."

Adrien smiled because now he understood that his father feared him, feared what he could do to him, what he was becoming. He would never have ordered Adrien's death first, not when he could have inflicted more suffering by killing Lily or even Josh first.

Father, he telepathed, pushing into Daniel's head. *Shall we find out what you've really created in me?*

Did he hear shrieking in Daniel's mind?

"Use the blade and take his head! Now!"

Adrien opened his eyes and embraced all that his life was, including all that Daniel had given him as his father.

Adrien saw the sharp edges of the blade rise high above his head, the executioner's hand steady, the man ready to obey Daniel.

But as the blade fell, Adrien lifted his fingers, focused his power, then released. A stream of energy flowed down his shoulder, through his arm, and outward in a powerful thrust from his hand. The blade flew from the executioner's grasp, sweeping in a high arc that took it out of the Pit and beyond the surrounding seats.

Cries from the spectators flooded the arena.

He focused the same power within his body: his chest, arms, and legs. He flexed his muscles and one by one the wrought-iron links snapped and the manacles on his wrists and legs fell away. He heard the whirring of a long battle chain ready to strike. A guard came at him swiftly, the chain spinning. He reached in and plucked the chain away from the guard. At almost the same second, he flipped the chain toward two other guards. The chain wrapped around both necks and bound them.

The remaining guards backed up.

Adrien moved in Daniel's direction, but he called out, "Kill the woman and child! On pain of death, *do as I say!*" He threw Josh in the direction of the guards. His words carried enthrallment power, and once more the guards, now glassy-eyed, moved to obey.

Adrien had a decision to make. He could go after Daniel right now and slay him, removing the scourge of his life from his world for all time. But if he did both Lily and Josh would die.

Or he could save Lily and her son.

But he couldn't do both.

There was no real choice to make. In the same way Lily had refused to turn the weapon over to Daniel, Adrien refused to follow Daniel and take his vengeance.

As Daniel switched to altered flight and vanished, Quill and Lev following in his wake, the blades descended on Lily and Josh.

Adrien split into his two selves and with the greater power and speed of his Ancestral status, he destroyed the guards in quick succession, flinging the killing blades away, breaking bones, snapping necks until he was alone in the Pit with the woman he loved and her son. He reformed quickly.

The assembly of Ancestrals broke into an uproar of shouting, at least those who either believed Adrien and Lily guilty or served Daniel. But Adrien also heard a lot of cheering as he broke Lily's manacles.

He knew that even as he released Lily's chains, some of the guards would return to do their duty. He had to get out of the Pit and get away now.

He took Josh in one arm and Lily in the next.

With the barest thought, he set them flying with his greatest speed ever, to his most secure residence in South Africa.

Within seconds, he stood in the living room, his aston-ished housekeeper staring at him as he held Josh and Lily in a tight embrace, mother and son weeping, the son fi-nally enfolded within his mother's arms.

CHAPTER 16

Lily led her son to the couch in the living room, then sat down and took him into her arms once more. Adrien moved into the hallway and she heard him on the phone talking to Gabriel and making arrangements to add to the security of the South African system.

She could be at ease now, at least where their safety was concerned, so she turned all her attention to her son.

She tried not to weep, but her tears escaped anyway, and she felt Josh's emotions give way at the same time. For the next hour she let herself grieve and let Josh do the same, until finally they were both spent.

She reminded herself that this would be a long road, especially for Josh, so she reined in her emotions and focused on him, on what she felt coming from him, on what he was feeling.

There was a kind of blankness, almost an emptiness, as though the years of separation had robbed him of part of his personality, of who he was. And why wouldn't they have?

At last he drew back and looked at her, his large hazel eyes a mirror of her own, but his nose and strong jawline like his father's. "You were gone so long, Mom. I didn't think I'd ever see you again."

"Two years, sweetheart. But during most of that time, I didn't know what happened to you. I didn't even know you were alive."

"You weren't there, the night they came."

"I was visiting my sister, your aunt, in Oregon when it happened. Do you remember? Can you tell me?" She wasn't sure if the questions and timing were even appropriate, but she had to ask, had to know what he remembered so that she could help him.

He nodded. "The vampires came. I heard screaming."

"From inside the house?"

"And from other houses. The next thing I knew, the vampires were in my room. One of them said, 'Is this the one?' The other nodded. They took me away. When I asked about Dad and Jessie, Mr. Kiernan said they were dead. He said you were alive, though, and that one day, if I was very good, I'd get to see you again. I tried to be good. I did. I guess I was good enough because here you are."

"Oh, Josh." She drew in another deep and much-needed breath. "Did you cry?"

"Yes," he said slowly. "A lot at first. I don't cry much anymore, except tonight, with you."

He seemed so serious and maybe a thousand years old as he looked at her. "Did you cry, Mom?"

Tears filled her eyes. "Yes. Often. Every night for months and months. Oh, Josh, I can't believe you're here and I'm trying not to cry all over again."

He put his hand on her shoulder. "I'm here, Mom. And I'm not going away. I'm here."

Oh, God, her son was comforting her when she should be comforting him. She turned more fully toward him, so that she could pull her boy back into her arms. She held him for a long, long time, his thin arms holding her as well.

When Adrien appeared in the doorway, his expression solemn, she shifted to telepathy. *Will Daniel come for us? Are we safe here?* She had her son back and didn't want to lose him again.

Daniel doesn't matter now. He may come after us and if we have to, we'll go into hiding as several of the Ancestrals have done. But Lily, I promise you, I'll do whatever I need to do to protect you both.

Josh's gaze shifted to look at Adrien as well. "Is this your home?"

Adrien nodded. "And yours and your mother's as long as you need."

Josh looked back at Lily. "I had someone with me, Mom, someone who took care of me. I think she might be in trouble, too."

Lily smiled and squeezed his shoulder. "Tell us."

"Her name is Claire. Mr. Kiernan called her my caregiver and she helped me a lot. We lived in a small house at the back of Mr. Kiernan's property. I just hope she got away okay."

"What do you mean?"

"She said she was going after a vampire named Lucian. She told me to be brave, then she left the house. I heard the dogs go after her, but I think she got away. She said she was going all the way to India to find this vampire."

Lily stared at Adrien once more. Adrien opened his hands and shook his head. *I have no idea what this means.*

Josh put his finger on Lily's single-chain beneath the double one. "Claire had a chain like this. She was wearing it when she left."

"You mean it looked just like this one?" Lily held it up and Josh peered closely, examining it.

"Just like it. She said she got it from Mr. Kiernan's safe."

Lily's brows rose. "Then she must be one clever young woman."

"She is," Josh said, smiling. "She's a lot like you, Mom. You'd like her."

"Oh, I have no doubt of that. She took care of you. For that, I owe her everything."

He glanced at Adrien. "Do you think you could help her? I saw what you did when they tried to kill you. Claire told me a lot of things about vampires because she said she's been around them for years. You have a lot of power. Could you help her?"

Adrien nodded. "I think I know where's she's headed. You see, Lucian, the one she's after, is my brother."

Josh's eyes brightened. "He is? Then you can help her."

"I'll do what I can. I have powerful friends who can go to India and watch for her."

Josh released a deep breath. "That would be great. I'm really worried."

"I can see that."

Lily understood then that her son had formed a critical bond with Claire, another mother–son relationship. She gave his shoulder another squeeze. "We'll both do what we can to see that she's watched over, to find out what happened to her."

Tears filled his eyes. "Good." He pressed his fingers to his eyelids. "She took care of me."

"I know."

Lily had to work all over again not to become enraged by all these circumstances that had brought so much pain into her son's life. But once more, she took her emotions in hand. She could give vent to her feelings about the situation later. Right now, however, Josh needed her just to be his mother, to be there for him, to make him her priority for as long as needed.

She remained quiet, therefore, and let him deal with what he was feeling, in whatever way was necessary. That he wept again, this time probably for having lost Claire, didn't surprise her.

After at least another hour, with Josh leaning against her shoulder, he said, "I can't believe you're here."

"I can't, either, but somehow we made it, and now you're here, too."

Josh sat up, pulling away from her as he looked around. "What is this place? This must be one of the cavern systems that Claire told me about. It is, isn't it?" He shifted toward Adrien.

"Yes, in South Africa."

Josh nodded. "I'd like to know more about your world." How old he sounded, but then he'd lived a lifetime and if anyone understood what that was like it was Adrien.

Lily watched as Adrien pulled up an ottoman and sat down in front of her son, answering question after question, anything Josh wanted to know, leaving very little out. Josh often referred to Claire and all that she'd done for him and told him during his time at Kiernan's home.

One day she'd want to thank the woman for what she'd done for Josh, because it seemed to Lily that single-handedly Claire had saved her son.

When Josh's questions finally stopped, at least for now, Adrien had his housekeeper prepare a light meal of one of her fine soups and homemade breads.

Lily ate as well, as did Adrien since it seemed to them both that otherwise Josh wouldn't have eaten. The housekeeper had prepared him a room, and when Josh's eyelids grew heavy and he was weaving in his seat at the dining table, Lily finally agreed it was time for bed.

But she hated to let him go. Now that she had him back, she didn't want him out of her sight. She tucked him in and sat in the chair next to his bed until he was sound asleep. She would have stayed there as well, but she needed to be with Adrien as well, to talk everything over with him and plan their next steps.

We won't be far, just down at the end of the hall. Adrien cupped her face with his palm. *This compound is well hidden and fortified for security. We need to plan where to go next, and he needs to sleep after all he's been through.*

Lily shifted her attention to Adrien. The new double-chain intensified what she sensed from him. She felt his love and his appreciation for her as Josh's mother. She also felt his profound gratitude that she'd donned the second chain.

She smiled at him. *I understand that and I will comply. But just a few minutes more?*

Of course.

Adrien's heart had never been so full, not in his entire life, not in four centuries of hard living—and a woman had done this.

Three days ago he'd been chained to a cavern wall; now he was free, powerful enough to stand up to Daniel and to protect his family, and he had a woman in his life who he loved with all his heart.

In a way the boy had brought her to him, and for that reason alone he would cover Josh with a shield of his protection so that no one would ever get to him again.

Though he'd started a war tonight against Daniel, he might not be the one to finish it. His first priority had to be Lily and Josh and he knew that Daniel would come after all of them with a vengeance. Daniel had been denied a kill and he'd been humiliated in front of an assembly of Ancestrals. Above all things, he'd want Adrien dead.

While waiting for Lily, Adrien made his call to Gabriel. Together, they decided on a hiding place deep in the Amazon, in a cavern system hidden behind multiple layers of Ancestral disguising skills. Gabriel and some of his closest Ancestral allies had unequaled disguising skills and they'd successfully hidden away a number of Daniel's enemies, keeping them safe until the vampire world could figure out how to unseat the most powerful despot ever to take hold of the Council of Ancestrals.

Lily. He called her name. She turned toward him a little, but her body still faced Josh's bed. Her fingers were pressed to her lips. Her eyes glistened with tears.

Telepathically, he reassured her that they were together now and would stay that way, which brought a deep sigh flowing out of her and her shoulders finally loosened and lowered.

Only then, when she was sure Josh would be safe, did she move toward him. He opened his arms and she stepped inside the circle of his embrace as he held her fast. "I swear," he whispered, "that I will protect you and your son, above all things, even above the vengeance I want to bring down on the head of my father. I owe this to you, on behalf of my people, to do this for you."

The chains vibrated heavily. It was as though a wave crashed through Lily, and she began to sob. He carried her from her son's room to his bedroom, now their bedroom.

He sat down on the side of the bed and held her in his arms for a long, long time, and let her cry it all out, the years of separation, the years of believing Josh was dead, and the horror of having gone through a near-execution with her son as a witness.

He felt her pain because of the chains and because he knew what suffering was. As she wept, he also felt her begin to heal, and in her healing he was healed as well.

Lily rested her head against Adrien's shoulder. She fingered the lapel of his finely tailored tux. She felt emptied of emotion, yet full, so full.

She released a sigh then another, heavy exhalations of all that she felt, the relief that she was safe and that Josh was under Adrien's roof, hidden in a cave protected by Ancestrals.

Safe. She was safe and so was Josh.

And though Adrien held deep concerns for his brothers, she and Josh were his priority.

"What about Lucian and Marius?" She rubbed the fabric between her thumb and forefinger over and over.

"Daniel won't kill them. Their deaths right now couldn't serve him at all. He needs them to form tracking pairs."

Lily frowned. "So Daniel can't use Quill and Lev?"

"No, neither of them has that ability."

She shifted to look up at him, her head cradled in the nook of his elbow, his hand rubbing her bare arm. "But you're worried about Lucian and Marius."

"Yes. And no. Before I met you, I'd thought of little else than helping to keep my brothers safe. At the same time I felt powerless. Then you arrived and changed everything. You created this enormous miracle in my life and now I'm trying to think about Lucian and Marius in those terms—that maybe something will come into each of their lives to change their futures as well."

She shifted to stroke his cheek with her fingers. "Like Claire? Do you think she intends to form a bonding pair with Lucian?"

Adrien nodded. "I believe so. Why else would she have

told Josh the things she did. She must have learned about Lucian's chain and schemed to steal it. I'll alert Gabriel so that he can keep an eye out for Claire. Hopefully that will give Josh some peace as well."

"What if Daniel is waiting for her and decides to use her like he used me? Maybe you should try to intervene?"

He leaned down and kissed her. "I can't answer for what is about to happen to Lucian or Claire, and I wish I could go to him, but you're my responsibility now, both you and Josh."

She wanted to protest, her guilt rising, but he kissed her again and a soft smile curved his lips. "No guilt, Lily. I don't know exactly why events unfolded as they did, why you were brought into my life, but you're here. Lucian and Marius are men, very powerful vampires, and what I trust in the most right now is that each will figure things out, how to survive.

"But there's something more. Gabriel is working behind closed doors with other Ancestrals, and intends to create a counterforce against Daniel. He wants to retake the Council, and in time he will. So I will trust in that, in those vampires of Ancestral status, like Gabriel, and those aligned with him, to do what needs to be done."

"But you should be with them." More than anything in life she didn't want to be a hindrance.

He shook his head. "If Daniel knew he could find me, he'd turn his attention toward me. The Ancestrals want his attention fixed on my brothers and on still hunting for the extinction weapon. They can track him better."

"Did you give Gabriel the location of the weapon at the Black Cavern system?"

He nodded. "They've been there and destroyed it."

"But it's not over."

He shook his head. "There were several groups experimenting at the time. Gabriel and many of the Ancestrals believe there was more than one weapon, and some of them in pieces, hidden in different systems."

"That would explain why, when I thought about the weapon, I'd get so many readings, all over the globe at the same time. But Adrien, shouldn't you and I be looking for them, perhaps now more than ever?"

He caught her hand and kissed her fingers. "In one sense, yes. But Gabriel and I both believe, as do many of the Ancestrals, that Josh should be our focus. I know that won't make sense, but Josh, a mere child, didn't deserve to become embroiled in what is essentially a vampire problem. He didn't deserve to lose his mother, or his family. If I go with you both now, we can atone to you and Josh to some degree for what was taken from you because of my father. Please, don't protest. The decision has been made. We're going to the Rain Forest Caverns."

Lily felt his determination and knew he wouldn't be moved, which also gave her a tremendous sense of relief. She rested in what appeared to be a group decision to let her, and her tracking ability, disappear into the jungles of South America.

With her biggest concerns laid to rest, she looked into Adrien's beautiful flecked teal eyes and finally began to relax. Josh was now safe, the future settled, and she could focus on the miracle that had become the man, the vampire, cradling her in his arms.

She pushed her fingers into his hair, shoving the beautiful strands away from his equally beautiful face. Love flooded her heart, an intense love, surprising and miraculous, because of the chains that bound her to Adrien. Tears filled her eyes all over again.

"Don't cry."

She chuckled softly. "These are just tears of profound joy and gratitude. I didn't think we were going to make it."

"But we did, didn't we?"

"Incredibly, yes. With Josh."

He nodded. "With your son." He dipped down and kissed her, this time a lingering kiss. "Oh, Lily," he murmured. And he lifted her to her feet, took her in his arms, and kissed her again.

The feel of his lips removed the last of her worries.

She was with Adrien, in his South African home, and he was going to make love to her.

He searched the recesses of her mouth and drew her tightly against him, all her velvet and crystals pressed against his fine black Brioni.

The physical strength of him was what she felt, the latent power in his muscled physique, the way his biceps rippled beneath her hands, his thighs flexed against her legs.

He drew back then dipped to kiss her neck, a series of plucks against her vein, a reminder of who and what he was.

She felt his blood-need rise, a tremor that passed through him and sent a strong vibration through her double-chain.

"Yes," she whispered, "I need that as well. I need you to take from me. Tonight, you've given me so much. You've given me everything."

He licked her neck repeatedly so that her breaths grew light and shallow, longing for him.

"I want to do something with you, Lily. Something I've never done before, but this new level of power tells me I can."

Her mind flowed back and forth, loose with desire. Through the chains she could sense his desire as well, like a dull wonderful ache. "Anything, Adrien. My God, anything."

He kept plucking at her neck. Chills rippled down her chest and arms, even her back. "Mmmm," she murmured softly. "What do you want to do?"

"I think it's better if I just showed you."

He shifted her back to the bed and set her down on the edge. Her fingertips gripped the sides of the silk comforter. She trembled now as he knelt on the carpet. He took her burgundy skirts in hand, pushing them up her bare thighs, higher and higher.

"Lift your hips," he whispered.

She obeyed and he shoved all that fabric up behind her, then spread her legs. She wore a black lace thong, the barest scrap of fabric.

"Lie back." His deep voice worked like a hypnotic drug and she eased down on the bed, her dress a lump under her back—but it really didn't matter because he was kissing her low, and using his finger to play with the lace, which gave her two sensations at once. He rimmed the edge of her thong with his tongue so that the fabric tugged on her while his fingers played and his tongue spread a layer of oh-so-welcome moisture over her skin.

"Unh," came from between her lips, a soft moan. She shuddered when he gripped the sides of her thong and tore the fabric apart.

"Oh, God," she said, a whisper against the air.

His tongue covered her in long wet swipes, sideways over her bare mons then moving lower and lower, teasing her labia, all swollen now with tingling desire.

But when he began to work her between her lower lips, her body arched and a deep moan fell from her throat.

Lily.

Telepathy. Beautiful. I love your voice in my head.

I'm going to do that thing now. Be ready.

She might have groaned, she wasn't sure. *I'm ready.* She closed her eyes and waited. He never stopped taking care of her very low but after a moment a familiar vibration began, the kind that happened when he battled in two places at once.

The thought of Adrien becoming two entities at the same time forced another long moan from between her lips. He sucked on her low as the vibration intensified.

She felt a strange movement all around, more vibration, and her chain sang against her skin.

Open your eyes.

Though she felt Adrien licking her low, now he was also, at the same time, staring down into her face, stroking her cheek.

She gasped. "You separated."

I did. Are you enjoying this?

She nodded.

Good.

Are you able to speak?

He shook his head, then leaned close and kissed her.

Lily thought she might have just died and gone to heaven. *More of Adrien*, that was what she thought as he worked her low and kissed her mouth at the exact same time.

Two Adriens.

The love she felt for him expanded as she slid her arms around his neck and embraced him. He deepened the kiss, searching the recesses of her mouth, but to feel two tongues at once caused a shiver to chase up and down her body in exhilarating waves.

Her hips responded to the flick of his tongue low and she groaned against his mouth at the same time. She slid her fingers into his thick hair, caressing as he kissed her. Using the same hand, she drifted her fingers down his back, then shifted to the second Adrien, stroking his face and feeling where his soft tongue played along her labia.

I like that you're touching my tongue. Adrien's voice in her mind, as well as two bodies she could savor and enjoy, strengthened her rising need.

Adrien, I don't know how much more of this I can take. His lips shifted to suck her finger, then back to her clitoris, flicking his tongue quickly until she rocked against his face. At the same time, he kissed her with swift erotic plunges of his tongue that left her gasping.

Being tended to in both places at once brought pleasure rising sharply, and she cried out against his mouth. Lower, he sped up so that one sensation piled up on another, his tongue in her mouth, flicks down low, the feel of one body beneath her right hand, and a second set of shoulders beneath the other.

She writhed beneath him, hungering, reaching for more, rushing toward ecstasy.

Lily, he whispered within her mind. *I love you so much. I love feeling you beneath me like this.* One set of hands caressed her breasts, her arms, her shoulders. The other squeezed her hips and stroked her thighs. So much incredible sensation.

A string of cries left her throat. *Adrien, I'm coming.* Other words might have traveled along the telepathic link but she wasn't sure since she was so caught up in all that she was experiencing. Pleasure exploded as his tongue pummeled her mouth, as two sets of hands traveled her body, as the other Adrien kept pleasure spiraling through her low. He sucked and flicked until she trembled, ecstasy rolling in waves, one after the other.

At last, panting, her body began to settle down. When she finally lay quiet, he leaned back once more and smiled. *Good?*

Perfect.

He nodded. I love you so much.

I love you, too.

Down low, the second Adrien kissed her repeatedly just above her clitoris, then the first Adrien kissed her mouth again.

I'm going to re-form now.

She watched as he drifted back to himself, wavy lines in the air like a blur, and at the same time rose from the carpet. He leaned over her, his hands planted on the bed, on either side of her. "How was that?"

"Oh, my God. Adrien, to feel you kiss me while you brought me between my legs. Heaven." She rubbed his neck.

"More?"

"A lot more. I need you."

He nodded and began to undress. But he took his time as he held her gaze. She leaned up on her elbows, her legs dangling over the side of the bed, her toes just touching the carpet.

And now he was taking his jacket off, folding it up and laying it across the bench at the foot of the bed. He unhooked a pair of ruby cuff links. He set these on the nightstand. They rocked back and forth, two small spots of red, bloodred.

Her heart beat harder, her gaze drawn to him as he worked at his shirt. He opened the front, eased the soft white fabric down his back, and let it fall to the floor. The vampire had a magnificent body, thick, built pecs, shoulders that went on forever, muscled arms.

And he was hers.

She touched the double-chain at her neck and her heart swelled, knowing that this man belonged to her now and forever.

He took off his shoes then slipped his pants off, as well as black silk boxers.

And there he was. She felt heated up and dizzy. Her heart raced now and it wasn't just his body, it was all of him, who he was, his tenderness with her, his concern for Josh, his commitment to keeping them safe from Daniel. He overwhelmed her with his character, his presence, and yes, with that body standing in front of her, his cock firm and ready.

But the earlier tremor rolled through him and she felt his need for her blood. She moved to the edge of the bed, her legs parted wide. She tilted her head, presenting her neck.

He groaned and fell on his knees. She felt his hands on her waist through the velvet. The chains vibrated continuously now so that she felt connected to all that he felt.

He moved swiftly, making a quick strike with his fangs, then sealing his lips over the wound as he started to suck down her blood.

The sensation sent chills down her abdomen all the way to her sex, firing her need for him to plant himself between her legs.

He held her close as he continued to drink her down. She felt his blood-hunger begin to ease, and when it dissipated at last, he released her neck.

He rose up from the floor, extended his hand to her, and drew her to her feet. She thought he would take her gown off. Instead, he pulled her into his arms and kissed her again, plunging his tongue into her mouth.

She whimpered beneath the vast sensations that pummeled her, of his warm skin beneath her fingers, the thickness of his muscles, the pressure of his hard cock against her gown. Her hands grew restless and greedy. She slid them up and down his back, reached in front and stroked his abs.

He gave her just enough room and she drifted her hand low. She cried out as she touched the tip of his cock and found it wet.

"I need to get inside you," he said.

"I want that, too. You've given me so much pleasure. Now it's your turn."

He nodded, holding her close as he reached back and pulled the comforter off the bed.

* * *

Adrien didn't quite comprehend all that he experienced right now. The sheet was ready to receive the treasure in his arms, but for just a moment, as he held Lily with one arm, her legs dangling, he was unwilling to let her go. He warmed up his vision so that he could really see her hazel eyes, her head leaning back just so. With his free hand he cupped her chin then kissed her.

Love, desire, passion all swirled together, whipping up a tornado in his mind, round and round, driving into his chest, whirling around his heart and pulling at him. His soul strained toward her.

Oh, Adrien, I can feel what you're feeling. It's so beautiful, like watching the wind blow clouds across the sky at a maddening pace. Adrien. My Adrien.

Lily, my darling.

Yes, that was what he felt, that in these few nights together, she had become *his darling.*

He settled her on the bed once more, then stretched out on top of her. The part of him that was now Ancestral felt the power he held over her, and with his knee he pushed her legs apart maybe more forcefully than he normally would have.

But her whimpers told him what he needed to know, how much she wanted him.

He positioned himself at her opening, and as she slid her hands up his chest he began to thrust, pushing his way inside her beautiful wetness. His hands found her waist and he squeezed as he thrust, which caused her body to undulate in a sensual roll of pleasure.

He loved this part of sex, building toward a strong orgasm, watching his woman writhe and feel so much. Her feminine scent worked in his brain as well, hardening him that one degree firmer so that she groaned this time.

I won't last long. You feel too wonderful.

I'm close again as well, she returned.

He moved faster, pushing hard, letting his new power, Ancestral power, leach into every muscle of his body. He sensed her pleasure mounting.

He thrust hard now and she began to groan, her hands caressing his buttocks. She cried out repeatedly, muffled sounds against his throat. At the same time he could feel her tugging low, and maybe it was that movement, that he knew she was coming, that brought him, or maybe the nails digging into his ass. Whatever it was, he came hard, the sensation of love he felt for Lily tripling the pleasure.

The moment of ecstasy rolled as he thrust, as Lily continued to moan, her hips pushing against his, grasping for each last bit of ecstasy.

When at last her body settled down, his body at almost the same time, he watched her smile, her lids at half-mast, her hands roving him still, caressing his shoulders and arms, his back and waist.

"Unbelievable," she said. "That was incredibly erotic, so pleasurable." She met his gaze. "Thank you for that, Adrien. Thank you."

He leaned down and kissed her. "We both needed this." He kissed her again.

"Mmmm," she murmured.

With Adrien still on top of her, Lily held him close, her arms around his neck. She sighed deeply. She didn't want to let him go. She had never expected all of this, so much man and so much love.

And of course she'd never done a threesome, never would. But that was her experience with him tonight, a twosome that was a threesome. Yes, more man than she had ever thought to have.

At the same time, the beauty of love, intense, extraordinary, wondrous love, flowed through her.

Love.

Sweet love.

Irreplaceable love.

She thought back to the moment of washing Adrien clean in that makeshift tub in India, and putting the binding chain on him for the first time. How long ago that seemed; an entire lifetime ago. Now he was here, lying in her arms, beautiful, powerful, renewed.

She stroked his back with her hands and played with his hair with her fingers. She sighed and smiled, smiled and sighed.

"I love you, Lily."

She sighed again and smiled a little more. "Who would have thought when we left the Himalayan cavern system, bound to each other by the first set of chains, that we would have ended up here?"

He drifted his hand over her side and caressed her breast. He kissed her and with her heart so full, she kissed him back, willing him to feel all that she was feeling.

He drew back, looking down at her. *I've never been so happy in my life*.

His words soothed her and expanded the love in her heart.

I'm so glad that I make you happy.

Adrien hardly recognized the sensation in his body, but he finally defined it as an unqualified ease. The heavy muscles of his fighting body were lax, his lips parted instead of stretched taut in a hard angry line, and his breathing slow and even.

But mostly, it was love that he experienced, a flow of affection and adoration for Lily that moved through his blood and over his body in steady warm waves, as though washing away all that had been ugly in his previous life.

He was made new, born of the chains that had bound

him, the physical ones and the more invasive chains that had kept his mind locked into his hatred for his father.

All that was gone, made new by love, Lily's love for him and the love he felt for her, the healing of his heart that he'd never known before, not in his long four centuries of living.

He thought of the boy, of Josh, who had essentially brought Lily to him. For that he would spend his life doing all that he could for Josh, whatever the boy needed, and whatever Lily needed for her son. This was the solemn depth of his commitment.

He lifted up and said these things to her, which brought a new round of tears streaming from her eyes, flowing to the sides of her face and into her hair.

But she smiled and he kissed her.

He made love to her again and again,

He used his splitting skills and worked her up in a dozen different positions until he wore her out with her muffled cries against different parts of his body.

As dawn broke, she fell asleep in his arms and he watched her slumber, unwilling to end this first time with her as his true woman, as the one he would spend his life with. He didn't know how long he would have with her: The double-chain would increase her human life but not as long as his. Despite this reality, he would savor every moment. Rather than think too much about the future he would treasure the present and the tremendous gift that had been delivered to his feet.

He released a deep sigh, one that came from so far down in his body he actually quivered. The sensation brought her partially awake.

"Happy?" she asked, a slight foggy sound to her voice.

She couldn't even open her eyes, and before he could say anything she drifted off once more.

Was he happy? More than she would ever know.

The vision came to him, a roll of sensation first, then clarity, a perfect image of Lily and Josh, but in the future, though how far forward he couldn't tell. Josh was a man, fully grown, human-perfect. He held a woman's hand and she was a vampire.

Lily, forever siphoning his power, hadn't aged at all. She beamed her smile, all her goodness radiating over her son and his fiancée.

Adrien's heart pounded because he was in the vision as well, his arms wrapped around Lily much as they were now, and Lily's stomach was very swollen with child, his child.

The vision faded.

"What's the matter?" she asked. He'd awakened her again. Of course she would sense that something was wrong.

"Nothing."

"You're shaking."

She turned in his arms to face him, and there she was in the glow of his vampire vision, his Lily, the woman who meant the world to him. He smoothed her hair away from her face and kissed her. "I love you so much."

Her fingers went to the chain around her neck. His vibrated heavily. No doubt hers did as well. "Me, too."

"Do you want more children?" he asked, suddenly afraid of the answer because of all that she'd been through.

"I didn't think it was an option, or not much of one."

"But if you could have your heart's desire, would you bear another child?"

Her lips curved. "If we are speaking only of what we wish and not what we expect, then yes, of course, especially if I could have your child."

"Why my child?" He could feel how far his brows rose.

This time she laughed and smoothed her fingers over his brow. "Because I love you, Adrien, more than words can express, and because you deserve to be a father, to have that joy in your life."

That was all he needed to hear. He kissed her hard, to which she responded by whimpering and easing her arms around his neck.

"We should practice, then," he said. "A lot. Just in case it could help our genetics kick in and we can make a baby together."

"I'd love nothing more."

Despite his earlier conviction that she needed her rest, Adrien rolled Lily onto her back and made love to her again, but she didn't seem to mind as she cooed against his lips.

He didn't tell her about the vision. Those images were meant just for him, in the same way his initial vision of her in a burgundy gown had been the start of all this goodness way back in the cavern.

How long ago that seemed, even though only a few nights had passed. But that was now his former life, a life that had ended when Lily arrived, when she came to him bearing her bonding chains and set them both down this impossible, miraculous, and ultimately love-filled journey.

Don't miss Lucian's story!

CHAINS OF DARKNESS
By Caris Roane

Coming April 2014 from St. Martin's Paperbacks